Gladys & Jack

A Historical Novel

Beverley Hopwood

GLADYS AND JACK
BMD Series #1
Copyright © 2012 by Beverley Hopwood

ISBN: 978-1-77069-527-6

Word Alive Press
131 Cordite Road, Winnipeg, MB R3W 1S1
www.wordalivepress.ca

WORD ALIVE PRESS
Just Write!

Library and Archives Canada Cataloguing in Publication

Hopwood, Beverley, 1952-
    Gladys & Jacks / Beverley Hopwood.

ISBN 978-1-77069-527-6

    I. Title. II. Title: Gladys and Jacks.

PS8615.O68G53 2012   C813'.6   C2012-903466-5

Dedication

To my grandparents: Gladys Hannaford Bailey and Jack Bailey who, with their own writing, inspired my story.

table of contents

acknowledgements

I FIRST NEED TO THANK MY GRANDFATHER JACK BAILEY FOR WRITING HIS MANY speeches, poems and letters. Without them, I wouldn't have found the desire to share the family story. Although he died when I was an infant, I feel I have gotten to know him and some of our ancestors well. My gratitude extends to my grandmother Gladys Lavinia Hannaford Bailey for being the inspiration behind my grandfather's writing, for saving all his letters and poems, and being the kind of grandmother to make me feel special. Her essay on "Dogs I Have Known" was interspersed throughout the twentieth century section. I wish, as so many of us do, that I had had sense to ask more questions.

Rita Bailey, second cousin once removed, has been a wonderful historical, geographical, and family history guide for the Bailey side of the tree in Hyssington, Wales, and Bishops Castle, Shropshire. A special thanks to her for editing that section. Sherry Bailey, third cousin, needs recognition and thanks for allowing me to include parts of her interview with her grandfather Percy Bailey. Her foresight made this possible.

I wish to acknowledge historical bits gleaned from TORQUAY & PAIGNTON The Making of a Modern Resort by Henry James Lethbridge, published in 2003 by Phillimore & Co. Ltd., Chichester, West Sussex, England used in chapters two through four, and the Loman <u>Pocket Scottish History</u>, edited by Dr. James Mackey, published by Parragon Books in 2002 .

Without the detailed maps included in the <u>2001 Road Atlas: Great Britain and Ireland</u>, published by the Automobile Association in Britain, I might not have found my way to the correct branches of family, who, although they migrated only short distances before coming to Canada, had many names in common with other branches of the family. <u>The Penguin Atlas of Britain & Irish History</u> published in London, England in 2001 provided early historical background for all areas of Britain.

In Canada, the <u>Vernon</u> and <u>Might's Business</u> directories for various years from 1870 to 1922 provided details of residences and businesses as well as an overview of Hamilton between the censuses. Between the years 1880 and 1922, many headlines and stories were used in the characters' dialogue from *The Hamilton Herald*, and *The Hamilton Spectator*. In those days the articles were not identified by reporter, so I could only make a guess as to which items my grandfather wrote.

Besides archivists and records at The Devon Records Office, the Torquay Library, Devon, The Hexam Library, Northumberland; The National Archives in Aberystwyth, Wales; London, England; Ottawa and Toronto, Ontario, a thank you needs to go to Findmypast.com and Ancestry.ca for continuously adding files to their resources which were invaluable in the research process.

editorial acknowledgements

LARRY HINCKS HAS GUIDED ME THROUGH A THREE-STAGE EDITING PROCESS. HIS historical knowledge and his command of the English language have been excellent resources which helped me turn a 'family tree' into a 'historical novel.' His assistance has been invaluable to the editing process.

Thank you also, to friends who read early chapters, daughter Pamela McManus, technical advisor and editing assistant, daughter Adrianne Hopwood and Kay McManus, readers.

foreword

A BOX OF UNLABELED PICTURES, LETTERS, AND DOCUMENTS STARTED A FIFTEEN-year journey through records offices, archives, internet sources, and libraries on two continents. The thrill of finding ancestry headstones overlooking the green hills of Hyssington, Wales, or East Allington, Devon fired my desire to share the family story. Once retired, I became determined to organize the material I had been collecting and put it into book form so that members of the family could read a comprehensive format.

Thus began a two-year journey with *The Word Writers*, two or three false starts, and with encouragement and assistance from Sara, Brian, Donna, Heidi, Ruth, Mandy, and Sue Ellen, I got going on the historical novel you are about to read.

The dialogue has been added for readability, but I hope that it remains as true to the facts available to me as possible. Many branches of the families early on had to be cut for clarity. The remaining characters built themselves, although with more research, they might grow and change. Many questions remain unanswered, and I am sure that because more and more records are being made available, this historical novel could be in the process of being written forever;

however, here is the cut-off point. May I humbly present <u>Gladys and Jack</u>, the story of my paternal grandparents?

PART ONE

Hannaford
FAMILY

one

Edward Hannaford = Sarah Ryder
(1767-1837)

Sarah	Robert	Edward	**John**	Sarah	Mary Ann	William
(1798-1805)			(1806-)		(1812 -1825)	(1815-1816)

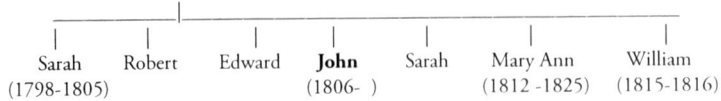

John Hannaford=Mary Miller
(1806-)　　　(1805 -)

Mary	Thomas Miller	William	Elizabeth Ann	John	**Robert**	James	**Alfred M**
(1830-)					(1844-)		(1851-)

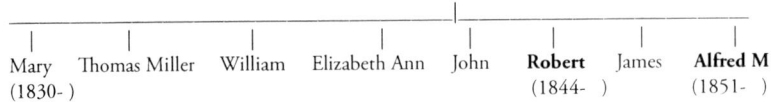

St. Andrew's Anglican Church, East Allington.

The exterior of the church.

ANXIETY, AS MUCH AS ROUTINE, AWOKE JOHN HANNAFORD JUST BEFORE DAWN. Today was the day he and his family would leave the familiar East Allington cottage. They had been in the village as far back as he knew, and it was out of near desperation that he was moving his wife and children to the bustling seaside town of Torquay. There was not much choice really. Alfred, born in 1851, was their eighth child and most of them still lived with him and his wife Mary in the cottage next to his brother, Edward and his large family. John's oldest brother Robert and his wife Mary still lived nearby, although their children had moved south to areas around Dartmouth.

John quietly pulled on his outer leggings trying not to disturb Mary who had baby Alfred curled in her arm. He stepped cautiously around the sprawled forms of his oldest two sons who were sleeping more heavily than usual. After having worked a full day over at Morley, they had tiredly struggled the seven miles home in the absolute dark. He'd let them sleep while he said his goodbyes.

John waded through the heavily hanging pre-dawn fog, just in time to catch Robert and Edward on their way over to the farm. Normally John would have been with them, working dawn to dusk, collecting few wages from the grim landowner.

"God speed, John," Robert hoarsely whispered.

"Don't forget yer roots," Edward admonished.

They each silently clasped the others' hands and John patted the backs of his brothers he would never see again. John then watched as Robert and Edward turned down the earthen path on their way to labour.

The Fortesque family dominated the town and provided most of the labourers with work in either agriculture, or cattle, sheep, and swine husbandry. John's heart still thrilled at the sight of mist blanketing the lower dips of valleys between the gentle rises on all sides of the town. Sheep dotted the hillsides, resembling loose stones scattered over small, green feeding grounds. Long before his grandfather's time, low stone walls had been strategically stacked, allowing some shrubbery to grow atop the winding ridges which outlined fields of green grasses or reddish-brown earth. He stood now, surveying the well-known territory, offering his final goodbyes to his ancestors.

Subdued by a sadness mingling with reserved hopefulness, John turned to head up the hill to the churchyard. Work for his growing sons was getting sparse. There were only two shopkeepers, a mason, a blacksmith, an innkeeper at the Union Inn, and a few that did carpentry in town, but most of the population provided labour for the surrounding farms. Small farmers were struggling, and jobs were getting harder to find. For the past decade crop rotation had improved the production, but mechanization and other events seemed to be against the labourers.

"This 'ave been the wettest summer I saw yet," complained Robert to his father and brothers in 1842.

"Aye, and we're bound to lose the Corn Laws and 'ave things opened up with this Free Trade thing. The farmers aren't getting their price for corn and the wheat crop t'aven't been good this past two year. I think we're in for hard times in our town," responded his father.

The population of the village itself had been greatly reduced since 1801 when the total was 468 persons. John's sons Thomas and young John had had to venture over to Morley to work as servants for two farmers. John wanted his family together, as did his wife Mary. Besides, the boys would soon need wives and the girls, husbands. Many were leaving the village, now only 250, searching for a better life, and therefore the choices were limited if they weren't to marry cousins.

John turned his gaze to the steep path towards the parish church. Saint Andrew's was a solid gothic stone structure; its square bell tower at the west end could be seen from all directions. A deep path had been cut through the hill from the lane towards the south side of the church, and five-foot stone walls lined this path through which he now made his way. Above the stone wall rose the graves and tombs of ancestors and friends. The few markers visible from the burrow-like path poked out among tall grasses rising up on the south side. John's father Edward Hannaford and four of John's siblings were buried there. He and each of his siblings had been forced to bury at least one of their own children. It had always seemed to him a mistake somehow, that God deemed the young die before the old. He pictured the ancient stone baptismal font and the newer one under the bell tower at the back of the church. He and his brothers and sisters had been baptized there, just as all of their children had been.

Recent restoration works had sharpened up the loose and crumbling mortar inside and outside of the church with clean, white lime. Where cracked black and red tiles had erupted in uneven patterns up the central and side aisles, now new ones smartly lined the floor between polished wooden pews. A low, dropped ceiling had been removed to reveal gracefully arched wooden beams lining the ceiling above each aisle. The heavily carved pulpit and ancient dark wooden choir screen could be admired by visitors and brought the parishioners' attention to the front at a Sunday service. Until lately, there had been no caring wealthy patrons to restore the church building to its sixteenth century grandeur. As John turned in the dim light towards the altar, he saw the vicar rising from a kneeling position.

"Oh, pardon me, Vicar. I didn'a mean to disturb you."

"Ah, John, come to say your goodbyes, have ye? Our families have been in these parts for a long time," reflected the rector.

"Yes, as long as I can remember, and we're sad to be leaving, but there is so little work around here that we just can't manage."

"Well, we'll miss ya," the Reverend Fortesque said, then added doubtfully, "You'll come back if you can?"

John shook hands self-consciously and headed out the door, replacing the floppy hat on his head.

He watched from the hillside as the carter pulled to a jiggling halt at the front of his cottage. He allowed gravity to pull him quickly downhill, watching as the older boys loaded the heavy cooking pot, packed with pottery and pewter in straw, onto the cart. He had promised Mary, his wife of 22 years, some real pottery as soon as they settled. First thing was to establish the family in employment when they moved to Torquay.

John could hear his wife's voice intensify as she followed her sons, instructing them about moving the one piece of furniture they owned: the sideboard which John had given her on their wedding. The cart appeared to already have a full load of barrels, but they made room, strapping things down with the carter's belting.

"John, work with Thomas. Quit trying to lift it all yerself," called out their father as he approached the cart.

"Ah, Pa, he's moving too slow."

"Quit yer complaining and be careful with that. We don't have another, ya know," chided Mary. She hurried back into the cottage for a last check around, but more to hide her sudden burst of tears.

"Robert! Stop hopping around, and help your sister get the food and belongings into the cart. Here young James, you can help me lift this barrel," instructed John. It took little time to load the few other belongings they were to take.

John hoped his sons' enthusiasm would be contagious. Robert found it difficult to contain his youthful excitement. The family was moving to Torquay, a newly developed seaside resort and spa for the rich. They were going the three miles with the cart to Blackhawton where all would rest and eat while the carter delivered some of his load to the public house, then on to Dartmouth, a ferry ride across the River Dart, and on to Paignton. Mother, baby Alfred, and Elizabeth would take a carriage to Torquay up the red coast line, while John and his sons would accompany the cart. Young Robert would miss his uncles and cousins, but was too eager to see wondrous new things in a big town to worry about the fact he might never see the family again.

"Hey, Pa. Canna we go by way of Totnes? We could see the castle and the red church and the clock bridge!"

"Nay, son. The way is too long and too costly by train. We've got young James, Alfred and the womenfolk to think about. We all want to get there as fast as we're able."

"Remember when I got to go with Thomas and William to the Tuesday cattle market? I remember the hillside street where the clock tower bridge crossed the road above us and joined the tall buildings," said Robert.

"Yes, and now you are going to talk about how the street sloped steeply down to the River Dart where an arched-stone bridge went across the river. But do ya remember me carrying you on my shoulders to least as far as Harberton where we could get a dry spot in a shed?" reminded Thomas.

Robert sheepishly looked with gratitude at his brother. "But it would have been fun climbing a tree and sleeping up off the wet ground. It was a long way home!"

"Yes, it was. And now let's get on with our journey, because it's a great deal further, and yer brother won't be carrying you this time!" Thomas said emphatically.

II

Mary's whole body ached and her mind had been a blur early this morning. She and her sister-in-law, Jane, had talked long into the night after making food preparations for the journey ahead. For two decades they had shared the workload of raising fifteen children between them, visiting back and forth, their spouses off early to the fields six days a week, and long into the evening in spring and summer. Mary's brother had lodged with them for some time, along with others during harvest or planting. It had always been a busy home, familiar faces all around, and now they were about to leave all that. Her heart ached.

"I need to put the last patches on and finish mending the boys' Sunday pants. I want my family to look neat and tidy when we arrive in the town," Mary had sighed, weary with preparation.

Jane was mending her own family's rough-spun clothes. "I've heard they hav' many fine materials, smooth, and colourful in lovely shop windows, and all the ladies wear hats with wide ribbon trim. They say they have very full skirts with layers of flounces. How can they do a day's work dressed like that?"

"I doubt the ladies dressed like that have to do a day's work," commented Mary. "There are other things I hear about. Shops with windows displaying Millenary, London goods and things for every room in the home line the shop windows in Paignton and Torquay. I hope we can get reasonable food. I will miss our garden. You'll take what comes up later in the summer, won't you Jane?" offered Mary

"Oh, ya, and be mighty grateful for it too. With ten mouths to feed, I can hardly keep up with the bread making."

Mary smiled, but her heart was sad in the knowledge of leaving her friends and family of a lifetime. Her own Miller family, too, would miss them sorely.

This morning, Mary looked around at the cottage she and John had shared since their wedding on August 31, 1838. This morning, the bundles of bedding, the pot of crockery, and now the sideboard were loaded onto the cart which Doggery had brought to a noisy stop out at the front. Jane was looking at her with a wistful sadness, perhaps wishing she too could move to the big town. Her boys and husband had long been gone to the fields, so she and young Henry were helping to send John and Mary's family off.

"We'll miss ya terribly, Mary," lamented Jane. At the parting moment, they gave an awkward embrace, grasping hands in a final farewell.

"I'll send ya word with one of the carters who come to the village just as soon as we've settled in."

Had Mary been able to write more than a few simple words, Jane would not have been able to read them anyway. This would be their final good bye.

two

LEGGINGS DROOPING AND SHOULDERS BENT, THE TIRED FAMILY ROUNDED THE last cliff-side and viewed Torquay in all its nineteenth-century grandeur. New buildings were being constructed, carved into sides of the steep hills. Lanes and roadways were active with shiny carriages drawn by smartly prancing horses. Upon reaching Paignton, Mary had changed her mind about getting on the crowded carriage with Alfred and Elizabeth.

"No, John. I've decided we all need to stay together. There are too many people milling about, and those fast horses make me nervous. Besides, I believe we are going to need to save the expense."

The excitement of the busy bustle of a developing town was not lost on the younger members of the Hannaford clan. They stared in awe at fancy dresses and suits, rows of stone houses, hotels, and six-foot high stone fences that seemed part of the cliffs as they girded the streets winding up to the top. The "tor" in Torquay actually referred to the seven hills around which the town buildings clung like barnacles on a ship.

"Pa! Pa! Look at the castles up on the hill! Look out at those sailing ships! Alf, look at those wagons with all the piles of wood and boxes," Robert exclaimed in awe, swinging his head from one thing to another.

"We're looking son, we're all looking." John, himself exhausted, wondered how the young lad kept up his energy. He was pleased to see all his children looking about with enthusiasm, keen on taking in their new surroundings with pleasure. John observed that Thomas's eye seemed to linger on the smart looking young ladies with heavily draped hats, boldly coloured gowns trimmed in ribbon and frills, and layers of smooth, colourful capes over their bodices. Young John must have noticed Thomas's glances as well.

"Wait till yer've got yer top hat there, Thomas, afore you start choosing a lady," John joked. Thomas jabbed his elbow deep into John's ribs.

"Quit yer gawking yerself there, brother."

"Take heart, Mary. You'll soon have a stool to sit on and a bed to lie in," encouraged Mary's husband with tender concern. "You'll see in no time at all, things will be settled." John took her arm, as every time a shiny horse-drawn carriage whizzed past them, she gave a start and shivered.

Mary's firm resolve to hold her head high in her new surroundings had dissolved in little dips, bit by bit. Their Sunday best was plain and rough, though they were clean and newly mended. Their boots were loose and dusty from walking beside the cart for nearly two days. It would be obvious to others that they were plain, country folk. She was now thinking she would use the money saved from the cost of the carriage to help purchase new, finer fabric. She was already planning ways to collect a little more money to clothe the entire family in more modern designs, perhaps with a bit of ribbon for the girls, with longer, more up-to-date gowns for their Sunday best. What was East Allington's Sunday best would be Torquay's everyday work clothes.

II

Robert glanced down fondly at his two little brothers to see if they were appreciating the splendour of a street filled with carriages, people, and fine mansions. There had been hills in East Allington, small narrow lanes with low stone fences and hedgerows, but the hills of Torquay were grooved with steep lanes and wide roads. They seemed to go up and up, twisting and suddenly making a downward turn, before continuing to rise again before them. His older sister Elizabeth took turns minding Alfred and James, while soaking in all the sounds and sights of a town with more than 11,000 inhabitants.

They had gone slowly by Cockington Court, peering between hedges and trees at the grand home of the Mallock family, eighth generation in residence. They passed the rail station in operation only a few years. They passed the new Catholic church, The Church of the Assumption, and the Torre Abbey estate, which the influential Cary family had held for several generations. There were new developments everywhere.

Elizabeth, who was as impressed with the flora as the boys were with the women exclaimed, "Oh, look, Ma, through those stone gates you can see the bushy trees in the outer garden, and there! Look at all those bluebells and white hyacinths." The formal inner garden was not visible from the road, but it provided private pleasure and food for the Cary household.

People with money came to holiday and picnic near the town which overlooked Babbicombe Bay. Others came for the mild climate in winter. Torquay was situated between Exeter in the north of Devonshire where the politicians and businesses governed the county, and the famous Plymouth to the south where mariners and sailors had been trained for centuries. Sir Francis Drake had sailed from there, and the navy had often set out from the port for war with Spain, France, and the New World.

The boys knew some of the history of Torquay from a few lessons their old school mistress gave to enhance their knowledge between the learning of figures and letters. Now they felt they were arriving in a location where real history had taken place.

"Do ya think that might be where the pirates hide their contraband and ships from the excise, Pa? When do ya think we can see the quay and what about the caves? When do ya think we can go down to the seashore?" Tall tales of pirates plotting in the bay were also heightening their first viewing of Torquay. Walking along the Strand which bordered the sea and was open to the harbour, they could see the quays which made it a year round haven for shipping.

Seeing palm trees, Thomas remarked to those listening, "They call this the *Italy of England.*"

"I hear that a lot of people come here for their health, mostly those with the consumption. I've heard it called the *Belle of Health Resorts,*" responded his sister, Elizabeth.

"Pa, why do we have to pay at those little round houses?" asked James.

"Well, son, those are toll booths and that's to help pay for the turnpikes. They pay to keep the roads better." John doubted the sense of his own words, thinking he and the neighbours in East Allington had worked together with their own carts and tools to keep the roads in better shape than these turnpikes.

"Now there's a wonderful looking terrace of houses!" exclaimed John. He was referring to the Hesketh Crescent on Meadfoot Sea Lane. Their graceful curve had full view of the sea below them in an exclusive residential area meant for the rich.

"Wouldn't ya like to be seated at one of those windows Ma, with nothing to do but some needlework?" said John, trying to cheer his mother.

"Ah, quit yer jesting, John. Work in the laundry more likely," and Mary resolutely climbed down when the cart next stopped at the bottom of a very large hill. She watched anxiously as the sideboard swung from side to side, clunking against the barrels as the wheels skidded in six inches of thick mud.

The cart creaked and groaned to a weary halt at their destination.

"Well, this must be it, eh, Mary? We're at number two. We'll soon get to know our neighbours," John remarked.

"Oh, Ma! Look at that quaint, old thatched roofed cottage across the street," exclaimed a delighted Elizabeth. "And all the trees along the lane that goes right up the hill."

"We're lucky we don't have those steep cliffs facing our place like the cottages further along the curve," added Thomas, trying to imitate Elizabeth's optimistic tone.

"Well, I guess we may get used to this busy roadway right out the front door," conceded Mary.

With time they would become used to it. Theirs was the second of about a dozen in the row. A new way of life was beginning for them all.

III

Once there had been great massive oaks on these hills, but these must have been used for early ship building. There had been much tree planting on the hillsides since, and all in all, it was a beautiful town. The sea provided a taste in the air unlike the surrounding fields of home, and the elegant homes and gardens rendered a delightful setting. Thomas, who had shared with his family the idea of him becoming a sawyer, was delighted with the wooded areas to the north of St. Marychurch. John realized Thomas was feeling a need to be on his own soon, and settle down.

There were plenty of competitors for jobs in masonry, plastering, marble cutting, tile setting and decorating, but there was still work to be had. New hotels were being built once it was found that the seaside Royal Hotel, Belgrave and Torbay hotels were inadequate to accommodate all the wealthy wintering in town. It was an exciting time to learn the trades in Torquay.

three

Pope Family: Paignton, Devonshire: 1852

William Pope = Elizabeth Narramore
(1799-)   (1805-)

| | | | | | | | | |
Mary Narramore =Samuel Jerman   William   George   James   Nicolas   John   **Elizabeth Ann**   William
(1823-) | (1821-)   (1829-1846)   (1845-)   (1849-)

| | | |
William James   Edward   Sarah   Hannah Jane
(1847-)   (1848-)   (1851-)   (1852-)

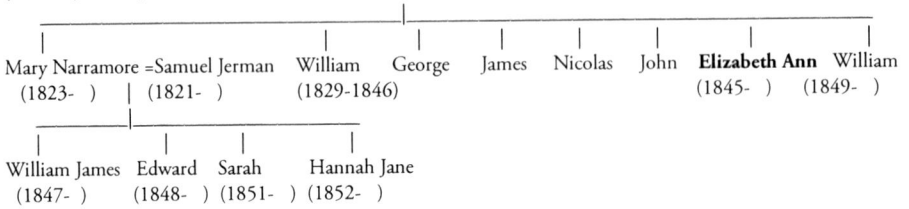

The beach at Paignton, Devon.

SOUTH OF TORQUAY, THE VILLAGES WERE NOT AS APPEALING AS TORQUAY. FEWER fashionable homes dotted the coast. Its hillsides gently meandered away from the coast, and along with it, the town of Paignton. Only the Torbay House stood firmly on the seashore. Once a hotel, it now slumbered as a boarding house. Nothing much had come of the plans to develop its harbour. Mary Pope Jerman was somewhat concerned with the lack of new construction and her husband's trade. Samuel and his father before him had been carpenters.

"Oh, Elizabeth Ann, can you get Hannah from her basket? She'll be needin' a change. I would just like to get this bit of sewing done for Mrs. Bridgeman before your uncle gets home if I can." Her sons William and Edward were rolling stones along the path in front of the cottage, on the lookout for their father's return. Seven-year-old Elizabeth Ann Pope from Torquay, visiting her sister Mary, seemed happy to supervise her nieces and nephews. She had the main care of her three-year-old brother at home, a task she took to naturally. Although there were twenty-two years difference in age between Mary and Elizabeth Ann, they had a special bond as the only two daughters of William and Elizabeth Pope. Six boys were between them, and William, the seventh brother, came after Elizabeth Ann.

"Ma put our brother George's name in the family Bible, Mary. It says he sailed out of Dartmouth on April 14, 1852. Does that mean he isn't coming back?"

"Oh, I don't think that is quite true. I'm sure that sometime Mother will hear from him. Life on the sea is dangerous though, and I think Mother will want to remember the date he left." Mary looked at Elizabeth Ann kindly. She was a contemplative young lass, unlike herself who was inclined to be more lively, more animated, until recently when her fourth child was born. She seemed so tired.

"Our father is quite busy with the road construction and he thinks there could be more work for Samuel in Torquay. It would be lovely to have you close," said Elizabeth Ann, rocking the cleaned up Hannah to sleep.

Mary smiled at her sister. The way she was feeling it would be wonderful to have an extra pair of hands to help. Mary had a growing concern with her health, and hoped it was just tiredness from having four babies in five years. She feared a cholera outbreak as there had been in Exeter not long ago, and wished for the experienced help of her mother. Yet Mary and Elizabeth Ann's mother was needed to help in her husband's business, and she had her own three- year-old son to care for.

"I don't believe Samuel will be thinking of moving anytime soon. His father did work for the lord of the manor in Paignton, George Templer, you know. There are always some repairs or construction projects at these large homes. Don't you worry now about your brother-in-law. He'll do just fine. He's a good carpenter," proudly explained Mary to her sister. Today, Samuel was down at the Crown and Anchor Inn where the Torbay area court was being held. His friend was being brought up for some misdemeanour which Samuel had felt was a falsified case by the neighbour, and he was there to offer support.

Mary grew wistful as she watched her two boys, who treated her so often with thoughtful gestures, that she soon forgot her fatigue.

II

In the middle of the night, Elizabeth tiptoed up the creaking steps to Mary and Samuel's room. She hated troubling her exhausted sister, but she just didn't know what else to do. She was dead on her feet herself, and could not get Sarah to settle. She had been crying and whimpering for hours. Now the hint of dawn was peeking over the horizon.

"Psst, Mary?"

"Come in, Elizabeth Ann. I'm awake. Hannah was hungry, but I think she's finished." Mary shifted the sleeping infant, covering her depleted breasts, and rose to accompany Elizabeth Ann, leaving the snoring Samuel with his infant daughter.

"I'm sorry, Mary, but Sarah just wouldn't settle. She's cried all night." Mary's weary eyes could hardly focus on her sister's exhausted face, but she gently put her arm around Elizabeth Ann as they made their way to the warm kitchen.

"It's nothing to do with you, Elizabeth Ann. She hasn't been sleeping well since Hannah was born. I wonder what sickness she might have. Are you feeling well enough to warm some milk for us all?"

The two sat and had small cups of warm milk, and tried to encourage Sarah to drink some as well.

"We have to get our strength up for the baptism today," cheerfully stated a revived Elizabeth Ann.

"Yes, we have to keep our strength up for the baptism," mumbled Mary.

Suddenly, she crumpled onto the floor. Baby Sarah was in shock, having slowly dropped to the floor from her mother's arms just as Mary collapsed. Then she let out a holler that woke Edward, bringing him out of the back room.

"Go and get yer da, Edward. Yer mother's fainted. Hurry!" Elizabeth had to direct a confused Edward towards the stairs.

"Mary, are you awake? Are you all right?" Elizabeth Ann bent closer to her sister, a screaming Sarah in her arms.

Mary groaned. She didn't want to alarm Elizabeth Ann, but she needed a doctor. Surely Samuel would allow a doctor's visit this time, despite the cost.

"Just take care of Sarah. Can you do that, Elizabeth Ann?" and Mary's head fell weakly to the side.

Samuel entered the room carrying infant Hannah. Edward followed slowly. He had been frightened to see his mother and baby Sarah lying on the floor.

"Edward, go and wake your brother," commanded his father. "Elizabeth Ann, what happened?" Elizabeth Ann began to blubber incoherently about Sarah, milk, and Mary falling.

"Don't be anxious, Elizabeth Ann. This has happened before. She will soon wake up. Here, Edward, take Hannah and hold her by the stove, and William you add some coals. I'm getting the doctor," and without adding more than a shirt, Samuel was out the door gone for the doctor.

Both Hannah and Sarah had settled down somewhat when Samuel and the doctor arrived. Mary was still lying on the floor, but moaning now. Elizabeth Ann didn't see how they were going to be able to have the baptism now.

"She shouldn't try to walk, Samuel. Your wife is in a severe state of exhaustion. I don't like her colour." The doctor turned to Elizabeth Ann. "Can you make everyone a nice cup of tea, dear? Thank you."

The doctor pulled Samuel over to the doorway on his way out. They talked in low tones. Samuel gasped, but turned before Elizabeth Ann could hear anything further. When the doctor left, Samuel kept his back to them all for a few moments.

"The tea is ready, Uncle Samuel. I thought the doctor wanted a cup of tea so I used the good cups," explained Elizabeth Ann. She felt she needed to be older at this moment, but didn't know how she would be able to grow up quickly enough to meet this adult situation. She couldn't possibly look after a sick Sarah, an infant Hannah, and her sick sister as well as William and Edward, although they were good boys.

"Oh, that's fine, Elizabeth Ann. We'll have tea, and hope Mary here revives a little. Let's put a shawl on her, Edward. I'll get my sister Jane the moment it gets light. William, here let me hold Hannah," and Samuel pulled his shoulders up and sipped his tea, praying that Mary would soon revive.

III

Later that morning, with the help of Jane and a neighbour friend, they managed to get Mary into a small open carriage. Mary held Hannah on their way to the baptism at the nearby parish church. Samuel held Mary's arm over the side of the carriage, Jane carried a slightly fevered Sarah, and Elizabeth Ann took the hands of William and Edward, following the cheerless procession. Hannah Jane Jerman was baptized the fourth of August, 1852.

Jane and Elizabeth Ann were up preparing breakfast for the boys the following morning, when Samuel came down the stairs slowly.

"Jane, I'm getting the doctor. Will you see to Hannah?" He passed the infant over to his sister and headed out the door.

"Shouldn't you hurry, Samuel?" she inquired, but realized the situation when he slightly turned his shaking head.

Elizabeth Ann was stricken. She suddenly realized the state of affairs and turned to hug Jane for some comfort.

"We must be brave, Elizabeth Ann. The family will still need their breakfast, and we must see if Hannah will take any gruel. If she refuses, we may have to try to find a wet nurse temporarily. William and Edward, wash your hands, please." The boys were playing roughly in the hall, but came immediately to do as their aunt commanded. Elizabeth Ann thought, I wish they listened and obeyed me that quick.

IV

Elizabeth Ann was still with the Jerman family along with Jane two months after Mary's sudden death, when Sarah began getting worse. Her fever could not be brought down, so the doctor was called yet again.

"This child may have a contagious disease, Jane. We can't be sure of what Mary died, but this little one will soon be joining her mother. Best to keep her isolated and the children away from her," he said looking directly at Elizabeth Ann. "Only go in when you think necessary."

Elizabeth Ann was about to go flying after him. She wanted to pound on his back. How could he let this happen? She took one glance at her aunt, and stopped herself. She wanted then to weep as never before, but heard her aunt's voice speaking to her.

"We need to be brave, Elizabeth Ann", so she straightened up her shoulders and turned to look after baby Hannah.

Later that afternoon, Jane sat down beside Elizabeth Ann who was having some success in feeding Hannah gruel.

"You've had a big responsibility here Elizabeth. I know it's been hard, but you are such a big help," said Aunt Jane, putting her arm around Elizabeth Ann's shoulder. The doctor had just left after sadly handing Sarah's death certificate to Jane.

"I wasn't a big help when my s-s-ister asked m-me to take care of S-s-sarah, was I?"

"Oh, Elizabeth Ann, you did the best you could, but little Sarah was already sick before you arrived. She's in heaven now with her mother, God rest their souls. I believe your sister would think you have been doing a fine job. Now what do you think about taking William and Edward home to Torquay with you for a while? Then I can help your uncle try to manage things here. He loved your sister very much, you know, and he will need help."

four

HANNAFORD FAMILY: ST. MARYCHURCH-TORQUAY, DEVONSHIRE: 1856

John Hannaford = Mary Miller
(1806-)   (1805 -)

| | | | | | |
Thomas Miller =Sarah   Elizabeth Ann   John =Mary   **Robert** = Elizabeth Ann   James =Elizabeth   **Alfred M**

| | | | | | | | | | |
Mary Elizabeth William John   James Robert George S.T   Emily Louisa   **Charles**   John
                                                    (1866-)   (1865-1866)   (1870-)

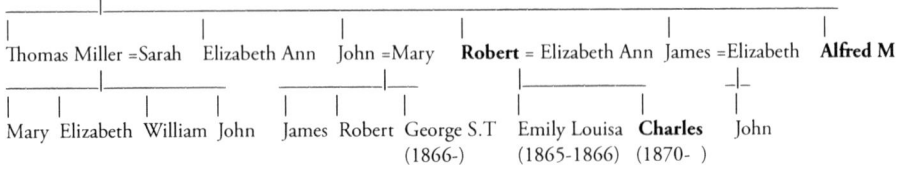

#2 Daizon Cottage, Torquay, Devon.

"Pa, we need to take Catto Road then St. Marychurch Road to get to church, or it means walking a long way down the hill and then back up to the church," instructed young John.

"Yes, we would hate to have to walk up any more of these steep hills than needs be, now would we? My legs twitch and ache at night enough to keep the devil himself awake," joked their father. One thing John noticed about going anywhere in St. Marychurch or Torquay were the steep hills, everywhere. Walking was difficult, but carriages had no easy time of it either, swaying violently from side to side in the ruts.

"Did ya know this used to be an ancient Saxon settlement, and the church is the third one built right on the same site?" Robert apparently enjoyed his ability to remember facts taught at school. The family, except his mother, were on their way to Sunday Evensong.

"There's Thomas and Sarah, Pa. Can I go in with them?" pleaded Robert. John nodded, and Robert, quickly followed by James, running back to the gate to walk with their brother Thomas and his new wife Sarah. The entire churchyard was fenced. The back gate through the graveyard was the closest to their homes so it was the one most frequented.

"Where's Mother, young feller?" Thomas asked. Robert paused briefly, glancing at Sarah's bulging middle and explained to his brother.

"She had some stomach pains, and Pa thinks she should rest this evening 'cause she's been working so much. She and Elizabeth have been washing and scrubbing heaps of clothes for folks."

The family gathered near the side entrance of the church where a number of the congregation were talking exuberantly, discussing the bishop's attendance today at St. Mary's. John Hannaford stood slightly apart, listening. Two of his sons were hoping to work with one of the parishioners, William Smith, as labourers and later apprentice for the plasterer. The congregation was friendly, but not yet familiar. The church building was grand, but not comfortable. Young Alfred was only five and held John Hannaford's waistcoat as they entered the church.

II

Pope and Hannaford Families: St. Marychurch- Torquay Devonshire: 1865

Robert told his mother his news first, privately.

"Elizabeth Pope and I are getting married, Mother. After all, I'm twenty-one."

"Seems quick, son. Is there a child on the way?" she asked sternly. Robert held her gaze and didn't answer. There wasn't as far as he knew, but he also knew there could be. He had promised her marriage months ago and he knew she would make a loving and capable wife. He would really like to have Elizabeth with him in their own bed instead of having to find excuses to be together. He worked long hours plastering new buildings being constructed and wished to spend his other time with Elizabeth Ann.

"I'm working steady now, Ma. The plastering business is going well. We can afford to rent a little cottage soon, but could we stay here for a bit? You'll like Elizabeth when you get to know her. Can you tell Pa?"

"No such thing. You'll tell him yerself and see what he thinks." She felt he was somewhat impulsive, suddenly coming to this decision, but perhaps it had been in the planning for some time and she just didn't know about it. "I'll ask God to bless you, no matter what," she said giving her son a reassuring smile. He was such a hardworking lad so she didn't foresee any real problems. John was enjoying his grandchildren so he would be happy with more. Whenever they appeared, he greeted each with a big hug and smile. He even played games with them at times. She was almost jealous of his ability to have fun with them while she fed and cleaned them.

"Your father had to work so hard when we lived in East Allington. I mean he works hard now, but at least at the end of a job he gets some pay. He doesn't have to work 14 hour days. I hope you don't feel he should have spent more time with you," said Mary. "You had as much attention as anyone."

"Ah, no, Ma. I had a good time as a lad. Do ya think Pa seems to be tired and coughing more in the past week? I know he says it's much easier than being a farm hand, but I think he works too hard. He's always got somewhere to go to work up a garden, yet I'm glad we moved, aren't you?"

Mary paused only briefly. "Yes, of course I'm glad. I couldn't have earned a living as a laundress in the village. It's great to be able to put such plentiful food on the table. I still miss the family though."

III

Over on Fore Street Elizabeth Ann Pope called into her mother's room. The young lady had blossomed in the years since she helped to take care of her deceased older sister's family.

"Ma, there's a gentleman here to see ya about a shipment of lime." Elizabeth Ann's father had been a contractor for repairing the turnpike roads and this had provided employment for the family until his death in 1857. Since then, his wife Elizabeth had continued to sell lime, her son William Henry and grandson

Edward Jerman assisting as carters. Elizabeth Ann had the main responsibility of running the house, now three rooms above the stores on Fore Street.

"I hope that brother of yours is not wandering off with his cousin Edward instead of making his deliveries." Elizabeth was tempted to start dwelling on her daughter Mary's death, but knew that Mary and Sarah's deaths had upset Elizabeth Ann who had help nurse them. Edward was an everyday reminder of Mary.

"Thank ya, Elizabeth Ann. I'll see to him right away. I know you'll be wanting to ge' yourself ready to see that young Hannaford boy this evening. Can ya finish those ledgers for me before ya go, and I'll see ya later?"

Elizabeth Ann hummed while she finished the bookkeeping for her mother, smiling inwardly about the prospects of seeing Robert again this week. Once finished, she untied her soiled apron, smoothed her hair back in its traditional bun, part in the middle, and hurried down the steps to the street. She enjoyed the bustle of people coming and going, the neighbours chatting in the street as she headed to the largest tree in the churchyard where she and Robert would meet.

She might be early, but she was keen on discussing more about the Plymouth Brethren, the Wesleyan Methodists, and her Baptist chapel. She viewed the Church of England building with its thick, cold stone walls, tall steeple, and surrounding grounds. Their little meeting house for Baptists was really a cottage, but the members were joyous in their singing, plain in their dress, and friendly in their outreach. She was secure in her self-disciplined approach to life and strong sense of duty.

Elizabeth Ann became anxious when Robert didn't appear. She peered up and down Fore Street and through the churchyard until it was too dark and damp to wait any longer.

IV

Thomas motioned to his mother Mary who was seated at his father's bedside, indicating that he would take over the night watch, although he doubted that it would be long now. Alfred sat in silence with his brothers and families. Robert was torn with awaiting his father's likely death, or going to meet Elizabeth Ann, who would by now be mighty concerned. She would understand when she found out, but he had no way of letting her know the circumstances.

"He's having such a hard time getting his breath, but I think his fever is down," reported Thomas to the family a few hours later. "I don't think he will last 'til morning, Robert. You should be ready to get the doctor."

Thomas sighed. He loved his pa. They had always had a special bond as father and oldest son. He had watched his father spin homemade wooden tops, or pick up stones while clapping his hands with the grandchildren. The rain rattled the window, and Thomas became aware that his father's breathing was even shallower than earlier. He knew that his father believed in that far off heavenly peace, providing God did not judge him too harshly, and his dear Mary would join him when God saw fit.

"Wa-ader," came a raspy whisper.

"Right here, Pa. Let me tip your head. Ya know yer've been a good pa to me and the boys." Thomas bent his head to listen and could not hear or feel breathing. He tried lifting his father's hand, but it was limp and heavy. He pushed the stool back from the bedside as he got up to inform his mother and brothers. Thus ended the tenth of June, 1865.

V

Two days later, Robert and his brothers were sitting in the kitchen with his mother, who, having finished weeping all the tears she had over the loss of her dear husband John, took a sip of tepid tea. Thomas' wife Sarah had made the tea, cut slices of bread and pieces of cheese for their afternoon meal. It had been a quiet funeral with just family present, the vicar saying a few words as the plain coffin was lowered into the red earth of the common burial ground.

Friends and relatives had been in last evening for the wake. John's body had been laid out in the front parlour, the boys all taking turns keeping watch nothing disturbed him. They helped themselves to small portions of port out of the bottle on the sideboard. Many friends John had worked with came to say their solemn goodbyes, then make a quick stop in the kitchen to express sympathy to the women. In East Allington the entire village would have stopped by and stayed longer than what was good for them. Nevertheless, it was late by the time Mary went to sleep. She felt she had aged greatly since just last week, but found solace in knowing her boys were good boys. They all worked hard to keep their own families fed and happy.

"I heard that Mallock finally is going to allow his relative to build on the estate, up on Seaway Lane," commented young Alfred.

"It's about time there was a little less control by the gentry. They're not going to be able to hold onto all their estate lands forever. The population is expanding, and more houses for workers are needed. I mean decent homes," replied Thomas.

"That may be true, but it's going to take time. I hear that Sir Palk is nearly ready to move into their Manor House on Lincombe Hill," said Robert.

"All this talk of the rich is only going to make you envious. You know we're plain folk and it's no good talking about the affairs of the rich." Mary was suddenly feeling contrary, and rose to get a fresh cup of hot tea.

"Ah, Ma, we didna' mean any harm. It's just talk. We're happy with what we got. We just like to be atop of what's going on in the town. There's something new going on all the time," soothed Robert.

VI

Robert grasped Elizabeth Ann Pope's hand. He thought what a coincidence it was that his younger brother, James, had married a different Elizabeth Pope, almost a year ago now. Robert and Elizabeth Ann had been having the discussion about where to marry for weeks, probably months. It was already halfway through the summer of 1865 and Robert had taken some time to get over his father's death.

"We could go away to Newton Abbot to the registrar's office," suggested Robert.

"I had hoped to have a preacher marry us."

"You know I can't abide that Baptist preacher you're so taken with. But we need to be doing something soon." Robert glanced down at Elizabeth Ann smoothing the folds of her dark dress over her enlarging belly. She so looked forward to having a home with Robert and this new little one. Both were twenty-one and of full age, so they could go to the registry office if that was what Robert wanted. She wiped the perspiration off her forehead, and slowed as they came to the crest of the hill.

Robert pressed her. "Let's get on the train and just go. I'll ask William for the afternoon off, and if you meet me down at the South Park Hotel with clean clothes we can leave by the two o'clock train and we'll be there and back before anyone notices. I would like the whole day, but Will's got plastering jobs lined up for months ahead for us. James, Alf and I are fortunate to be part of the trade now."

Elizabeth Ann agreed, both that they should marry as soon as possible and that Robert and his brothers were fortunate to be working with such an esteemed plastering business. Late on August the eleventh, they signed their names in the marriage register at Newton Abbot. Robert surprised Elizabeth Ann by taking her to a café for a light supper before returning to Torquay. He was concerned that her stomach might become upset without food, and he himself had had little to eat since breakfast early that morning.

"I think we might have Laurel Cottage to let shortly. It will be a good idea to get moved in so we can settle in before the baby comes. Thomas's Sarah wants to know if you need a few baby wrappings and nightgowns for December. She figures she won't need them for a while."

"Oh, that would be lovely. Please tell her thank you, and when she comes up to the shops, maybe she could stop in for a cuppa. I haven't seen Sarah in weeks. Ma will be pleased to see her."

five

ROBERT AND ELIZABETH ANN GREATLY ANTICIPATED THE BIRTH OF THEIR FIRST child. Elizabeth Ann knit little sweaters and leggings and hand-stitched little nightgowns while she waited. At last, Emily Louisa was born on a cold December day after much struggle to get into the world. Elizabeth Ann spent as much time holding her wee daughter as she could, but she could do nothing when illness struck and in September the following year, nine-month-old Emily died. Elizabeth Ann folded up the wrappings and nightgowns to return to Sarah. She didn't want them lying around as a reminder. The drawer went back into the dresser, and Elizabeth sluggishly went about washing dishes, shopping in the market, and mending clothes. She was tearful and lonely. She wanted company and awaited Robert's return each evening. After the evening meal one night, Robert came over to her with her father's family Bible. The thick, leather bound Bible was not a very grand one, only eight inches by six inches without picture plates in it. Impressed into the centre of the cover was a crest: SOCIETY FOR PROMOTING CHRISTIAN KNOWLEDGE 1698.

"I think it's time we made the entry for Emily," he simply said handing her a pencil stub. Elizabeth Ann looked at the first entry written by her father; *1834 December 25 William Pope His book*. She glanced to the opening in the middle of the first page inside the cover and wrote "*Emily Louisa Hannaford Died 1st Sept 1866 buried the 5th of September*." Tears welled up in her eyes as she thought of the gift of Emily's short life, and how numb she still felt this Christmas season. Robert gently took the pencil stub and closed the Bible's cover, replacing it carefully on the sideboard's lower shelf. He remembered the day his brothers had moved this sideboard from East Allington into his parents' cottage nearly a dozen years ago. How carefree he had felt in those days.

"We have a big job coming up at the new bank building down in Torquay. Smith wants me to come to the yard in Coomb Paffard to load the scaffolding boards and bags of lime. I said I would go early, at about half-six, so I need to get up a bit earlier. Bickel is having some difficulty with getting the quality of marble he wants for the floors and counters. With so much demand for marble these days it's hard to get what the big businesses are asking for."

Elizabeth nodded in agreement and picked up her mending from the wicker basket by her chair. She had given up knitting for the time being, having carefully folding the knitted jumpers, blankets, and nighties she had made for Emily in used brown paper, which she tied with a bit of string. Soon she hoped she would need them again.

It had been years since her sister Mary's death, yet she knew that her mother still thought of her daughter and her little granddaughter Sarah as well as two sons who had died before Elizabeth Ann was born. Their names were entered into the family Bible. Elizabeth Ann felt sad for her mother, for all mothers of the time who had lost not just one child, but so many along the years. Even the rich were not exempt from losing children during birth or to childhood diseases or accidents. She knew she must carry on and stop brooding over losses she knew were in the Lord's plan.

Alfred tapped on the door, somewhat out of breath. Elizabeth Ann and Robert looked up from their supper. Alf was all excited, his newly grown moustache bristling above his lips.

"Did ya hear? William Pengelly found some old human bones down in the Kent Cavern. They think they must be thousands of years old." Robert nodded in suppressed surprise, taken unaware by the news.

"Well, I wonder if that doesn't mean Mr. Darwin will be paying Torquay another visit. His views are heretical!" firmly exclaimed Elizabeth Ann. Robert nodded in agreement.

"There hasn't been this much excitement on the coast since the Paignton riots when the mobs were fighting for a piece of the half-ton pudding at the railway opening celebrations!" Alf, satisfied he had been the first to bring Robert the news, backed out the door, hat in hand.

II

Years passed before Elizabeth Ann gave birth, this time to a healthy, strong boy.

"I'd like us to call him Charles, if that pleases you," Robert said to his exhausted wife. She nodded. They smiled at each other in relief and hope.

"Charles Henry, then. Thank ya so much, Bessie." Elizabeth Ann spoke to a large woman bustling between the kitchen and bedroom with baby wraps, hot water and wet bedding.

"Ah, lass, the pleasure is mine to be sure, and you be taking your ease now. Come on, Robert, out with ye to the water pump for fresh water to make us a nice cuppa'," answered the Irish midwife.

Elizabeth Ann sighed, content to be alone with her beautiful son who was already hungrily nursing. Tears of relief and exhaustion dripped down her cheeks. She had watched over the past four years while so many of her nieces and nephews were born and survived. Both Robert and her brothers had all added to their families. The delighted looks on the grandmothers' faces were a painful reminder of what she was lacking. Now, however, she lovingly gazed at the sleeping bundle she held, and dreamily thanked God for the wonder of giving birth, as she drifted off to sleep.

Robert entered their two room cottage and quietly peered into the bedroom. He looked with pleasure at his healthy baby Charles, and prayed God would see him through to old age. He imagined briefly the potential lineage that could be recorded in the family Bible, documenting life and death in years ahead. Baby Charles cried, breaking Robert's moment of reverie.

"He looks a bit like me, but I think he will be more handsome," he whispered to his slumbering wife. Robert was working long hours these days. William Kitson, who was in charge of the Palk estate, was one of the men with enough sense to plan for town development. Kitson had his hand in banking and was also a lawyer. He had survived the collapse of a Newton Abbot Bank in days when banking was a risky business. He did help developers and contractors with loans from his Torbay Bank, as well as selling the land of Sir Palk. He tried to ensure they were quality homes that were being built, and skilled tradesmen had flocked to the area, but despite his desire for growth, he did think a public bath for the workers was unnecessary and extravagant.

Robert was concerned there might be a slowdown in the construction business soon. No new turnpikes had been constructed since the Belgrave Road of 1860. Apparently, from the newspaper reports he read, the population in Devon was down. Many had been flocking north to the industrial towns of the Midlands, or the city of London for improved business prospects. Farming methods had improved a few decades before with crop rotations, but still there seemed to be fewer labourers needed in farming districts. Robert was not sorry his father had brought the family to Torquay. He quite liked the place. His brother Alfred, though, could talk of nothing but the business opportunities in Canada.

"Alfred has gone to apply for his passport this afternoon," offered Robert.

"Well, I hope he enjoys the journey. I hear so many get sick and there are so many that die on the way over."

"Things have improved with the steamers they have now, Elizabeth. It takes less than a month and the berths, I hear, are quite comfortable." Robert left it at that for the time being. He hoped to join his brother soon and start up their own plastering business.

six

HANNAFORD FAMILY: TORQUAY, DEVONSHIRE: 1870S

ELIZABETH ANN WOULDN'T HAVE GIVEN MUCH THOUGHT TO EMIGRATING, BUT she had heard of many others who knew someone leaving for North America, Australia, or New Zealand. Looking at her tiny garden and familiar lane, she knew it would be a difficult change; people talked of huge gardens and vast space in Canada. They talked of modern homes with indoor water closets. They talked of bountiful business and building opportunities for new immigrants. They never mentioned cold, harsh winters, or mud-filled streets.

"Robert, I've been thinking for the last little while that maybe I should agree to go to Canada. I know how much Alfred would like you to join him."

"Elizabeth Ann, dear," was Robert's cheerful reply, "I've already made our passport application in the hopes that you would soon agree. I think you might want to inspect this young lady Alf talks so much about. She and her parents only recently emigrated themselves. How soon would you like to go?"

Elizabeth smiled and ruffled the tawny hair of their four-year-old son.

"I'd like a few weeks to try to get down to Dartmouth to see my brother and family. Then we will need some time to pack these things up. How much can we take with us?"

"I think we're limited to one trunk, so the furnishings will have to stay. You might see if any of our brothers or their wives wants anything. We will have to make do to start, but I want to build us our own house and run our own business. Alf says this is the opportune time for beginning our own plastering business. Toronto, from what I hear, is booming."

Elizabeth began immediately to plan what things to take. The first things in the trunk were a few baby items she would hopefully need in the future. Then some extra pieces of fabric and bedding were carefully arranged in the bottom. Long before she had completed packing, the trunk was full to overflowing. She hated to ask Robert to pay the extra expense of shipping an additional trunk, so she began further sorting. She was torn between her grandmother Pope's shawl and her father's baptismal gown. There were so many things she had grown to depend on using; she almost didn't know what to leave, and what to keep. What would she need?

Her mother entered the room with the family Bible in her hands. She placed it in Elizabeth Ann's hands and tried hard to keep the quiver out of her voice. Elizabeth Ann thought perhaps one of the boys would want it for their boys to pass on, but her mother had given it to her. Perhaps when she saw William next, she would ask him if he would like it. He might not remain a widower forever.

"I suppose you might be needing all your warm woollen undergarments. I hear it's mighty cold in that country." She regretted Elizabeth Ann and Robert's move, but even more so, she would miss young Charles. He had a great deal of liveliness in him, and was such a joy to the household.

"Grandma, can you come with us? We can make room in Canada. It's a big, big country and we'll go on a big, big boat. Can you come?" he asked, only slightly deflated when she shook her head. She didn't care for the idea of winters where snow fell on the ground and actually stayed around for weeks. How would her family bear it? They might even encounter native Indians, or those wild, drinking Irish men.

II

HANNAFORD FAMILY: ENGLAND TO MONTREAL TO TORONTO, ONTARIO: 1870

The journey across the ocean to the harbour at Montreal was not as terrible as Elizabeth Ann had feared. Their family arrived safely, passed through the busy but cheerful immigration officers and health inspectors, and were soon on their way to rooms in Toronto arranged for by Alfred, Robert's youngest brother. They were delighted with the gas lamps which lit the streets. Union Station, where the Grand Trunk Railway and Northern Railway of Canada converged in the city appeared new and very grand in scale. Canada had been a nation less than five years, but every effort to make Toronto an outstanding provincial capital was being made now that Ottawa was the official national capital.

Their first social engagement was to meet the parents of pretty Caroline Cornell, Alfred's bride-to-be. Not long immigrated themselves, they were happy to meet Robert, Elizabeth Ann and young Charles.

"Well, Elizabeth? What do you think?" inquired Robert of Elizabeth Ann back at the house.

"I think she seems very sensible, and being four years his senior is probably a good thing. She certainly has turned his head though. I hope marriage won't be too much of a shock for him. When will you view the house on Lumley Street? I hope there will be enough room for all of us."

"You will be surprised how big the house is. Compared with any house we ever lived in over in Devon, it is a palace. It's nearly new, has two levels and a root cellar, and a cellar for coal and wood, as well as a front and back garden where Charles can play. We will get to view the inside next week which is the week before the wedding. They celebrate Dominion Day here on July first. You need your rest now, and my, but it is warm, so while I go with Alfred to seek out some job prospects, you could lie down. I'll take Charles with me."

Robert and Alfred lost no time in finding their niche in the construction world. They were amazed at the number of individual houses with yard between them. Most of them had full basements or at least a belowground cellar. The streets were wide and they were straight. There were no centuries-old pathways to have to follow and the town planners had placed most of the streets on a grid. Youge Street was the town centre and business nucleus for the whole area and stretched to Barrie, miles north of the city. Roads which were often still impassable with mud made shipping most important.

Caroline, or Carrie as most of the family called her, and Elizabeth Ann quickly became friends, sharing the food preparation, laundry, housekeeping, and shopping. On market days Charles was happy to be with his mother and aunt, but other days he wanted children to play with. His wish was finally granted, but he was disappointed that when she arrived, she was so small.

"She's too small to play with. She smells," Charles complained. Mary Elizabeth Ann had been born into a cold, miserable November day. Her mother and aunt had plenty of bedding prepared, so she was cosy, but not yet a suitable playmate for Charles. He was making friends with other British immigrant families, and was so delighted with every snowfall that he soon forgot Bessie was too small to play with.

"You'll be having your first baby at a sensible time of year," commented Elizabeth. Carrie was very excited about her baby's expected arrival. Her cheeks glowed, and she was the picture of health. She and Alf smiled so frequently at each other, Charles gave to comment, "Pa, why are Uncle Alf and Aunt Carrie always looking at each other so funny?"

Robert smiled, but only cleared his throat.

III

"Oh, you have a big, healthy boy!" exclaimed Elizabeth Ann on the eighth of May 1874, only hours after Carrie had gone into labour.

"Alf will be so happy. Oh please let him in and he can see for himself," begged the perspiring Carrie. Alfred was indeed pleased, so much so that he started planning their next move.

"They say up the coast is even prettier, and the towns are a little smaller. We could use a little more space now, and a bigger garden."

Carrie and Elizabeth Ann looked at each other with mock horror, their eyes met in agreement; two young babies to look after and now the men already had a bigger garden planned for them!

"At least give Carrie time to recuperate after childbirth, Alf. Birthing is hard work," chided Elizabeth Ann. Within another year and a half, Elizabeth Ann and Carrie each held another new baby boy. Now there were five children between them. Elizabeth was concerned that her son William James, born two weeks after Carrie's Frank Arthur, was not gaining weight quickly, but soon after the births, the men found a house in Burlington, Halton County. The two Hannaford brothers' families happily expanded into the extra space of their new house. Bessie, nearly two, was babbling happily to year-and-a-half old Alfred, Charles was clamouring to be taught to read, and the babies all were exercising their lungs wanting to be fed. Sharing daily chores made time pass quickly for the women, and allowed the men time to focus on their business.

seven

HANNAFORD FAMILY: BURLINGTON, ONTARIO: 1875

Robert Hannaford = Elizabeth Ann Pope
(1844-)   (1845 -)

Emily Louisa	**Charles Henry**	Mary Elizabeth	William James	Arthur
(1865-1866)	(1870 -)	(1873 -)	(1875-1876)	(1877 -)

Alfred Hannaford = Caroline Cornell
(1851-)   (1847-)

Alfred Edward	Frank Arthur	Emily Louisa	Caroline Elizabeth
(1874-)	(1875 -)	(1877 -)	(1879-)

IT HAD BEEN A BUSY WINTER, WHEN TRAGEDY AGAIN STRUCK ROBERT AND Elizabeth Ann. William James, just over four months old, was not strong and succumbed in January of 1876 to what Doctor Richardson had identified as *enteritis*. With sadness, they buried his tiny body in the church graveyard, marked by a simple cross. Robert turned gently to close the whitewashed picket fence gate behind them, studying their infant son's resting place among many headstones. Someday he might return to place a marker.

Their home in the new town of Burlington was none-the-less comfortable and they all lived compatibly with the four busy young children supplying entertainment much of the time. Robert and Alfred were beginning to get contracts for a few larger buildings as well as homes. The new style of plastering required skilled labour to which they brought much practice. Recent immigrants often made do, or were pioneers in doing jobs themselves, still not able to afford luxuries such as paying skilled workmen to plaster. The Irish Catholics were now the largest ethnic group in Toronto, but the population that had been sprawling along the shore of Lake Ontario and creeping toward Hamilton, was mainly English. Villages were expanding all along the bay and down toward Welland, the canal, and the peninsula towards Niagara.

"Am I going to walk to school by myself today?" asked young Charles.

"I'm on my way to Aldershot today, so you'll get a ride to Central School. You need to come home sooner than yesterday young man. No stopping to pick apples with your friend on the way home," replied Robert.

"Ah, but those were good apples and we didn't have to climb up far to get them either. James's mother makes great applesauce and apple tarts. Can Mother make some?"

"We'll see. She and Aunt Carrie are busy with baking bread, preparing meals and keeping our clothes clean. You come home and help with the youngsters." Charles's shoulders slumped just a little, since he had been looking forward to fresh baked apple tarts. He would pick just a few more today after school, then his mother would have some to cook.

Alfred had convinced Robert to accept an invitation to join the Odd Fellows, one of the many new organizations created by the expanding population. They had turned down an invitation to join the Protestant Orangemen, the Foresters, and the Sons of England. Tonight they were just visitors, but it gave Elizabeth Ann and Carrie a little quiet time to sit and visit while mending.

"When do you think you might be due?" asked Carrie of Elizabeth Ann.

"I'm calculating about the middle of September, maybe the third week. I'm anxious, Carrie. I can't help but think of little Emily and William."

"I know you are, but we just have to pray that the good Lord will be willing to bring the next babies into the world safely." Carrie smiled self-consciously when Elizabeth raised her eyebrows interrogatively. Carrie continued.

"I wasn't going to say anything just yet, but I think my time will be around November. Won't we have a house full then! Maybe Alf is right in thinking we will need a larger place of our own, although I will sorely miss you. You're truly like a sister.

II

Two more healthy babies added to the joy of the 1877 Christmas season. Robert was proud of his new son Arthur, and Alfred was equally thrilled with his new daughter Emily Louisa. Seven-year-old Charles was somewhat curious about the infants that seemed to preoccupy everyone. He though, was a school boy, and enjoyed learning his letters and figures. He was thrilled with the new cloth-bound coloured booklet he had received as his sole Christmas gift.

"Can you listen to me read Papa?" He had eaten every bite of his Christmas goose with potatoes and dressing. He had extra caramel sauce on his Christmas pudding, and maybe needed to sit and rest up while reading his new book to his father.

"Alfred, can you hold Emily while I help Elizabeth Ann with finishing up the dishes?" Carrie entreated. Robert and Alfred pulled chairs from around the kitchen table and moved them and the children and babies into the sitting room where they could discuss business. Charles sat and read to his sister, Bessie.

"I have been taking a look at the new carriages they are producing down at the carriage factory. If we were to purchase our own, we could get out to some of the jobs in Freeman and Port Nelson. Brown's Wharf at La Salle Park doesn't seem as busy as last year. What do you think about the wharves at Wellington Square?" Alfred asked his brother.

"They seem to be shipping out a lot more lumber than wheat lately. Aldershot melons seem to have become mighty popular these days, and the apples are being shipped out as well," Robert replied, shying away from discussion of a new carriage.

"I believe they are producing and shipping much more grain from western Canada. The farms there are measured in sections -- by the mile. Here, a hundred acres is standard and the farmer has had to clear it first before it's workable. It seems a shame to cut all those big trees down, but we saw that in Devon too. Do you think that it's time to move on again, perhaps around the bay to Hamilton?"

"Things are comfortable here, Alfred and we've got to think of the womenfolk. I'd like to wait a year or two before we make any move. If you want, I can scout out the business directories for Hamilton and Niagara at the Mechanics Library and see what the prospects are."

Alfred twirled his moustache, now a thick, well-groomed handlebar under his nose.

"I think you're right. Things are going well. I know we need a little more living area than we have room for here and with six little ones it's a busy space, but I think the women have adjusted to the harsher weather and Charles seems happy at school."

"Did you hear how the population in Toronto has nearly doubled since we arrived in Canada less than five years ago?" continued Robert's relaxed conversation with his brother.

III

Summer was a happy time for the Hannafords. Cool breezes from the lake freshened the humid air, and walking became a pleasant past-time. The women had been anxious to get the family out for a stroll through the summer resort in the Brant House Park. Twenty acres of gardens, croquet lawns, ice cream parlours, and dance halls were a source of entertainment for tourists, or inhabitants. Being Baptist, the family shied away from the forbidden dance halls, but on this occasion they indulged in flavoured iced cream while strolling along the water's edge, watching folks row along the shoreline and taking in the view of the freshwater lake. Somewhere nearby there was a band performing.

"I miss the taste of the salt, don't you, Robert?" asked Elizabeth Ann.

"And the sound of the waves pounding against the rocks. At least we have plenty of fresh drinking water. We can see the bay almost to Niagara, but we can't see right across the lake, that's how big Lake Ontario is," commented Robert.

It was a rare afternoon that the men agreed to take time away from their work, but they had agreed upon this half day as a holiday for them all. Tomorrow would be church at Calvary Baptist on Locust Street, and quiet reading and rest in the peace of Sunday afternoon. There was to be a Sunday School picnic the following month. Most of the churches had outdoor gatherings in the good weather, and the wicker baskets were packed solidly with plenty of fresh bread, cold sliced meats, boiled eggs, cold potatoes with pickles, and newly in-season peaches. There were no fancy extras at home, but there was always plenty of food in this new country.

There were several industries such as the wire works and the Canada Powder Company plant on Cedar Springs Road which made gun powder for the Canadian Pacific Railway. The Burlington Brand Canning Company and Tip Top Canners worked at canning local fruit and vegetables. The Glover Basket Works provided baskets for the pickers. In 1854 the railway had brought more business to the area with the exportation of wheat. The wagons used to line up at the wharves, and grain elevators were busy. At one time Wellington Square in Burlington shipped more wheat than Hamilton, a much bigger city. By the late 1870s more mixed crops were being grown in the area and fewer were being shipped for export.

Alfred and Caroline welcomed their fourth child, a little girl into the household. Caroline Elizabeth was born in the fall of 1879 and then the families began planning a move in the near future to Hamilton where Robert and Alfred could expand their plastering business.

eight

Hannaford Family: Hamilton, Ontario: 1880s

"Well, Elizabeth, what do you think? " Robert asked his wife as she entered the kitchen. There was piped water out of a tap. There were gas lamps in each room. The table in the center of the kitchen at 76 Merrick Street in Hamilton was being filled with young children bringing in wooden boxes or cloth bags of kitchen utensils, clothing and items of importance for their establishment of a new home.

"Charles, you're the oldest, so you can sit here at the end next to me." Charles, now a serious lanky lad of eleven sat straight up on the bench in the prized position next to his father who would sit in the chair at the end. Bessie, now nine, sat brightly at the other end of the bench nearest her mother.

"Bessie, you can sit here so you can help your mother. Arthur, you sit next to Charles." Arthur, a small lad for his five years, climbed up on the bench between his older siblings, and looked across the table at a large basket with his youngest baby brother Robert in it. The baby looked very pink.

"Where are Aunt Carrie and Uncle Alf and cousins Alfred, Frank, Emily, Caroline, and Alice all goin'a sit?" inquired Arthur of his father.

"Oh, they have their own house now on Walnut Street. It's right next to the shed where we are keeping the carriages and materials for our business. You'll see them plenty once we get settled."

Robert glanced at his wife who was searching out bread and meat for a luncheon. She had been very quiet this morning while they moved their things into the new home, and Alfred and Carrie moved their family and belongings into a house several blocks away. Robert hoped that the separation of the families would not be too painful for Elizabeth Ann. They could not find a reasonably priced house adequate for two families or two houses closer together. Robert did have a surprise in store for her later, though, which he hoped would soothe the detachment.

II

Robert returned punctually at six o'clock one night, having put many hours into labouring over buckets of plaster, trowelling the rough plaster over wooden lath or gypsum board, and then when dry enough, smoothing off the top coat of plaster until all was covered with white. Much of this had to be done on ladders and on scaffolding which Alfred and he now owned. Tonight was the surprise the two brothers had planned.

"Children, get your sweaters on. Charles, you hold on to Arthur. Come, Mother. There is a surprise in store for you." Robert cheerfully gathered his family at the front step and led them down the street. Charles hoped it was ice cream or some other such treat. Elizabeth hoped it wasn't too far as her feet were aching and she was tired. They marched along a few street blocks, past large brick homes, past the church, and turned down Robinson Street. Ahead they could see Aunt Carrie and Uncle Alfred with the cousins. Elizabeth Ann became more and more curious as the row of homes turned into empty lots where weeds slumped wilting after a dry summer.

"What are we looking at, Pa?" wondered Arthur.

"Well," Robert answered, looking at Alfred, "this lot is going to be your new home someday and right next door Uncle Alf and Aunt Carrie and your cousins will live. We have plans to share the verandas as the two houses will be attached. Our houses in England were mostly attached, not separated like here."

Carrie and Elizabeth Ann clutched each other's hands with growing pleasure, and the children began to wade into the overgrown lot.

"If you approve, we just need you ladies to go down to the Registry Office where the High Bailiff of Hamilton, Peter Belfour, will sell you the land for five hundred dollars each. We will supply you each with one hundred dollars and they will hold the mortgages. You can choose which side of the lot you wish," offered Alfred.

"Oh, you make the choice, Carrie. It does not make the least bit of difference to me, as long as we are next-door neighbours."

The paperwork was completed on October 1, 1881. Caroline signed for the east half and Elizabeth Ann for the west half. Although it was years before the double house was actually built, the lot was trimmed up and gardened every summer. By this time Alfred and his family were living at 100 Robinson Street, so they were getting closer, they felt, to having their own home.

Suddenly, Robert John took sick at 16 months old. His mother did her best to nurse him back to health, but the doctor's visit gave no hope. Robert, desolate about this son, knew now he would have no namesake to continue the family. Elizabeth Ann refused to grieve this time. She remained stoic and placed all her attention on her three other children. She felt she could not weep for the young lad or a flood of grief would overwhelm her, sapping her of all strength.

III

Robert received a letter from his oldest brother Thomas, written by their oldest daughter, Mary, in neat, scholarly cursive. It was to inform them that their fourth born, John William, would be arriving on the *Phoenician* at the Port of Halifax. Within days now he would be arriving in Hamilton. Robert had promised he would board any newcomers to Canada. John could certainly find employment in the growing city. Business was steady for the Hannaford Brothers.

John William Hannaford, tall and lanky, was polite and independent. His family would soon be following him. Having been trained as a carriage maker, he shied away from the plastering business. Letters were scarce as few of his generation wrote or read well. Robert pried him for information about the family in England.

Soon Elizabeth Ann had her own letter from the old country.

"Robert, I've had exciting news! Read this letter from my brother William," Elizabeth Ann exclaimed the moment Robert entered the kitchen. He wiped the plaster dust his hands and sat down at his chair while he waited for his dinner.

"Well, he's finally made the decision to move here to Hamilton with his son George. You must have been very complimentary about the city to get him to leave his homeland. Where will he be staying?"

"Well, he's not coming alone. Apparently John and Susan Eden and their six children are coming as well. You know that John Eden and William are business partners now, so they have decided they will make the move next year in 1884. It will be so wonderful to have him here and George too. He'll be 14 by the time they get here."

IV

On October 8, 1884 Elizabeth Ann was waiting for the children to come home for a noon dinner. She was taking in the fresh air and sunshine at the doorway, when she thought she heard some sort of explosion in the distance. There were a few moments of reverberation, and then when it continued to be silent for the next few minutes, Elizabeth Ann shrugged her shoulders and returned to the kitchen.

"Elizabeth Ann," called Robert from the front hallway as he hung up his hat.

"In here, Robert," answered Elizabeth Ann.

"The Canada Powder Company in Burlington has blown up. There was a fire, and then the explosion. Four people were killed. Come on outside. You can still see the black cloud." Elizabeth Ann dried her hands on her apron and followed Robert to the street where other onlookers were facing northeast in the direction of Burlington. Some remaining puffs of the black cloud lingered.

"Well that is most likely the end of the Canada Powder Company. No doubt, though, the CPR will be using the dynamite explosives that have been developed," predicted Robert.

V

Every two years Caroline gave birth to another healthy baby girl. After baby Caroline in 1879, Alice Gertrude, Adeline Beatrice and Ellen Almyra made their appearances. This brought the number of children up to eight, and a busy household it was. Elizabeth Ann and her daughter Bessie often went to help out as did their Scottish friend, Mary Smith.

"I am worried about you, Carrie." Elizabeth anxiously sat by the bedside while Carrie nursed baby Ellen, born in 1886. "What does the doctor say is wrong?"

"He thinks there is an abscess on my lung that is not clearing up. I don't want you worrying Elizabeth. Alfred is doing enough of that. I don't know what I would do without you and Mary. I just feel so weak," she replied, softly patting Elizabeth's hand.

A few days following this, Robert came home later than usual. "Alfred looked grim when I met him at the door. It won't be much longer by the sounds of it. She's having difficulty breathing, and the doctor says there is nothing to be done but to make her comfortable. Mary is a godsend. She just takes those children under her wing as though they were her own. There is no doubt about her being a Presbyterian Scot though. She doesn't take any nonsense from any of them. Young Alfred and Frank are not sure how to behave. They know how seriously ill their mother is, yet they are trying to take it like little men. I would almost rather see them go in to her and have a good cry, than walk stiffly about holding in their dismay. Alf is not going to get over this easily."

Alfred had purchased a plot in the Hamilton Cemetery, and the family stood around the earth beside their mother's coffin as it was lowered into the earth. Robert's family intermingled with them around the open grave. Alfred's shoulders shook as he inwardly wept in the hot July sun. He had lost his dear wife, Carrie.

nine

Alfred Hannaford = Caroline Cornell
(1851-)   (1847-)
_____|_____ (con't. below)
| | | | |
Alfred Edward Frank Arthur   Emily Louisa   Caroline Elizabeth Alice Gertrude
(1874-)   (1875 -)   (1877 -)   (1879-)   (1881-)

                                    Alfred Hannaford = Caroline Cornell
                                    (1851-)   (1847-)
          (con't. from above)_____|_____
                                    | | |
                                    Robert   Adeline Beatrice Ellen Almyra
                                    (1882-1882) (1883-)   (1885-)

Charles and Robert (foreground) Hannaford.

CHARLES FELT HE HAD HAD ENOUGH SCHOOL, AND HIS FATHER WAS MORE THAN grateful for the extra pair of hands in the business. Alfred tried to keep busy, but he was beside himself with grief, and in the end made their friend, Mary, his wife. The children accepted their new mother with wide eyes, still grieving themselves, and somewhat unsure of what to expect. Within weeks, however, Mary was truly the woman of the house for all but Alfred Junior and Frank, who felt they didn't need a mother if they couldn't have their own. They made no complaints to their woeful father and in time accepted Mary as much as their loyalty allowed.

The plastering business was reaching a peak. There were more than a dozen plasterers in the city. The Hannaford Brothers were now incorporated, but still worked out of 76 Merrick Street where they could keep a carriage and their supplies.

"Well, Mother, what do you think of our advertisement?" Fifteen-year old Charles handed Elizabeth Ann the Vernon's Business Directory, showing her a half-page spread on page three of the 1889 edition. The population of Hamilton had risen to 60,000 by this time, and Might's, as well as Vernon's, was creating a Business Directory for each of the major cities in Ontario. Businesses were given the opportunity to advertize.

"*Hannaford Bros., Contractors and Plasterers*" she read aloud. "*Centre Flowers, Brackets, Enrichments, Panel Ceilings, Cornices, Capitols, Bosses, Blackboards, Etc. Modelling executed to order. Every description of plain and ornamental plastering done to order.* Isn't that wonderful? I like the medallion pictured. I wonder if your father can put one of those in our dining room at the new house." Charles smiled. He was glad to see his mother looking forward to the completion of the house down the street. Now that they were within a block, it seemed more real.

Elizabeth Ann had perked up somewhat when the two families moved into the new, double house. Alfred and Mary and their brood had expanded, totalling ten children for Alfred. Ethel Victoria and William Stanley Preston were now two and three-years- old, so there was always activity going on next door to distract Elizabeth Ann.

One evening after the dinner dishes had been cleared, washed and placed on an open shelf above the sink, Elizabeth Ann got out the letter from her brother James about the wife and children of their deceased brother John. She had just received it in the post.

"Robert, I just received news from Torquay. My sister-in-law Selina has died and now the youngest two girls, Harriett and Rosina, are in the Sydenham Terrace Orphanage in Babbicomb, St. Marychurch. Their sister Henrietta is working at the rectory in Siddington. That's way and gone up in Gloucester. Those poor girls. I'm so sorry we aren't there to help out. I hate to think of them without either of their parents and living in a horrid orphanage."

"Well, be grateful they are thirteen and fifteen, old enough to cope and they are together. At least they haven't become one of the home children, sent to Australia, or New Zealand. They would all be separated and placed in we don't know what kind of conditions. I've seen a few of the orphans from the Barnardo Home in England, and they are not treated too well out in the country. More like free labourers, although some are given decent living conditions. Probably preferable to what they came from."

Robert filled his pipe with fresh tobacco and pondered the situation. Here they were, parents with only half of their children living, and there his nieces were, children without parents. It was a cruel world. God had his plans though, and they were to go along with them. Not that a person didn't question the purpose of those plans sometimes. Robert thought he needed to change the subject.

"Did I tell you Alfred is thinking of running for the city council?"

"Really? He is so involved already, what with the lodges and so forth. How will he find time to run for council?" Elizabeth wondered. Men seem to have more time for these organizations than women, not that she was keen on joining anything. Helping with food preparation and missions support at James Street Baptist Church was enough to keep her busy.

"I'm quite certain he will step down from some of his offices. He won't be running in this upcoming election anyway."

II

HANNAFORD FAMILY: HAMILTON, ON: 1890s

"Father says we can take the whole day for the Sunday School picnic. Are we taking the train Thursday, Mother?" asked Arthur.

"Yes. We will need at least two hampers to carry the food, and the throws to sit on. Elizabeth is bringing umbrellas for the sun and your father is bringing two folding chairs. Aunt Mary and Uncle Alfred and the girls as well as Bill will be coming with us. I believe your uncle is having Alfred Junior and Frank take care of the shop for the morning. We'll flag down the train at Queen and Herkimer streets so we won't have too far to carry all of our things. I hope the weather will be sunny and warm. Ainsley Park can be breezy and cool."

"Can I bring the feed sacks for the races? Arthur asked.

"Yes, that's a good idea. Why don't you get them now so we don't forget them?"

""I won't forget them, Mother." Arthur scrambled off to the back shed.

Elizabeth Ann smiled at Arthur, knowing how much he looked forward to their church picnic. It was a break that most of the three hundred members of James Street Baptist church looked forward to: a day where extended families and friends would gather for speakers, food and games. The women had been baking and cooking for several days now in preparation for the big event on Thursday.

It was a beautiful day, just as the Reverend Boville had predicted. Alfred, Mary, the six girls and young Bill gathered at the front steps waiting for Robert, Elizabeth Ann, Charles, Arthur, and Bessie to join them. Other neighbouring Baptist families were already making their way to the nearest street crossing of the Hamilton-and-Dundas train. There was a festive atmosphere with everyone moving along with their hampers and belongings, looking forward to a church outing with the entire family.

Alfred Junior had finished up some paperwork and was helping his younger brother Frank clean up some buckets before they left to tidy themselves up and then join the family at the picnic.

"Come on there, Frank. Get a move on. We want to catch that 12:40 train or we'll miss the picnic," urged his brother. The train was already in sight when they came running up to the intersection at Herkimer, and then stood close to the tracks. The boys waved to friends in the third carriage, but they did not signal the driver to stop. Girls in wide hats with bows and ribbons laughed, and teenage boys whistled and shouted to each other.

Alfred suddenly made a leap to get on the train and Frank was about to follow suit, when he realized with horror that Alfred had missed his grasp, slipping under the carriage. Frank blinked with terror, dashing for his brother, just missing him, as Alfred made a few futile flails with his hand and went limp. The engineer stopped the train, horrified by the accident. Frank bent over his brother's broken body, now lifeless and still.

"I couldn't reach him. I couldn't catch him in time. I couldn't ...I couldn't save him!" Frank repeated hopelessly.

"They weren't signalling to stop. I didn't think they wanted to get on. Oh, God forgive me," moaned the engineer. Shocked faces peered out the open windows. A few younger children began to howl, anticipating delays, and sensing that the joy of the occasion had instantly changed. Several of the men from the group of picnickers got off the train and carefully lifted the body onto a picnic blanket, wrapping it carefully to prevent bystanders gawking at the bloody mess. They carried it down Queen to 232 Robinson Street while a few others gently led Frank by the shoulders towards home. He wanted to follow Alfred's body into his uncle's house, but they led him towards his own and stayed until the family could be notified.

At Ainsley Park, the Hannaford family clustered tightly together after people from the train gave them the terrible news along with their heartfelt sympathy. In numb confusion the Hannafords returned home. Alfred Sr. was most anxious to be with Frank, to find out what had happened, and to console him with what little emotional reserve he had. The Reverend Boville, Henry New, and Wilf Somerville returned from the park and went to 230 Robinson Street hoping to be able to offer solace to the shocked family.

Frank was beside himself with grief and guilt. Though everyone kept telling him it was not his fault, his mind kept replaying the sight of Alfred slipping under the wheels, the emphatic thud, the crunching of bones breaking, the squealing of steel against steel. Had he been accustomed to strong drink, he would have turned to it, trying to numb his nightmares that way. He eventually returned to the shop to try to relieve his heavy heart, but it was months before he had a full night's sleep.

Robert kept the Friday, July 11, 1890 *Hamilton Spectator* to himself where on the front page a full length column described the gruesome details. Elizabeth Ann and Bessie tried to help with meals and laundry while the family grieved and visited with friends who called on them offering sympathy. Robert and Charles tried running the business as usual. By now a number of young men were often employed to labour for the skilled workmen. Charles was keen to apprentice and Frank was trying his hand at it as well, though mostly to please his father. He had found life difficult since Alfred's death, and could not stop blaming himself.

ten

John Hannaford = Mary

Thomas = Sarah	John = Mary Towel	**Robert = Elizabeth Ann**	Alfred = Caroline
John William	George Samuel T.	**Charles Henry**	Frank Arthur
(1863 -)	(1866 -)	(1870-)	(1875 -)

Robert Hannaford at the corner of King and Dundurn, Hamilton, ON, 1905.

ROBERT HANDED ELIZABETH ANN A LETTER FROM TORQUAY. HIS OLDER BROTHER John's boy was immigrating to Canada and he needed a place to stay.

Elizabeth Ann gave her husband a half smile. "I don't mind having them stay here. They need family to get a good start, and you know how full Alfred and Mary's house is at the moment. Oh, I was going to tell you at supper tonight that Bessie has gotten a job at a dressmaker's. I wish she wasn't bothered by her headaches so much. It will be good for her to get out though. I can manage the meals and housekeeping quite well. Thank you so much for the new wash tub and mangle. It certainly speeds up the washing."

Weekly, tubs of boiling water with soap and lye were set on the wood stove ready for towels, bedding, children's clothing, undergarments, and last of all the work clothes. Once the hand scrubbing had been done, the clothes soaked in the tub, the tub was removed to a rack where two rubber rollers could be turned to press first the soapy water out, then the rinse water. The clothes were then hung on lines in the kitchen in winter, or racks outside in summer. By using a stick to lift things out of the water and between the mangles, Elizabeth managed over time to reduce the rawness of her rough, red hands.

The children had the full back yard to run and play in as well as the front veranda. The street was a quiet one that dead ended in a field. There was talk of forming a cricket club in the empty lots. Elizabeth Ann thought it might be interesting to watch the men in white. The girls next door would probably take quite an interest in the activity of a cricket club. Back home, she and her family wouldn't have even thought of joining a club meant for the higher classes, but immigrants here broke those old barriers the minute they had enough money.

Queen Street was becoming congested at times, but it was still convenient to get to the butcher, and not too much of a jaunt to the Hamilton Market right in the central part of the city. The trams and trains made transportation simple, although the dust from the earth-packed roads induced choking in dry weather. Things were increasingly busy in the Hamilton area. Dundas, Stoney Creek, and even Ancaster were thriving as small towns and growing each month, both towards the city center and further out into the country. As immigrants moved into the area, new businesses seemed to open daily.

Alfred thought now that the youngest of his brood was nearly in school, he might have the time to be involved in the next election. He had been discreetly warming the field as he liked to think of it, being sure that businesses which Hannaford Brothers dealt with would know his name. Lately, he had discussed the upcoming election with his brother and decided that this would be a good year to run.

II

After the election he gathered his family and a few friends together.

"Well, gentlemen, thank you for your support. I thought we should have a little toast. Here is to new times for the City of Hamilton, new improvements," and Alfred raised his thick stemmed sherry glass of apple cider. As Baptists, he, his brother, sons, and friends did not imbibe alcoholic drinks. Neither did his Methodist friends, most of who belonged to either the Royal Templars, or the Foresters. George Hannaford his nephew, on the other hand would have preferred wine, but was quite satisfied by having his debonair Uncle Alfred on city council. He hoped one day that he too would be involved in politics.

"Tell us, Uncle, what big plans do you have for the city? Do you support the treatment of sewage, and how will you raise the funds?" challenged George. The group of men laughed. Alfred twisted the ends of his moustache and straightened his stiff round cornered collar. The shoulders of the heavy wool suit with their exaggerated slope and narrow collar closings just above the sternum were the typical close-fitting style of the decade. It emphasized his slimness.

"My plans will remain secret until the council meets and begins voting procedures. I have no intention of making enemies before I have begun," he responded, "although I am hoping to get onto the water board."

III

Alfred hurried up the steps of City Hall just before eleven o'clock on January 15, 1894. Council was to meet to form the special committee which would strike the regular committees. An attempt to amend the Striking Committee was moved by Alderman Hall, but was voted down with five yeas, and sixteen nays. It meant that Alfred was on the committee. After resolving the motion that all meetings of the Council, its Standing Committees, Sub-committee Meetings, and Special Committee Meetings be open to the press and public, the Council adjourned until seven-thirty that same evening.

At the evening meeting, Mayor Stewart introduced the three aldermen representing each of the seven wards of Hamilton. McGillivray, Frid and Hannaford were for Ward Three. Alfred was the chairman of the Water Works Committee as he had hoped.

On the twenty-ninth of January Alfred read his report of the Waterworks Committee.

"To His Worship the Mayor and Aldermen of the City of Hamilton:

Gentlemen,
Your committee passed and forwarded to the Finance Committee for payment accounts amounting to $2,722.50.

Your Committee considered a petition from John J. Seitz *et al* for a six inch main on Wilson street, between Stephen and Wentworth streets, to take the place of a one inch pipe already there which is left over for inspection and an estimate of the cost.

Your Committee received an estimate from R.G. Olmstead for repairs of the fountain at the John Street Wood Market for the sum of $25.00, which it is now recommended be accepted on condition that Mr. Olmstead repair the entire structure, including the lamp, without further extras.

Your Committee asks authority to advertise for the usual annual supplies and report to this Council.

All of which is respectfully submitted, Hamilton, January 29, 1894.

A. HANNAFORD, Chairman"

IV

Alfred's second report on the 29th of January was much lengthier. He felt that the council's attention was lagging by items one and two, but when it came to the committee's recommendation to restore "the chattels of John Doherty, recently seized for water rates, and now held by the Bailiff", they began to squirm. He enjoyed keeping them on their toes, and didn't mind that there might be some argument over his report by a few of the councillors. If they remitted the water rates to the first of January last, it would amount to $12.90 for John Doherty to pay, and then his belongings could be returned. He had known some of these men to spend that much on an extravagant gift for their wives, while others were struggling to put food on the table.

The list and cost of supplies for service brass work, lead pipe, pig lead, street hydrants, and castings was unremarkable and most would have stopped listening carefully after the first five items. Alfred was pleased to be on the waterworks committee because Hamilton could boast some of the cleanest water and best-treated sewage in the province.

PART TWO

Lyon

FAMILY

eleven

LYON FAMILY: HEXHAM, NORTHUMBRIA: 1774-1840

```
Sylvannus Lyon = Isabella Kell
(1776-  )        (1776-  )
_____|_____
|          |          |          |           |
Sarah    Cecilia    Robert     Matthew      David
(1796-  )                                   (1815 -  )
```

Hexam Abby night stairs, Hexam, Northumberland.

SYLVANNUS DETERMINEDLY PULLED THE HEAVY CART TO THE STALL IN HEXAM market. The blue veins in his neck emphasized sinewy muscles that stretched across narrow shoulders and down to his small but strong hands. He strove to be first with the wool fibre that would bring a good price at market. Roger James was not surprised to see the young man arrive so early with such a load, knowing of his desire to become a renowned weaver, mostly to prove himself to his grandfather. When Sylvannus' mother Margaret married William Anderson a number of years ago, it was never said he was Sylvannus' father, which kept Sylvannus wondering, Who was my father?

Sylvannus had been born in mid-winter 1774 in Hexham, east of the city of Newcastle-on-Tyne. The well-known market border town of Hexam was dominated by the ancient abbey beside which the market stood. Large herds of sheep, cattle, and swine were driven to market by the farm hands from the surrounding countryside.

"Sylvannus, tell your mother there's a fresh lamb stew for her when she comes to the shop," called a kindly looking old woman with few teeth. Sylvannus turned his head away slightly because he knew that when his mother did go to the shop, the stew would be a greasy, days-old left-over that he would be forced to eat because "wilful waste makes woeful want" was his mother's motto. He was glad his mother was thrifty because it would allow him to apprentice in a trade at which he could handily earn his living if he worked hard, and it kept him from the coal mines around Newcastle; however, the stew did not appeal to him.

"Thank ye, Aunt Celia, I'll tell her," thinking instead, if he delayed long enough, perhaps there really would be a fresh pot simmering over the smoky fire.

"What ye say we go rabbit hunting this afternoon?" called Robbie who stood at his father's stall of butchered meat. The smell of raw meats and dried blood wafted from the stall. Sylvannus really had no interest in hunting. He would rather pay someone else to hunt so that he might experiment with the dyes that he had been harvesting over the summer.

"Not today, thanks, Robbie," answered Sylvannus as he pushed past the rotund female servants who were searching out suitable produce for the tables of their masters and their families. Some young ones were with child, but many were just fat. 'Trying out too much of their own cooking,' thought Sylvannus.

"Where ye been, lad?" interrogated Roger as Sylvannus pulled the cart up to the half empty stall. "The sun'll soon be poking its full face over those clouds, and then half the buyers will be gone home for their breakfast!" Sylvannus never knew whether to take Roger seriously in his criticisms or not. The dawn was barely breaking over the hills and the dew remained heavy on the roadside grasses.

"I 'aven't heard the toll of the bells yet, sir!" exclaimed Sylvannus with a smile and a shiver from the chill, damp air. "I had to pick up the rovings from Mrs. Carder first, and she did want to tell me about the visit of Lord and Lady Patrick Bowes up at the new Georgian manor. I tried to hurry away as fast as I could without being rude. You know how she dislikes doing business without a bit of a gossip. I brought my new coloured dye lot sir, if you care to have a look." Roger nodded his positive impression as Sylvannus showed him the dark green, hand-spun yarn with which he was so pleased.

"Well, we need to get weaving if you are to really learn your trade. I imagine that lass of yours will be wanting a fine sample before she agrees to marry you," laughed Roger.

Sylvannus smiled, mostly to himself. He was just as determined to marry Isabella Kell as he had been to get to the stall through the crowded morning rush.

Just as Sylvannus safely got his cart emptied and was about to stand behind the stall, a dashing figure on a jet black horse thrashed his way through the early morning crowd, setting people scurrying, hens squawking with wings flapping, and forcing frightened young women into hastily pulling their children out of his pathway. The figure was cursing the crowds, and flailing those around him in anger. Sylvannus paled, his face growing grim, because he knew of this mean-spirited, self-centered type of young noble, who felt the rest of the town owed him respect and cowering courtesy simply because of his station, and the fact he was in a hurry.

He himself ducked as the towering figure throttled his way through the busy market. Suddenly, a young crippled lad lurched near the noble's horse's legs, almost falling under them. Sylvannus watched, frozen to the spot, as Widow Hooper screamed at the back of the escaping figure on horseback, while helping the young lad to his feet.

"May God judge ye as ye deserve to be judged! May He curse thy descendants to the last one!" Sylvannus feared reprisal from the noble, and leapt forward to silence the woman and to help to lift young Duncan to a bale where his cuts could be cleaned.

"Widow Hooper, ya needs be careful of what you say in the hearing of the likes of him. Ya know their power," admonished Sylvannus.

"Aye, lad, I know their power, and their selfish ways. They 'ave no time for the likes o' Duncan, here," patting the lad's matted hair.

Besides resentment between classes, the Jacobite uprisings had caused trouble in the Borderlands during much of the first half of the century, leaving many bitter hearts among the Highlanders and northern English. Even as far south as Hexam, though it had not often been in the centre of the Scottish raids and rebellion because the English had pushed the Scottish border as far north as they could, even here politics were unsettled.

Sylvannus still felt somewhat wary of weaving the clan tartans when requested by some of his private customers. Even though the *Disarming Act,* which had forbidden the making and wearing of tartans, was lifted in 1782, for another ten years there were still people being fined by ruthless soldiers who searched houses for signs of rebellious, tartan-owning Scots.

Sylvannus organized the stall. He preferred the feel and smell of the clean wool to the smoother, finer texture of the flax others used for linen. Hawick to the north was fast becoming established as an important woollen-manufacturing town, but Hawick seemed a distant land to Sylvannus in Hexam.

"How far do you suppose it is to Hawick?" asked Sylvannus out of the blue.

Roger frowned, thinking perhaps Sylvannus was looking to the north where the steam inventions of James Watt and William Symington forged ahead in the textile industry.

"Although not so far by miles, the remains of Hadrian's Wall runs in a thin line across the north of the town of Hexham. Then thar's the thick Northumbrian border forests which 'as slowed the making of roads and industry. Where the forests thin, thar's the edge of the Cheviot Hills just before the border town of Hawick. It's just about the same distance again to the city of Edinburgh. You weren't thinking of making a move as soon as I got you trained now, were you?"

"Oh, no worry there, Roger. Isabella and I plan on staying in our little market town here. Our families are here. What would I want with a lot of big, noisy machinery?"

Hawick was where his grandfather David Lyon's family had lived. He was now in Hexham and although Sylvannus and his mother had lived in a cold, deteriorating, wing of the old manor until he was seven, he only saw his grandfather when invited. While Sylvannus's grandfather treated him reasonably well, Sylvannus knew his grandfather resented his mother having "fallen" without the benefit of the promised marriage. No word as to who his father might be, Sylvannus had learned as a young lad not to ask questions. He knew others that had no father, and many were worse off than he and his mother. The lesser gentry were susceptible to frequent instances where minor noblemen wanted guarantees that there would be an heir to the line, sometimes testing the waters in more than one stream, leaving distraught, pregnant young women to flounder along on their own. His grandfather David often talked of the Lyon family who went back generations to the fifteenth century and Sir Patrick Lyon, the first Lord Glamis.

II

Many seasons later, in the same street, Sylvannus hurried through the fifteenth-century stone entranceway into the abbey where he and Isabella were to be married. His good friend Thomas MacKay was slightly behind him, trying to keep up to Sylvannus's anxious gait. He was to witness the occasion. They passed through the slype which served as a covered entrance, turned right through the main door, past the ancient night steps which ran up the south side of the transept, then through the crossing where the pipes of the organ lined up, pointing skyward in the most ancient part of Hexam Abbey. He hoped to be there before Isabella so he could watch her enter in the excellent cloak he had woven for her, a hint of blue in the fine woollen fabric. Though he was working in a small steam-powered factory setting, he still enjoyed the hand loom at home where he could experiment with colour and design.

First born was Sarah in 1796, followed by several other children. By the time David was baptized in February of 1815, Sylvannus and Isabella were quite comfortable in their home, furnishings were modest, but of good quality, and David was encouraged to continue in school.

The area was being industrialized by this time. Improved roads had joined Carlisle directly to the west of them with New-Castle-On-Tyne directly to the east of them. Both these cities had busy ports. Tartans were now freely being manufactured, although Sylvannus had to laugh at the idea that everyone in Scotland could or would wear a clan tartan.

"Robert, my friend, what do you think of the new catalogue that Black Watch Colonel Stewart prepared? What are they thinking of by glorifying the savage Picts of the Highlands?"

"Well, it was the king's visit to Scotland that instigated that. That romance novel writer, Walter Scott, encouraged him no doubt. They have a tartan for every family name they can find."

"I just cannas' imagine George the Fourth in full garb, kilt and all," contemplated Sylvannus.

"The newspapers were full of the festivities. The chieftains and clansmen were as happy as the Scots can ever hope to be. I think it was all a big public stunt to improve the crown's image in Scotland. The Highlanders were quite happy enough to go along with it."

Industrialization had taken its toll on home industries, and employment became difficult for many of the younger people of Sylvannus and Isabella's children's age. As a skilled tradesman, Sylvannus maintained steady employment although Russian immigrants and other former serfs from Europe flooded the countryside looking for any kind of work. Their freedom from serfdom had left them hungry and unemployed in their own land, so in Scotland and Britain where industry was booming, they searched for work, often undercutting the wages of locals.

"Well son, I had 'oped that you at least of all my boys would be takin' advantage of the Scots' open door at St. Andrews, or Edinburgh, or Aberdeen. It's an opportunity that the ones with talent should look carefully at. You sure you won't reconsider it, my boy?"

"Father," David responded, he hoped respectfully, "I'ave my heart set on metal work. You know fine metal work for jewellery and watch-making. I know cousin Thomas Lyon has gone to the university, but he is to be a solicitor and he has to. I need to apprentice," he concluded.

By the time he was twenty-five, David had followed his brothers Robert and Matthew to the city of London and established himself at St. James Clerkenwell, Finsbury, leaving both of his parents, now in their sixties living in Hexam at Gilliesgate.

twelve

DAVID'S BROTHERS MATTHEW AND ROBERT, AND ROBERT'S WIFE ANN MOVED south to the big city of London in hopes of finding adventure and a better way of life. They began their journey by coach, but a new train line took them from the city of Birmingham into London as far as Paddington Station. They were amazed at the number of people, the grand buildings, and the busy River Thames' traffic of scows, barges, and small crafts. By 1841 they had found work as oil leather drapers, a process in the tanning of hides, David followed them to the city, establishing himself at St. James Clerkenwell.

David, though somewhat self-conscious of his northern English heritage, fit well into the cultural and social circles of a developing middle class. He was honing his skills and connections in the metal trade, often dealing with watchmakers and jewellers. He had a keen eye for judging the purity of metal even without chemistry and tests. When he became alert to the speech patterns of Londoners and adept at taking on a more southerly accent, he noted fewer Londoners were snubbing him simply because of his birthplace. He made many friends, and also enjoyed the company of his older cousin Thomas, a solicitor.

"Thomas, are you available to attend a lecture at the Islington Literary and Scientific Society? It begins tonight at eight o'clock."

"Well, yes I can. Perhaps you could join Ned, Edward, and Harry at my club beforehand for a little dinner. Do you know what the topic of the lecture will be?"

"I thought you might take particular interest in it because it's a fellow who was with Dr. Livingston on the first trip he made into the heart of Africa. I certainly wouldn't mind mingling. My boarding house is very quiet and the quarters are quite confined. In order to have a room to myself, I had to take a third-floor garret, which can be positively stifling. I can easily take the omnibus from the office if you wish to meet for dinner." David always enjoyed a ride on a horse drawn omnibus in the evenings when he needed to travel a distance within the city. The busy streets and traffic still gave him a thrill, even after being there for several years.

Since David had come to the city, he had been corresponding with a young woman born near his hometown of Hexam in Northumberland. He was so pleased that Isabella had agreed to visit him in London. He met her at Eustan Station. Isabel gazed intently at David as he took her gloved hand to assist her in stepping off the train carriage. She brought him news of Hexam.

"Your father was so thankful you made the trip home to see your mother late last winter. He is quite lonely without his beloved Isabella, and since April, he has been nearly despondent. Matthew returns to see him often, but he is always asking about you and how you are doing."

"I know that he misses her. I do too."

"Oh, ay, your ma was a lovely person. Ee, David, the streets are grand. I canna' believe all the carriages and gas lamps on the streets. Were you going to take me to the theatre as you wrote so much about in your letters?"

"Oh, Isabella, do you think you would like to live here? I hope that you don't have strong Northumbrian ties, and I would like you to make it a permanent change. Does your sister Jane still object to our friendship? I had hoped that I made it clear at our last visit that I had no feelings for her, other than being friends, that it was you that I cared about."

Their courtship was brief and by the fifth of June the two signed the marriage register. David's cousin Thomas Lyon and Isabella's friend Mary Ann Burrell were witnesses. After the birth of their first child, Thomas Stokoe, in 1847, Isabella's younger sister Jane came to live with them, assisting during the birth of their second child, Mary Isabella, born in 1849.

II

"Papa, do you think we'll see the Queen and the Prince? Can we go to the steam engines first? How did it get built, Papa?" David was wondering if he had been wise in bringing his young son, but the two older children of Victoria and Albert had attended the Exposition, and that had opened the door for the attendance of well-behaved children accompanied by their parents. It was too rare an occasion to miss.

"Will there be live animals there? Will I see a tiger? Or elephant?" Four-year-old Thomas Lyon grilled his father with questions as they walked hand in hand down Bayswater towards the entrance of the Crystal Palace in Hyde Park.

"I don't know if we will see the royals. They have already been to the opening three weeks past, and I'm sure they can go any day they wish. So you think the steam engines would be interesting, do you? Let's wait until we get there to decide what we will view first. Do you see all the people heading in the same direction?" David pointed out the horse drawn carriages, and all the people like themselves on foot hurrying in the same direction towards Hyde Park. They wanted to get there early to make full use of a day pass.

"Papa, do you think Mama wanted to come?"

"Your mother and I will come again. She will be interested in different things than you."

Excitement had been building in the city of London for months, during the construction of the Crystal Palace. Many had helped pay with subscriptions to subsidize the building of this amazing achievement.

"What happened to the trees that were in the park, Papa?"

"Well, no one wanted the great elms to be cut down, so they built the palace around and above them. When we get inside we can see them." David was hoping the crowds were not as heavy as the first three weeks, but there was a lengthy queue behind which they had to line up. Just looking at the ceiling of the glass walls and observing all the variety of people was enough to keep young Thomas interested. Here and there small groups of foreigners could be heard speaking in other languages. David hoped Thomas would remember this event for the remainder of his lifetime.

III

Ten years into their very happy marriage, David was struggling with sadness. He knew that he soon would lose his wonderful wife Isabella, and for the three children, their mother.

"Mommy isn't well, is she?" asked five-year-old Sarah Jane. Her furrowed brow warned David that she was close to tears.

"No, she isn't very well, Sarah, and that's why we need to be quiet just for now." He didn't see any point to appease her with untruths. He estimated he would be a widower within two weeks, if not sooner.

"Is that why Auntie Jane Stokoe is staying here?"

Young children did like to ask so many questions, thought David. He felt weary himself, and longed for a peaceful night, but knew that Isabella's illness would not allow it. He was thankful that Thomas and Mary seemed to be taking this more in their stride. He was coping, but worried about the effect on the children.

"Yes, and I think she may need your help in the kitchen," giving her a gentle pat on the head of bouncing curls, which she took as a cue that her father needed to be alone.

David hoped to be able to remain in this particular lodging because there was an extra room where he could have a study, which was large enough that he could carry on business if needed. The fact that it was on the main floor was an advantage. The street was quiet, and he could take the air if need be. They had moved four times since he married, which, he supposed, was usual, but things had to be broken in again in a manner of speaking, to be made comfortable.

thirteen

LYON FAMILY: LONDON ENGLAND: 1860S

```
David Lyon = Isabella Stokes
(1815-  )    (1809 - 1860)
        |
  _____|_____
  |          |           |
Thomas Stoke   Mary Isabella   Sarah Jane
(1847 -  )    (1850 -  )    (1855 -  )
```

AFTER HER DEATH, ISABELLA'S UNMARRIED SISTER JANE REMAINED AS A housekeeper and managed the children's affairs. A cook came in to prepare the main meals, and with her one morning came a surprise.

"Well, will you look see what I did find, just there on the back steps? The poor wee thing is hungry!" And cook brought in a bundle of gray wool wrappings with a slip of paper tucked in the corner. It might have been torn from a daily newspaper.

"Lookee here, Miss Stokoe. It says *Deverill*. I think we have ourselves a wee babe to look after."

"Well, that we can't do, what with three children in the house already. Here, let me see," and Aunt Jane took the light little bundle in her arms and before she knew it, she was rocking her.

Cook was delighted. "We'll call her Barbara, shall we miss? That were me ma's name, and a right fine name it is."

Jane nodded her consent. She had an idea that Cook had arranged the baby's arrival and was not telling them all she knew about the wee babe. Still holding the baby, she frowned at Cook.

"I have no idea what my brother-in-law will say to this, but you let me speak to him when the time is right." Two days later when the censustaker came rapping the door knocker at the front entrance, three month-old Barbara Deverill was on the register at 43 Upper Victoria Road, Islington, along with David, widower, Thomas 14, assistant to his father, Mary 11, scholar, Sarah 6, scholar, and Jane Stokoe, sister-in-law, housekeeper.

II

It had been a year since Isabella had departed this earth, and David was concerned that the children needed a mother. He needed a wife, as disturbing as the thought had first been when it came to him. David spent considerable time browsing the shops in the neighbouring streets, and was very pleased to find out that the young lady he had observed in his favourite grocery was single, although how someone as lady-like and so obviously well-bred as she remained unattached, he did not know.

"You will find the quality excellent and the ripeness to your liking," she tactfully told him of the melon he was handling, perhaps excessively.

"And do you think the flavour would suit someone such as myself?" he asked somewhat sheepishly.

"It is very sweet," she responded, her eyes dancing with merriment at her own boldness. He handed the melon to her to be wrapped as he pulled out the two pence needed for it.

"I don't suppose you would know of any interesting entertainments in the near vicinity, would you miss?"

"I would imagine that someone from the north, such as yourself, might find the follies at Collin's Music Hall to be of interest, or there is a new display of pencil sketches by the artist who has recently illustrated the book cover for Stevenson's novel *Kidnapped*. It's at the library just around the corner on Tottenham Road."

"How did you know I was from the north?" She shrugged off the question, not wishing to reveal that she had been talking to her employer about him, learning that he was a widower for a year now, and had three children.

"My name is David by the way, David Lyon. I don't suppose you might be enticed into joining me for a viewing of the sketches on your day off, Miss...?" he asked, hoping she would pick up his cue by giving him her name.

"Miss Meeks it is. I suppose that I might be enticed, as you say, to go and see the illustrations." She neglected to tell him that she had already spent a substantial amount of time one morning in studying the sketches, but felt his presence might make them all the more interesting at a second visit.

The next week David entered the shop just at the stroke of one. Miss Meeks was removing her apron and carried on pinning her black, smartly draped hat to her very full head of auburn hair. David assisted her in getting her lightweight wool coat on and they exited the shop holding on to hats and flapping coat tails, which were being buffeted in the March wind.

Some discussion ensued regarding their religious commitment. Although a Church of England member, David was willing to begin a new life without painful reminders of Isabella. Annie was insistent, so the two were quietly married at the Wesleyan Methodist Liverpool Road Chapel. It was now becoming quite acceptable for the middle and upper classes to join one of the non-conformist religions which were spreading rapidly during the second half of the century. Knowing she was no longer needed, sister-in-law Jane Stokoe quietly returned to Hexam to look after various family members in various stages of life; some were just beginning families, some were aging and needed nursemaids. She kept in touch each year with a card created just for the Christmas season, but passed on to her greater reward at the age of fifty-five.

III

"We should call him Henry David Meeks Lyon, should we not?" questioned Annie the next July after the birth of their first child.

"I would prefer just David Henry Lyon. He only needs one middle name or one surname if you look at it that way. I don't want the boy to be encumbered with a name which might indicate any kind of timidity the way *Meeks* might." Anne had wanted the boy to be named after her father whom she had lost at a young age. She was still upset that David had returned to the Church of England, insisting that the baby be baptized there. She felt she would have to join him, or cause an irreparable rift between the two of them.

"You name our next child," placated David. Thomas was in a hurry to get to work. The birth of a young half- sibling hardly interested him at sixteen. He had been happy when the baby Deverill had been returned to her parents, but Mary and Sarah were fascinated, although somewhat shy of their new mother and her new baby.

IV

The move from 18 Victoria Road to 59 Arundel Square began uneventfully. The moving men loaded two carts up with furniture and trunks while the family rode in a cab to Cousin Thomas Lyon's home for tea while the movers reassembled their belongings as best they could.

"Look where they have placed the buffet!" exclaimed a very pregnant Annie when stepping into the new hallway. The hot weather was irritating and she still had another month to wait before delivery. She suddenly gripped the edge of the buffet as she felt her knees buckle under her. Thomas tried lifting her by the elbow, but thought better of it as Annie began to moan. David, Thomas, and even Cook worked together to get her up the stairs and onto her bed.

"Run for the midwife," David instructed. Although this was his fifth child, he hated the delivery process. The baby was not expected for four weeks yet. The helplessness some men felt at this time was a frequent emotion among his friends, and he knew of some who would have two or three scotch whiskies to dull the sense of sound. He quite enjoyed children after they were five, and more so after they were ten.

Mary and Sarah were busy keeping two-year-old David distracted from the moans and groans of his mother. Cook went to the new kitchen to set a kettle of water boiling, if she could locate the kettle. She prayed the midwife would hurry.

"Here she is nearly thirty-eight, and this only her second child. The first didn'a come easily so Lord help her if this baby is early," she muttered to herself.

Little Annie Iphigenia Lyon only lived five weeks before succumbing in the heat to *cholerine diarrhoea*. David who was with Annie at his wee daughter's death felt he hadn't known sorrow before this time. Three days later he took the doctor's certificate to register the death at the Islington office. He was sullen and morose with his wife and children.

"Father, I think we need to get in to work today. I just heard from George that Edward King wanted an order filled as soon as possible. With him, that means yesterday." David nodded in agreement so he and Thomas got an early start the next day. Work did fill in the days for both Annie and David. The four children were busy, the younger ones needing tending, and the new house and business needed attention.

A move to 53 Ellington Street was planned well ahead of the next birth, so that Louisa Jane's appearance three years later was not such a struggle.

"Ee, Mam, you have a stout baby girl there. Listen to her exercise those lungs." Cook smiled affectionately while returning the clean baby to Annie. David was touched by his wife proudly holding their newborn daughter in a fine long nightgown. Her dark hair splayed across the white linen covered pillows fluffed up behind her, and the mahogany headboard gleamed in the sun. She so enjoyed fine things and Annie and the baby looked beautiful. He must try to have more patience with the children and Annie. He knew she did try and please him. It was just that he couldn't help make comparisons to Isabella's sunny disposition and Annie's more perfunctory manner.

In another year and a half, Lavinia Cecilia was born, this time in the middle of winter. David had asked that his own sister's name, Cecilia be included. Young

David was fascinated with his younger two sisters, and his older two took their roles as nursemaids seriously. Thomas was keen to get to work every day. He and his father enjoyed each other's company because Thomas was keen to learn from his father about metals, and from watchmakers about machinery.

fourteen

David Lyon = Isabella Stokes
(1815-)   (1809 - 1860)
_____|_____
| | |
Thomas Stoke   Mary Isabella Sarah Jane
(1847 -)   (1850 -)   (1855 -)

= **Annie Iphigenia Meeks**
(1827 -)
_____|_____
| | | |
David Henry   Annie Iphigenia Louisa Jane **Lavinia Cecilia**
(1862-)   (1864 -1864)   (1867 -)   (1869 -)

David Henry Lyon.

Louisa Lyon.

Lavinia Lyon.

By 1871, David was taking a break from the younger five children—rather, the rest of the family were summering by the sea. Cook had retired not long before, so he had provided the assistance of a young girl at the house in Southend, Essex where Annie ran the house, and David employed a servant at the house in Arundel Square where he and Thomas could more easily reach work. His friend's mother, Elizabeth Schrivener who boarded with them, kept very much to herself with reading what David considered questionable Victorian writers such as Mrs. Mary Seacole from Jamaica. Trains now frequently ran across the country, so some weekends Thomas and David joined the rest of the family in the village of Southend, directly east of London. It was not as popular a summer resort as Brighton to the south, or Torquay to the west, but it smelled of fresh sea air, and was cooler by several degrees.

Louisa read her Aunt Louisa's letter of August 16, 1876, sent from Paris, France.

"My darling pet Louy,

One whole week I have had your letter on the table, hoping each day to find time to write to you but as I have no servant, I have so little time. Many thanks for your kind remembrance of my birthday. It is so nice to know my dear little nieces do not forget me though so far away. I am so glad dear to hear you have all got juried, and especially that David Henry has one for German, it will be so useful to him in the future. You become happy at school; I know the ladies you are with will do all they can to cause you to make progress, and you must remember you can never know too much. School here is a much more serious affair than in England. Both young men and women make education a real business, seldom quitting college before 19 or 20 but then they dress so simply so that parents find but little expense, but they work very hard and long, long hours to attain their knowledge. The heat here is excessive. I do not like it at all I assure you and thunderstorms are frequent. I am glad that sister Mary has got away for a change. She must need it having had no servants. I think she will like Bournemouth, but it is very expensive, do not think Mansua would enjoy it on that account.

I send you a photograph of cousin Mayherd in his school uniform. At Paris schools, both boys and girls are compelled to dress in uniforms so that the rich and poor are an equality. Mayherd is going to school of an evening. He begins to speak French very readily, has not yet commenced with German. He has fortunately leisure time to learn and master it if his health only gets stronger. Ernest has received a letter from Aunt Cooper. No news in it is directed from the City."

Louisa thought her father must have been complaining of the cost of education and there was a hint that their clothes were extravagant in comparison to their cousins who now lived in Paris. Louisa did not think her aunt was very up to date in the dress of young ladies in England. Aunt Louisa continued her letter with "Remember me to Aunt Lyon and to all friends, especially to sister and brother. With much love and many kisses, Remaining your affectionate Aunt Louisa."

Louisa was glad that she had at last heard from her aunt. She tried to keep in touch with the family as much as she could. She wished she had also known Aunt Sarah Lyon Irvine, her father's oldest sister. She sounded like such a grand lady, and very pretty from her father's descriptions. Unfortunately she had died in Scotland a few years before Louisa was born.

Annie had employed a tutor for the younger children so they were not idle. Fancy needle work such as lace making, tatting, and crocheting had become popular for young ladies. Sarah, at 16, enjoyed the needle work, and was already thinking about making a trousseau. Mary, somewhat limited, would probably never marry, had no interest in handiwork, but liked to dig in the garden, wash clothes, cook simple meals, and scrub floors. Together, there was relaxed harmony among the members of the entire family in the two locations for quite some time.

Annie enjoyed the Victorian way of decorating; furnishing the rooms with heavy drapery, over-stuffed upholstered furniture with dark wood trim, and ornamented china on every surface. Delicate white china cups and saucers marked with gold trim were placed in a glass-covered case. Most of these items were for show, not everyday use.

Thomas and Ellen married in Islington. After their first two children were born, they moved south of the Thames across the river to Lambeth. Thomas was now qualified as a machine maker, dealing in precision equipment. Science had improved weighting and measurements so much over the past few decades that precise equipment was now needed to manufacture nearly all machines. Precision meant speed. Speed meant improved production. Improved production meant increased capital, and that all meant gains in the Industrial Revolution.

"Father, I don't like the man's politics. Yes, the proletariat needs opportunities, but not every man is equal in what he does. That neighbour of yours does nothing to help himself. Every week he's down at The Swan with his pay, and the children hardly have enough to eat for the rest of the week. He complains when an employer fires him for not showing up to work on time or at all, after he's had to sleep off his medicine." Thomas had strong opinions.

"Well, the Temperance Society needs to get busy with weak-willed men like Nick, and get them out of the pubs. Some of them don't know any different. It was the way their fathers lived. But I say, Thomas, the International Working Men's Association is a growing organization. I understand the Association already has a socialist party in Germany."

"I won't join them, Father, and you should not be listening to their propaganda. That Marx fellow had it wrong. If I join anything, it will be the Fabien Society. They don't promote revolution or violence." David nodded in agreement over that point. At the moment he was mainly concerned with his girls.

David invited Samuel home with his daughter Sarah's interest in mind. Later, the family joke was David had always wanted money in the family, and now he would have it: Samuel Money that is. The suave watchmaker took to Sarah Jane and her to him. They married in 1878. Sarah invited her sister Mary to live with them after Albert and Percy were born. Samuel made a good living and the couple were active socially, not just with outings, but charity work as well. With supervision, Mary was a big help around the house.

fifteen

"ANNIE, THIS IS WHAT COMES OF HAVING TRAINING IN THEATRICS AND MUSIC, rather than a solid career," argued David.

"He just needs to find himself. He does have a flare for the theatre. He needs to take these smaller parts if he is going to get any proper training." Annie's nostrils flared as she breathed heavily, trying to keep the anger out of her voice.

"Well, he has six months. If he doesn't make a go of it by then, he needs to get down to Lambeth so he can work with Thomas. Now, there is a hard working young man," stated David with conviction.

"You never have given David a chance, have you? Thomas has always been the favourite son."

"That is not true Annie. I care about all my children equally, and I just want him to be able to earn a descent living, that is all. And did he really need to change his name to Harry? I didn't think David was a bad choice of name."

"If we could change the subject, I have some concerns about Mary Isabella's health. She needs to see Mrs. Frost about some stomach powders, or something."

"I won't have her visit that charlatan. She can go to the doctor if she is not well. She hasn't said anything to me."

"Papa, you mustn't be so angry. Mary is feeling poorly, and you have been too busy with your activities to notice." Louisa spoke with more firmness than the wide-eyed, younger Lavinia imagined was wise at the time. Their mother and father were having their differences, and their father could be immune at times to the needs of the household. Since his retirement, he had drifted from them somewhat, busy with other retired gentlemen at his club, but always keeping his hand in some business affairs, mainly to pay club dues, school fees, and reading material.

A few times a year he visited his daughter Sarah Jane and family in Prescott. He realized Sarah was becoming sharp in tone and impatient with most of those around her. Samuel, who often responded by grabbing his hat and coat, his walking stick or brolly, went stroling in parks. A few times he had asked David join him, but David declined, choosing to rest in the parlour with a newspaper. He found he disliked Samuel somehow.

David was in a sad state when he learned that his youngest two daughters and son had decided to side with their mother. He and Annie had become increasingly estranged and now, to prevent arguments he spent his time at the club, sending housekeeping money each week with a young runner to the Thorpdale Road house.

He spent a sorrowful six weeks in rented rooms on Horsey Road trying to get his daughter Mary Isabella stronger, but in August of 1887 she succumbed to the diseases she had suffered for two years. It grieved him that she had to be buried in unconsecrated ground. His younger three children could have been more helpful, but felt that Annie must have turned them against him. He wrote to his daughters trying to keep in touch, but he hated the fact that his letters were intercepted by the pinch-faced, interfering friend of his wife, Mrs. Flint. Somehow she felt it her duty to protect his daughters from their own father.

Sarah Jane was so busy with five children, having had another son Herman, and two daughters, Clarice and Beatrice within the last seven years, that she was little solace. Thomas had his own family and long hours of work to put food on the table and to try to educate the children, so they too might improve their way of life, and so David had little comfort but the simple things, such as a few good books, two good suits, and a warm overcoat as the chill seemed to be creeping into his bones these days.

II

David handled the card outlined in black.

"In loving Memory of Anne Iphigenia Lyon
Who entered into rest February 3rd, 1888.
Aged sixty years.
Interred at Finchley Cemetery"

"Finchley Cemetery; the same as Mary Isabella," he spoke aloud. So his wife had passed on without his knowing, and now a few days later Lavinia had sent him the death notice and a short letter.

David sat down with paper, ink pot, and quill. He had not written often, but appreciated the fact that Lavinia had sent him news of Anne's passing.

12 Jackson Road
Holloway Rd
February 1888

Dear Lavinia

I received you letter after some days intimating to me the death of your mother, you say she was a good mother to you. That I believe. I have been at the above address for some months. I have got most comfortable lodging a room well furnished. I have it entirely to myself. I had Sarah staying with me for a week before Christmas. I should be glad to see both yourself and Louisa. Bear in mind I am your father who has gone through a world of trouble; thank God I am very comfortable now, I have an easy situation till about 10 o'clock in the morning till about 5 in the evening in the city altho' the income is small, yet I can live well, and save a little, if you or Louisa will come and see me I can put you up most comfortable. Now Lavinia I must have your correspondence direct and not Mrs. Flint. I will after this have no communication with her she did me an eternal injury - I cannot imagine why you keep your address from me. I don't require anything from either you or Louisa but would be pleased to assist you. I have a lot to tell you about the death of my dear girl Mary will do so when I have a letter from you and will give you a memorial card and tablet both for her and your mother. I enclose my private card and send one to Louisa and tell her to write me. You can come and see me. It will be most convenient at any time and I will do all I possibly can to make you both very comfortable. On Jubilee day I met with an accident. The omnibus turned over in the Caledoman Road and I was on the top. Will give all particulars in my next. Now my dear child let there be no more letters through Mrs. Flint as I will <u>not</u> answer them. I give you my address, therefore I shall expect yours. Believe me my dear girl. Your affectionate and loving father David Lyon.

Lavinia turned the letter sideways to read "write for return if you possibly can" and tears dripped down her cheeks. She felt badly for him. It was obvious that he wanted her and Lou to visit. What injuries had he sustained in the omnibus accident? Perhaps she would ask David Henry if he had read something in the papers.

III

"Father, you need to see a doctor."

"Lou, I am quite capable of looking after my own needs. The doctor has done what he can for me. I would just like to have a quiet visit with you both and enjoy what little time we have together." David looked at his daughters beseechingly, and pointed to the teapot indicating the tea was brewed enough for them to begin pouring.

"The accident was on the Tuesday morning of June 21. So many people were getting on the omnibus because it was on the parade route of the Queen's carriage, and I suspect they were all hoping to get a glimpse of Her Majesty. People were milling about and there was a great deal of traffic. I certainly don't blame the driver, but as we were turning near King's Cross, the wheel caught in the railroad tracks, and the bus tipped sideways throwing all of out onto the street like so many potatoes!"

"Oh, Father!" exclaimed Lavinia. "You must have been terrified. Was...was anyone killed?"

"No, thank the Lord. There was a great deal of confusion, and blood, and the screaming was frightening itself. At first they thought three people might be dead, and quite a few had to be taken to hospital, but most, like myself, had terrible bruising and were in shock."

Louisa broke in, "And to think we were standing in that quiet crowd at the palace. People were cheering when the Duke of Cambridge marched by with the Horse Guards, but then it was very quiet while we waited for the Queen."

"I was surprised the Palace wasn't decorated, but then the Queen arrived in her carriage, and the horses! The horses were so large, and beautiful cream coloured creatures! Everyone began cheering then, and waving handkerchiefs, and flags, and throwing flowers. Oh, it was exciting!" exclaimed Lavinia.

"I thought the Queen looked rather anxious, even with a white bonnet on," commented Louisa.

David was sad that they would be leaving this evening. He really didn't like them traveling on such a late train, but as they were no longer dependent on him, he could do nothing to dissuade them to change their plans. Their talk of going to Canada upset him, but he would not think of that this wet August day.

IV

Their father was not well, but they did make an occasional visit together, trying to bring him fresh baked goods which they thought he might enjoy eating.

After their father's death in the fall, it was a sad and lonely Christmas. Their brother had decided to join them, though too briefly for their satisfaction. They made the best effort they could without any parents or close family nearby. They had thought that perhaps Sarah would invite them to Prescott to her grand home. Five young nieces and nephews would always brighten the atmosphere in any celebration. When Lavinia and Louisa visited there in the New Year, however, they realized that things were not very happy in the Money household, and perhaps Sarah's bitterness at Samuel's spending so much time in the business and basically leaving all the household management, schooling and discipline to Sarah was causing disharmony which although only an undercurrent at the moment, gave them cause to think they would not find a great deal of support in that realm.

Lavinia and Louisa had decided together that their mother's inheritance was not going to get them to Canada unless they soon made the move. On the fifteenth of January 1889, Lavinia and Louisa went to the registry office to file their passport application forms. Cousin Thomas had given them instructions to prepare them for the process. They soon had plans for a spring sailing and would be headed to Toronto.

"I will be very lonely, Topsy, but I completely agree that you will have a better life in Canada than you possibly could here," commiserated their brother, David Henry.

"Harry, you could come with us," pleaded his sister Louisa.

"No, I am very happy lodging where I am, and with the company that I keep. You have had your passports for two months now, and with the little money left you by mother, you can have an easy situation for a while before you need to seriously look for employment."

"I wish father had reconciled with us sooner. I do not understand why he would not accept Mrs. Flint as a go-between. Do you understand what happened that father was so set against her, Harry? It said in his last letter that she had done him an *'eternal injury'*" Lavinia said thoughtfully.

"I can only surmise it had to do with something that she passed on from Mother out of the context in which it was spoken. She did tend to interfere. Have you written to Sarah lately? She will want to know that you are immigrating to Canada. Have you thought of a location? I understand Toronto, the provincial capital is quite an industrious place and they even have some delightful theatres and music halls."

"No, we have made up our minds to go to Hamilton from Toronto," Louisa said, and Lavinia nodded her agreement. Lavinia was only a little distraught at leaving her brother. He was working on a number of parts for a new production, and though sad to see both his sisters leaving, he would have realized there were no fond memories in the distant, remaining family, no homestead where furnishings and decor would fill the gaps from the dozen moves around the city. The few items Lavinia treasured she meticulously packed in the steamer trunk ready for transportation to the docks of Liverpool. These included a set of gold trimmed, white china porcelain cups and saucers which had belonged to her mother. Upon embarking the *Parisian* which was headed for Montreal, she noted the seating plans for the dining room for the ninth of July 1891.

PART THREE

Hannaford and Lyon
FAMILIES

sixteen

THE TRAIN HAD TAKEN LAVINIA AND LOUISA LYON FROM MONTREAL TO TORONTO. Friends had recommended they both go to Hamilton if they wanted to find employment quickly. Hamilton was fast becoming a busy industrial town, and both secured jobs in offices within days of arrival. Their eloquent speech and refined appearance appealed to firms dealing with British businesses. For two years they worked and saved, going to the local Church of England services, and meeting other immigrants, some not as fortunate in being able to converse well in English. Many Italian and Polish families had made their way to the industrial city. They used the library, they enjoyed the theatres, and they joined the English Temperance Society. From there, friends introduced Charles Hannaford to the young women and he immediately took to Lavinia. In the fall of 1893 Charles came to his father with what he hoped would be good news.

"I think you'll approve of her, Father. She is very much a lady, but still," he smiled, "she is rather taken with me. Her mother and her father are dead; her brother is very busy in the theatre and music halls in England, so she and her sister came to Canada themselves. We thought we would marry at the end of November when work has slowed down. She has even agreed to change from Church of England to Baptist. Do you think Mother would mind if I brought her over?"

"Are you planning to live with us? It might be a little frightening for a young lady to start her marriage off in our busy household."

"That was something that I wanted to tell you. I would like us to have our own little place and I found one on Wentworth that would be just right. We can rent it from the beginning of October so I thought I would move in then and after we marry Lavinia can join me. Her sister needs time to find a suitable apartment for herself. How do you think Mother will react to me moving out?"

"I think with both George and John lodging here, she has plenty of work to do. With your sister Elizabeth off busy dressmaking, she has all the housekeeping to do. We know you all have to make your own way sooner or later. Mary and Alfred are right next door. I'll approach your mother with your news if you like and we would be delighted to meet Lavinia soon."

Charles made plans discreetly, but it was difficult for his mother not to notice his increasing excitement.

"Where did you say Lavinia was born, Charles?"

"She was born in the north-western part of London, England, Mother. Don't worry. She is used to working. She isn't royalty you know. She does have a brother in show business, and her half-sister is married to a jeweller, but their father had some disagreement with their mother before she died, and they were quite upset about it. She hasn't said, so please don't ask."

"Of course not, Charles. I will try my best not to embarrass you."

"Oh, Mother," replied Charles affectionately putting his arm around her ample waist. "I know you won't. I might be more likely to embarrass you," he teased.

II

Elizabeth Ann had been hoping for grandchildren and when she saw the size of Lavinia in late August of 1894, she suspected there would be more than one baby born in September, and she was right. Lavinia had a long and somewhat difficult labour, but two living babies emerged. Robert Henry Hannaford was quite a bit smaller than his sister Myrtle Irene, but the parents proudly displayed them to visitors.

Charles decided that their photographs should be taken to go along with his and Lavinia's wedding day picture. In the spring Lavinia, her sister Louisa, and Elizabeth Ann the grandmother, took the babies down to the Farmer Brother's Studio on King Street. The two babies sat wide-eyed, nestled in a sheepskin which had been placed over a broad wicker chair. When Elizabeth Ann and Robert had first come to Hamilton, they had coloured portraits painted by J. F. Smith. Elizabeth Ann thought it was much easier for the children to be photographed. They would definitely not sit long enough for any sort of painting, although, sitting still for the photograph to be taken was long enough for babies as young as these. They were so pleased with the results.

seventeen

HANNAFORD FAMILY: HAMILTON, ONTARIO: 1895

Robert Hannaford = Elizabeth Ann Pope
|
Charles Hannaford = Lavinia Cecelia
_____|_____
| | |
Robert   Myrtle Irene   **Gladys Lavinia**
(1894-1895) (1894-)   (1895 -   )

Gladys and Myrtle Hannaford.

CHARLES AND LAVINIA WERE HEARTBROKEN WHEN TINY ROBERT SUCCUMBED TO *capillary bronchitis* in August of 1895. Myrtle continued to thrive and then two months later on Halloween night, Gladys Lavinia was born. Her eyes were pale blue and alert. Lavinia thought the baby would look better when her hair had grown long enough to cover her ears; so flat and pointed were they that she appeared a little elf. They were frequent visitors at 232 Robinson Street, often spending the whole afternoon and sometimes sharing a light supper when Charles, Arthur and their father returned from their work. They had been busy transferring saw horses, building supplies, plaster compound, buckets, trowels, wheel barrels, and scaffolding to their next job. Arthur, never strong, had become expert at doing corners and delicate cornices, although he was shy of a ladder. Charles, who was assisting at all levels, including some of the business end as well, enjoyed working on the walls the most. His white coveralls never looked flakey or soiled as some of the crew's work clothes did.

"Well, Mother, you were right," Charles said facing his mother squarely. "Cousin George has finally proposed to my wife's sister, Louisa. How did you know that was going to finally happen?"

"Just that feeling a woman has, Charles. Always take into account a woman's intuition, even for business decisions. We have a broader view of life than you men. How does Lavinia feel about the marriage?" asked Elizabeth Ann.

"Oh, she is relieved I think. She was beginning to wonder if George was just dangling her sister by his side, but I think he was just waiting to get solidly on his feet financially. Louisa enjoys fine furnishings and well-made dresses, you know. They will be Church of England, of course. Lou can move out of that boarding house and into his house on Charleston. It will need a few things done over with a feminine hand. George and Lou both agree they should purchase only good quality furnishings. Lavinia, thankfully, is prepared to wait for the finer things in life, although her tastes run a little higher than mine. I don't mind, though. She deserves good quality, and it's not that we can't afford them. She is too busy to think about that with those two girls of ours."

Next door another type of conversation was taking place between Frank and his father Alfred.

"I just need something different to do, Father. You know how miserable I've been since the accident and I've been giving it plenty of thought. Now that cousins Charles, Arthur, and George are in the business, you can do without me for a few years. I will be back. I've already signed with Nelson to be one of their traveling salespeople. I'll have a chance to go all across the United States."

Frank put on a determined look, prepared for argument with his father, but was somewhat relieved when Alfred stood quietly, pulling on his long side-burns.

"You know Mary will be so sorry to hear this. We do need you in the company. I was counting on you to take over someday," Alf finally responded.

II

When it came time to leave, Frank had a smart looking case full of product samples as well as a carpet bag of his personal belongings. One by one his sisters dolefully hugged him good-bye. Eleven year-old Bill looked at his oldest and only brother from beneath furrowed brows and bowed head.

"I'll send you a postcard, old man," consoled Frank as he shook his half-brother's hand. Without looking back, Frank headed up the street to the train station which would take him across the border to the United States, and all around the eastern seaboard, selling his products. Postcards would arrive on a regular basis: Chicago, Detroit, Pittsburgh, Boston, Philadelphia, Boston, Raleigh, Boston, Atlantic City, Boston.

"Elizabeth Ann, will you join me for a cup of tea at the front when you are done hanging out the laundry? I have some news for you." Elizabeth Ann smiled at her sister-in-law, Mary, and nodded. Mary liked a little mystery once in a while. It seemed quiet for Elizabeth Ann now that Cousin John William Hannaford and his family had found their own place on Hess Street, her son Charles and his wife Lavinia lived on Wentworth, and cousin George Hannaford was at 275 Hannah Street with his new wife, Louisa. They had all been residents at 232 Robinson Street at one time or another.

After placing teapot, cup and saucers on the oval wicker table, Mary sat herself down on the wide veranda in the cool October afternoon. Elizabeth Ann so appreciated having another wonderful sister-in-law after losing Caroline. Alfred's second wife Mary's Scottish ways had softened only a little, but Elizabeth Ann felt she had done a remarkable job of keeping the household together.

"Well, I have a letter from Emily in Toronto. Apparently she has met a young man and they are planning on getting married about the middle of December, in Toronto. I don't know what Alf will say about his first daughter getting married, but she certainly isn't too young."

"I think Alfred will be delighted. You know how he likes being married," Elizabeth Ann teased, and they both had a laugh over Mary's short courtship. Although they had married for practical purposes, Mary and Alfred were extremely companionable and enjoyed all of their large family, supporting each other after Alfred Junior's death. Mary had felt blessed to have two of her own children with Alfred, but mothered them all equally. She secretly was delighted to have received Emily's letter with her announcement addressed to both herself, as Mother, and Alfred.

"Well, I'm very pleased for her. I suppose they will live in Toronto with them both working there. I don't remember ever thinking I would be working out of the house. Things have changed."

"By the way, Alfred wanted me to tell you that for Sunday's gathering we will be taking a photograph. A friend of John's is bringing a camera over to take a picture of the whole family. We wanted to do this while Frank was visiting, since he comes so infrequently. This will be a memorable centennial year, the turn of the century as they say."

"I must be off to see if I can be of help to George's Louisa. Little Ivy is somewhat fussy, and I think it helps if I can get some dinner prepared and just rock the baby for a bit. I remember how tiring it can be, and without any close family in Canada except her sister, it must be difficult. I'm sure Lavinia would help, but that Gladys is an active little girl. You must come and see Myrtle and Gladys's picture. They look like two princesses with their long-waisted white dresses and pink satin sashes. They have big white bows in their hair at the side, and ringlets. I don't know how Lavinia has the patience for that with Gladys. She won't sit still for long." Elizabeth Ann smiled at the thought of her bubbly granddaughter.

George and Louisa had their second child, Norman Morris, on the sixteenth of May in 1901. George was now doing most of the book work for the Hannaford Brothers and was extremely competent in ordering the supplies and searching for new contracts.

Another postcard arrived from Boston in the United States. "Married to Anna Josephina Nelson" was all the detail anyone received from Frank at the time. After the census of 1901, the numbers in the Alfred Hannaford household began to dwindle. Alfred's daughter Caroline was married the eighth of June 1904 to a lithographer, Andrew Simpson, and second-born daughter, Alice Gerty, was a witness to the ceremony. Six weeks later, she in turn married William Kleinstreuber of Gravenhurst, whose parents lived just across the street. He was a mechanic now that motorized vehicles were becoming popular. Studebaker had a manufacturing plant in Hamilton, and another was on the horizon, a sign that automobiles were becoming the craze in Canadian cities.

In 1905 a letter came announcing a new grandson for Alfred Senior, Alfred Edward Nelson Hannaford. Mrs. Anna Josephina Hannaford, of Swedish heritage, wrote in a very formal fashion, as someone not entirely familiar with the English language would do. None of the family had yet met her. On the envelope there was a return address and so Alfred sent a response enclosing a five dollar bill. He asked Frank to come back home to help in the business. Both he and Robert were finding the physical labour increasingly difficult. They were hiring more employees, but effort had to be made to keep up with the competition. Few were as well-known as the Hannaford Brothers in the plastering business. They had reduced the size of their ads in Vernon's Directory to just bold lettering in the alphabetical listing, and were still as busy as they wanted to be.

III

Within the year, Frank and Anna arrived in Hamilton, having left Boston two days before crossing the American border at Buffalo, bringing little Alfred Edward with them. He stumbled occasionally, but was making progress in learning to walk. Anna was due to deliver a second child in the next month, so Frank made urgent inquiries before finding a place at 323 Main Street. It was not too far away from the big double house on Robinson Street where the business started and ended its day. It was September before Frank had time to register the birth of his new son, Francis Nelson Hannaford.

By November of the same year Frank's younger sister, Bea, as Adeline Beatrice was called, was growing more excited about her own nuptials. Her linens, which she had painstakingly prepared, were ready. Her step-mother Mary had given her a serving platter and teapot. Her father had given her one of her mother's shawls. She had her summer clothing packed in the trunk which her uncle Robert and aunt Elizabeth had brought from England. She was preparing for her marriage to Richard McCreary and she was happy. Nothing was going to stop her now. Richard was a good twelve years older than she, and they were good years. He was an admired worker and had his own house. No immature debutante was she. The family might miss her bright cheerful smile, and she would miss them, but she would have her own family soon she hoped, and they could still visit. Cousins Gladys and Myrtle next door were very sad to see her leave.

"But you will still have Ellen and Ethel and Bill," she told the downcast faces.

"But it won't be as fun," objected Gladys, "and someday they might get married and then there won't be anybody but Uncle Alfred, Aunt Mary and Arthur and Mother and Father and Grandmother and Grandfather."

"That sounds like plenty of people around if you ask me. Besides I can bring Richard over and then when we have children you can come and help me look after them." Myrtle brightened at this prospect, but Gladys still frowned. She didn't like babies just yet.

Gladys was glad that her parents had moved back to 232 Robinson Street. She hardly knew life without grandparents, aunts, uncles, cousins and of course the workmen who came in to be offered a cup of freshly brewed coffee. She had been delighted when her grandfather made her a little wooden cradle. Her kittens allowed her to dress them up and put them in it. Her father thought it so funny that he had taken a photo, not of Gladys and the kittens, as she had hoped, but of the cats in the cradle, frilly hats on, looking up beseechingly towards Charles.

"Grandpa, why does Dot keep barking at the horse and mare while they're eating?" asked Gladys, who was sitting on a straw bale inside the contractor's barn.

"He's a small dog, see, so terriers like him, have to sound big. I think he feels that he's greeting them, but they've been hauling tools and material to and from the job all day so horse and mare are too tired to be bothered with her so Dot just keep's barking. She's been sleeping all day."

A few weeks later an incident took place which brought Gladys to tears. Myrtle was a bit more nonchalant about it and said, "We can get another dog," which to Gladys was cruel and heartless.

"But Dot was such a sweet dog. Why did Father have to go and ... and shoot her?" cried Gladys.

Charles entered the room at that moment and explained to his girls what had occurred.

"Your uncle Alf went out to feed the horses and Dot took a nip at him. Dot didn't recognize him. You know she was nearly blind. It's quite a nasty gash and will have to be watched so it doesn't get infected. We couldn't let anything like that happen to you children. Bill had a small nip from her last week as well. We'll think about getting a new pup in the spring."

Gladys rubbed her eyes with closed fists, and then curled up on the sofa to mourn.

Before Charles had time to replace Dot, his father came home with a black and brown spaniel named Don. Don was full grown and became Robert's constant companion. He would hop up on the seat whenever Robert hitched the horse to the wagon.

eighteen

ROBERT AND CHARLES HAD BROUGHT GLADYS OVER TO ALFRED'S SIDE OF THE house for a bit of evening discussion. Immediately, Gladys went over to the new upright piano and gently pressed the keys, experimenting with the high sounds and the low sounds. She wasn't sure why some of the keys were black and others white. There wasn't anything to distinguish them except the further to the right she went, the higher pitched they were, and the further to the left, the lower they were. Oh, how she wanted a piano. She loved to sing and she thought music was the most wonderful thing in her life right now.

Her father glanced over at her. "Maybe if you concentrate harder in school, you might be able to take piano lessons some day."

Gladys immediately pulled herself up in expectant pleasure, but then remembered the messy inkwells, and the smell of perspiration in the high-ceilinged classroom. Twenty double desks faced the front where the teacher's desk sat. They had to turn their heads to the side in order to copy the notes from the side chalkboard into their notebooks or onto their slates. She hated the place. Often the sun was streaming in the large, tall windows, reflecting all its glory right onto the words she was trying to read off the chalkboard. The students formed rows and rows of loops, letters, upper case and lower case, repetitive sentences in the hopes of improving their handwriting. She wanted to be out running, dancing, jumping. She couldn't sit still most of the time unless Miss Reed thwacked the cane on someone's knuckles or desk, and on occasion Gladys'. Gladys did like to read though, and secretly read modern adventures during the evening instead of practicing her figures.

"Do you want to look at my piano lesson book, Gladys?" asked her cousin Ethel. Ethel had been taking piano lessons for nearly a year now and was beginning to play well, Gladys thought.

"Can you show me where the notes are?" asked Gladys hopefully.

Thus began a joy for both girls. Sometimes Ellen would join them, and they sang together and played, gradually teaching young Gladys as they went. She was very quick to learn the notes and she could pick out a familiar tune easily. Young

Bill would tolerate listening to them, but he never joined in singing unless the whole family was gathered around the piano.

"Did you see the police report that the library had been broken into and $6.50 was taken from the till? I think we better look at a safer strongbox for the shop, or start making more frequent bank deposits. We often have a lot more than that just lying around in the drawer," Robert stated in what he hoped was a casual statement. He was concerned with the look of Alf this afternoon, and wanted to see what his appearance was after a bit of rest and the evening meal.

Alfred said, "It appears they'll go for any amount these days. Why would they go into the library to steal? They could sign up and borrow books if they wanted to make their minds richer. I see that Newbigging Cabinet got the contract for the shelving for the new east end library." By now Alfred was seated, discreetly trying to massage the pain in his side. His paleness was noted by Charles who in turn alerted his father.

"Thank God, Frank is back. I've worried about that lad, and now here he is with two boys of his own. Anna seems to have a very strong will; not quite the type I would have thought Frank would choose, but they appear to get along. He certainly adores her."

"You need to take it a bit easier now, Uncle Alfred. We've got George, Frank, myself, Arthur, and Bill all doing much of the work, so it appears you need a bit of a rest. Too much in the way of civil duty. Five years on council was plenty. At least you have four of your six girls married off. They seem to be thriving." Charles tried to lighten the worry of Alfred's health.

✓

II

The next evening Gladys was at the barn petting and grooming the horses.

"There he goes again! Howling every time we get close to St. Joseph's. He keeps it up until the bells stop ringing!" exclaimed Gladys.

"His former owners must have trained him to do that," concluded Robert. He was collecting some tools and left over material from a work site and had brought young Gladys for the ride.

"Oh, my! He is such a funny dog. Aren't you Don? And I don't understand why he gets so cross with the postman. The postman must have kicked him or something sometime. He is so gentle with everyone else; it must be the postman who's to blame. He's a mean man."

Robert smiled down at his bubbly granddaughter. She always seemed to have something to say, some comment to make.

Only days later, Charles entered the house of his uncle to be met with the tearful faces of his aunt Mary, and cousins Ellen, Ethel and Bill. Alfred had died in the night, and was to be buried the day after. Dodsworth and Brown were doing the funeral. Alfred was to be buried in the northwest corner of the family plot. Two small ornamental cedar trees grew on either side of the tall, pink granite monument.

A few weeks after the funeral, Robert went to the Old Hamilton Cemetery as it was now called. He wanted to check the engraving. *In Loving Memory of Alfred R Hannaford who died Dec 21, 1908, Aged 56.* Robert's long mutton-chop sideburns were whitening now, and they dripped with salty tears in memory of his younger brother. He remembered them playing in the garden of East Allington, and walking all the way to Torquay which had seemed like such an adventure. They had shared so much: emigration, homes, business, even family. All their joys and sorrows were tied together in shared memories. The wet snow began to soak through Robert's shoes, so he strolled soundlessly down the path and climbed into the buggy where the waiting horse stomped around, anxious to be moving.

Down the street from 230 Robinson, Anna had decided that she and her husband Frank needed a photo of their two boys. She would then send her family back in the United States and Sweden copies of the photos. She studied their wedding photograph. Anna Josephina had gone to great lengths to find a suitable hat with a large ostrich feather draped elegantly around the wide brim. Her boldly printed dress fit her tall, smart figure, flowing out behind her as she stood ramrod-straight behind Frank. She thought her long feather scarf which draped over her shoulders might be what her mother-in-law would have called ostentatious, had she the vocabulary, but Anna was delighted with the latest fashion.

Mary may have disapproved of Anna's somewhat flamboyant ways, but Frank was enthralled. He sat pleasantly composed. His wife was competent, and clever. He had spent time polishing his boots before the ceremony, and had carefully smoothed his moustache and hair, adjusted his white bow tie, and placed the carnation in the buttonhole of his left lapel. He leaned back into the ornately carved chair, as Anna took her standing position slightly behind him, placing her hand on the armrest of the chair where Frank would make contact with it. Somehow by the time photos were sent to Sweden and the Nelsons, only this one was left for herself.

Now in 1909, Alfred and Francis posed beside the studio chair which had little ornamentation on it, although it did have curved arms and back. The boys smiled at the camera, thinking that dressing up in their outfits was a fine game to be playing. Their matching wide-brimmed sailor hats with ribbons at one side, coordinated with their white sailor dresses, high collars, low-waisted belts, and dark blue stockings. They had scuffled along in the earth as they were marched to the studio, and so their mother was horrified at the dusty boots on their feet when she first viewed the photo. Five year-old Alfred was blonder than his four-year old brother Francis Nelson. Anna looked at Alfred with special fondness, charmed by his handsome good looks as a youngster. Upon leaving the studio, she took their hats while they ran ahead across the Cricket Club at the end of their street. It didn't matter now if they were dirty.

nineteen

HANNAFORD FAMILY: HAMILTON, ONTARIO: 1910

Anna and Frank Hannaford.

Sons, Alfred and Francis Hannaford.

"BOYS! THAT WILL BE ENOUGH!" ANNA CALLED SHARPLY TO HER TWO SONS. THEY enjoyed being outdoors, but today was not a suitable day. Dark clouds had gathered and released snow showers making the ground too wet for sledding, though they rarely were taken on such adventures.

"Mother, can we go up the street to Grandma's house?" Alfred asked with wide-eyed innocence, knowing he might get cookies there, whereas he would not at home.

"Yes, Mother, please can we go?" chimed in Francis.

With four large blue eyes staring at her, Anna smiled and gave in to their request. They drew on their coats, left unbuttoned, and tied scarves around their necks as best they could. Albert was about to reprimand his younger brother for going out the door without putting on galoshes, but mid-way into putting on his first one, he threw it off knowing it would delay him and Francis might arrive first. He hurried after Francis before their mother could stop them. Off down Robinson Street they trotted, buffeted by a rising wind.

"Boys! Well! Come in, come in out of that cold," welcomed their grandmother. The fact that Mary Hannaford was their father's step-mother meant nothing to them. What mattered were grandmother's cookies and cheerful welcome.

"Are you going to make cookies today, Grandma, or do you got some already?" Francis led the way into the kitchen.

"What are you doing, Ethel?" Alfred asked when he saw his aunt bent over a pot on the cook stove, a tea-towel over her head while she breathed in the steam.

"Dere, you boys can 'elp me bring some more wood in fromb the shed for the stove. I have a bery nasty cold and need to steam up a bit to help the cough." Ethel continued to hold the towel over her head, coughing and sneezing periodically. The boys happily obliged and then sat at the table expectantly. Mary was arranging a few cookies made the day before on a plate and getting fresh milk out of the icebox to pour into two glasses. She and Ethel would have a nice hot cup of tea.

"Are you finished there, Ethel? I do believe you have been steaming long enough. I'll make the tea."

The two boys enjoyed a snack and visit with their aunt and grandmother. After Ethel went to lie on the sofa, Mary got out the wooden block puzzle with four different pictures, one on each side of the twelve blocks.

"I want to do the one with the milk wagon!" shouted little Francis.

"No, let's do the one with the horses in the field," argued Alfred.

"Well, perhaps I can make the choice so you boys don't argue about it, shall I?" Mary sighed. It was a delight to see their smiling faces. She missed her husband Alfred, even after two years. "The boys won't even remember their grandfather," she thought to herself.

They played until late afternoon, when Mary sent them home so that she could make dinner for Ellen and Bill. Ethel would probably just want some broth the way she had been feeling. Ethel hated to miss work. She had just started a job as a Bell telephone operator and thoroughly enjoyed the work, despite receiving the occasional shock through her headset. Her miserable cold and cough had kept her home for two days now, and she hoped that with rest this Saturday and Sunday she would be well enough to be understood at the switchboard.

"Goodbye, Aunt Ethel." Before she could stop him, Alfred had planted a kiss on her cheek, at the same time giving her a hug. She could only nod a thank you before a coughing fit attacked her. She waved goodbye as they headed down the street.

Anna was at the door the minute they arrived.

"You boys must have been having a fine time with your grandmother to be gone so long. What?" she exclaimed when she saw them without galoshes. "You will get your death of the cold and wet," she reprimanded firmly. "Get these wet shoes and stockings off immediately. Whose idea was it to go out without galoshes?" She searched their faces for an answer. Alfred weakened and couldn't help but look at his brother.

"Francis! You will not go outdoors again without your galoshes. Now go to your room," and Anna turned on her heel and took Alfred to the kitchen where she could warm his feet next to the wood stove while she made supper.

The next night Alfred made little effort to eat his dinner.

"Come, Alfred. Your mother has made you a nice dinner, so please eat it," pleaded Frank. He understood the boy's reluctance as the meal was a traditional Swedish dish that Anna liked to make for Sunday evening. Alfred had appeared sluggish in church, even during some of the liveliest hymns. Now he seemed flushed. Frank frowned as he put the back of his hand to Alfred's smooth forehead. He was definitely fevered.

"Anna, I think he has..." and at that moment Alfred sneezed. Anna immediately turned to Francis.

"Do you see what comes of not wearing your galoshes?" she demanded.

Alfred ran a slight fever for a few days and was forced against his wishes to remain in bed. Francis ran up and down the stairs as fast as his little four-year old legs could go with pillows, toys, papers, and treats. He had to go painfully slowly when carrying a drink, but wait on his brother he did without complaint. He had been the one to dash out the door without his galoshes and the guilt goaded him into action.

After the sneezing stopped, Alfred was allowed to sit bundled on the sofa. From here he could at least watch the horses and delivery wagons. On Wednesday, he took a turn for the worse. His fever rose and he coughed regularly. By Friday, Anna asked Frank to bring the doctor.

Doctor Wilcox arrived at the front door with a black leather bag at his side. After removing his boots at the door, he nodded at Anna to lead him to his patient. He took his time listening carefully to the young boy's chest, asked him to breathe deeply, which brought a fit of coughing. He nodded his head and glanced up at Anna who stood stoically by the end of the bed.

"I would recommend that you have him sleep alone. It is somewhat contagious. The infection is in both sides of his lungs. Try to get hot drinks into him, with lemon if you can get one. Honey will soothe the cough. He should rest, and keep him well-covered. If he doesn't improve in four or five days, come round to get me." The hunched shoulders of the doctor appeared to weigh him down. He had been out calling on patients for several days now, and the number of patients with pneumonia was distressing.

The doctor's visit on Tuesday evening brought little hope of recovery for Alfred. His mother walked around mechanically doing routine chores. Alfred had been stationed on a cot in the kitchen near the stove so that Anna might watch him closely. On Wednesday afternoon Anna was rocking the motionless lad as the doctor made his appearance. He took the limp wrist to seek a pulse, but slowly shook his head. He placed the certificate of death on the table beside Frank, who sat with his head bowed. Francis was hiding, not wanting to see his lifeless brother.

When Frank came to her door the next day, Mary took him in with her arm around his shoulder. She offered him tea which he refused and slumped to the seat in the kitchen where he had sat as a boy, where as a young lad he had grieved the death of his own brother, and where now he grieved for his son.

"You know that there is room in your father's plot for Alfred. I will make the arrangement if you like," offered Mary. Frank simply nodded, then hurried out of his chair towards the front door. He needed to be with Anna again, who would still be weeping, an uncharacteristic expression of emotion aging her features. He was surprised to see the tall, bearded figure of his cousin, John William Hannaford going up the steps to his and Anna's house. John's son Percy was waiting in the carriage at the street edge. It was a handsome carriage, one that John had made himself. Percy at the reigns, now a machinist, nodded to Frank who met John on the steps. John grasped his hand firmly; he knew the pain of losing a child and had come to offer his sympathy. The notice in *The Hamilton Spectator* had alerted him to the death of young Alfred.

Frank looked glum as he sat at the kitchen table having a cup of coffee. He vacantly watched Francis play with his dinner, who, not wanting to look at the empty space across from him, kept his head bowed. Frank didn't want to have to deal with Anna's hardness, but could do little at the moment to cheer her. She had been despondent since Alfred's death. It had been weeks now and all of them were exhausted both physically and emotionally. Frank wondered if he should take Francis with him to the sheds so he would at least have the distraction of the horses and his uncle Robert's black and brown spaniel, Don. Frank needed the company of his cousins right now, so off he and Francis headed to Merrick Street.

They met Arthur, who was doing his best to load the wagon with the morning supplies, a job that Robert had usually done. They all missed Robert since his death in July. He had always been working, quietly going about his business. He had worked every day until about a year before his death, and then he still came in to load up in the mornings, gently offering advice to the growing number of workmen who were now employed by Hannaford Brothers. Gladys and Myrtle missed their grandfather terribly. In his quiet, gentle way, he had given them affection and attention. He had made toys from scraps of wood, entertained them with training Don to sit on the piano stool in the backyard. Everyone carried on with daily tasks, but the pain lasted.

Two months later, after vomiting over the basin for the third time that morning, Anna chided herself for having allowed Frank to console her. God knew she needed someone to console her because she could not stop seeing the angelic face of little Alfred with his blond bangs dangling on his perspiring forehead. A new baby was not what she wanted at this time. She straightened herself, determined to get back to routine chores, to stop the mourning. The kitchen floor needed a good scrub.

II

"Are you sure, Anna?" questioned Frank, looking down at the round cherub face of his new daughter. He was so thankful it was a girl. Somehow another boy would not have seemed right.

"Yes," Anna declared firmly, "Alfhild Enid. We can call her Enid if you like." Frank nodded in agreement, not wanting to cause a row about her use of the Swedish form of Alfred.

The 1911 census takers were dispersing across the city, better educated than ever before. Most people had been informed by the local papers that such an event was happening. Vernon and Might both offered the city directories. The *Hannaford Brothers (Chas H & Geo) Plasterers*, printed in bold were now the owners and operators of the business. Coal and Wood was for sale by the W.A. Freeman Company.

twenty

HANNAFORD FAMILY: HAMILTON, ONTARIO: 1912

Alfred Hannaford = Caroline Cornell
|
Frank = Anna Josephina
_____|_____
| | |
Alfred Edward   Francis Nelson   Alfhild Enid
(1905 - 1910)   (1906 -)   (1911-)

Alfred Hannaford = Caroline Cornell
(1851-)   (1847-)
_____|_____ (con't. below)
| | | | |
Alfred   Frank=Anna   Emily=G Coffy   Caroline=A Simpson   Alice =W Kliensteuber
(1874- 1890)

(con't. from above)_____
                    | |
              Adeline = R McCreary   Ellen

Alfred Hannaford=Mary Smith (Alfred's second wife)
_____|__
| |
Ethel Victoria   William SP = Ivy Towers

230-232 Robinson Street, Hamilton, ON, 1889.

THE YEAR BROUGHT MANY CHANGES TO THE HANNAFORD HOUSEHOLDS AT 230 and 232 Robinson Street. Gladys and Cousin Ellen were sitting at the dining room table with their scrapbooks. They enjoyed cutting out poetry, pithy proverbs or pictures of the royal family, and more recently they added photos of each other they were able to take with their Brownie cameras. It was a serious hobby for the girls which lasted nearly all their lifetime.

"What's this, girls? Not out dancing?" Bill laughed in his enjoyment of teasing his sister and cousin.

"Yes, and partaking of alcoholic spirits too!" his sister Ellen quipped. "Don't mess those newspapers. I haven't finished cutting out what I need from them yet." Bill swooped up a bundle of papers and playfully tapped them on the table edge, causing several small bits of news cuttings to go fluttering out of order.

"Bill, stop that!" chided Gladys. "We've spent hours working on these. What are you so cheerful about anyway?"

Bill leaned over the girls' shoulders conspiratorially and asked, "Would you like to be the first to hear some spectacular news?" immediately catching their undivided attention.

"You can't let on you know anything, but if you listen carefully to my conversation with Mother in the kitchen, you will find out I got the answer to my question tonight."

"Ohh!" squealed Ellen, trying to smother her own excitement. Gladys didn't know what the question was or why Ellen was so excited. Bill pushed the dining room door open and found his mother at the sink peeling potatoes.

"I have my answer Mother. Ivy has agreed to marry me." Bill was so pleased with the news, Mary never let on she had overheard his quiet discussion with the girls in the dining room. Bill, Mary and the girls immediately began plans for a family celebration. There had been too many unhappy times, and now was a chance for celebration.

The lovely Ivy Margaret Towers, an artist, was introduced to the family in May and the date was set for a July third wedding. Plans for an outdoor tea with white table linens, cucumber sandwiches, and tiny fancy cakes were made with great anticipation. On the day of the wedding, Bill and Ivy sat down at the rectory office to fill out the marriage licence. It was the first time each had stated their full names before each other.

"William Stanley Preston Hannaford," Bill told The Reverend William Smith, glancing discreetly sideways to see Ivy's reaction. Her amused smiling eyes met his. "Aged twenty-three. Yes, we are both residents of Hamilton." After the brief ceremony, the foursome met the remainder of the family and a few friends in the backyard of 230 Robinson Street. The clouds provided just enough break from the scorching sunshine to make the day very pleasant. Mary and Lavinia sat comfortably in front of the silver tea service pouring tea and coffee. The service had been Alfred's twentieth-anniversary present to Mary, the last gift he had given her and one she treasured.

II

"Well, Lavinia, do you think you might like a holiday by the lake?" Charles asked of his wife. The girls clapped their hands in glee. They liked the idea very much and both would be able to take some holiday time before returning to school to enjoy the freshwater lakeside. Boating and fun in the sun would be delightful and it was close enough some of their friends could join them for the day or overnight if their parents agreed.

Charles had rented the cottage for a month. The hampers and trunk were packed and everyone piled into the carriage, including Laddie, their new black and white collie. The owners of the cottage lived across the highway from their cottage on a large farm. During the month of harvesting and haying, they rented out the cottage. Laddie loved to go across to the fields where he could run freely with the animals.

"Laddie, you are not to cross that highway. Do you see how fast those cars are going? They must be going 30 miles per hour!" Charles had the dog by his collar and was warning him not to cross, but excitement overpowered him one day and the inevitable happened. Laddie was struck by a fast-moving car when making a dash over the highway toward the farm animals. Gladys and Myrtle were heart-broken. They sat weeping in the main room, wiping their teary eyes with large linen hankies. Their mother made no comment as she was trying hard herself not to let her own tears drip on the bread for the sandwiches.

"No more dogs, girls," Charles stated after burying Laddie in the nearest field fence row. "You get too attached and upset when we lose them." By 'you' he meant 'we' because in his heart he knew that he became as attached as his kind-hearted wife and the girls.

Gladys was now working. She had had trouble getting down to serious study and her father decided she may as well be working. When Lloyd Freeman offered her a bookkeeping position in the fall, she was thrilled. She was able to walk to work, walk home for a noon dinner, return to work for the afternoon, and the rest of day and evening would be hers. No more studying after hours except for the piano. She now could pay for a few lessons herself and she was making amazing progress, having been told she had an excellent ear for music. It was always a thrill for her to pick out tunes, or read the music and play songs which were familiar to many, some whom might sing along.

Only slight twinges of regret surfaced when her friend Margery met her on the way to school occasionally, and Gladys saw her pile of school books, and carefree attitude, but Margery's parents were wealthy business people and expected their daughter to stay in school. There was even talk of attending finishing school in Switzerland or France; however, that did not interest Gladys at all. She was happy to have a few extra dollars a month for dress fabric, or the occasional pair of shoes after her mother took the housekeeping money. She had had no idea how much it cost to run a household until her mother sat her down and they did some practice bookkeeping. After that, Gladys was much more careful with her change.

William Pope had been around to the house at least twice to see his sister "in private" he said. Charles felt somewhat puzzled by his uncle's secretiveness, and hoped he soon would find out what it was all about. By the middle of September, he had his answer.

"Charles and Lavinia, I know you must be wondering what all the talk behind closed doors was all about, but William was afraid you might try to talk me out of it. Say I was too old. We're going back to England for a visit," Elizabeth Ann pronounced with resolve.

"Oh, Mother!" exclaimed Charles.

"Well, good for you both!" congratulated her daughter-in-law Lavinia. Gladys and Myrtle burst the door wide open, the door through which they had been eavesdropping.

"Oh, Grandma! How wonderful! When are you going?"

"Oh, that's simply marvellous, Grandma and Uncle Will. How long will you be gone? Are you going to Torquay?" Myrtle wanted to know.

"Yes, we are going to Torquay and to Plymouth. We leave on the 19th of October and will be gone for a month. My only regret is that Robert is not alive to join us. We had always wanted to return for a visit." Her excitement was tinged with ruefulness. Gladys was well aware of the reason. She had heard her father and grandfather talk of Torquay very often and could picture the hills, the sea, fancy hotels, and palm trees.

"You'll be glad you went, Grandma. Grandpa would want you to go. Can you take some pictures while you are away? You could take my Brownie camera." Gladys offered.

"No, no. I don't want to take your most prized possession. I wouldn't know how to use it anyway. These newfangled things confuse me. Maybe my brother's family or the Eden family can take pictures of us."

"Oh, you didn't tell us that John and Susan Eden were going. That will be quite fun!" exclaimed Myrtle.

"Yes, it was their idea that we make up a foursome. William and his son have lived with them since they immigrated to Canada. William and John Eden are business partners too. It will make the trip very pleasant. Our ship is the *Virginian* which apparently is quite a modern steamer. It is one of the first triple-screw liners of the North Atlantic and can sail up to eighteen knots an hour. We'll be among fifteen-hundred passengers. We take the train to Montreal where we board and we disembark at Liverpool." William stroked his chin somewhat nervously. He had studied the shipping lines carefully after the disastrous maiden voyage of the *Titanic*.

"I hope the weather will be good. You won't be going anywhere near any icebergs, will you?" asked Lavinia, also thinking of the *Titanic*.

"At my age, dear, I really don't mind the danger. I shall leave it in God's hands, and if He should see to it that we make a safe journey, wonderful. You can pray for our safety, but don't you be sorrowful if we meet with disaster," reflected Elizabeth Ann.

Charles had been about to protest, thinking of his mother's health and age, but thought better of it. He wished he had his mother's faith in God's protective hand in the matter. The trip would be wonderful for her. Although he was only four when he left Britain, he had fond memories of many aunts, uncles, and cousins, the salty seaside, and palm trees on rocky hillsides.

"I'll help you exchange some money into sterling at the Imperial Bank, mother. I'm acquainted with Glassco the manager," offered Charles.

twenty-one

HANNAFORD FAMILY: HAMILTON,ONTARIO: 1911-1912

CHARLES WAS READING THE EVENING *SPECTATOR* WHEN HE SPIED A NOTICE that Cousin John William Hannaford's daughter had married. He wondered if he could call John to offer congratulations, but there was no number in the telephone directory. More and more people were getting phones, but Charles wondered if not having one had something to do with John's religion, or perhaps he didn't like the modern invention. He and his wife were Christadephians, and he didn't know much about the religion. Charles knew they had five other children and a little girl who died when she was only ten. Now here he read, Olive was already married. He hoped his girls would wait a while, meet some sensible young men who were mature and responsible. He supposed that was every father's wish.

The girls felt something lacking at the house without a dog. Gladys usually walked with a friend through the Hamilton market on her way to or from the office. There were pups and kittens for sale sometimes. One day at noon they came across a stall of collie pups.

"Oh look at this one, Helen. It's just like a big fur football," Gladys cooed.

"Look at those dark rings around his eyes. They look just like spectacles against his gold and white furry body."

Gladys hurried back to the office and phoned her sister at home telling her all about the pup.

"How about if you work on Father's good nature. He'll listen to you. I just hope the pup will still be there tonight. Please phone me back as soon as you can."

Myrtle was swift to act. Her father agreed.

"I suppose there will be no peace if I don't say yes," was Charles' reply.

On the way home from the office, Gladys stopped at the stall in the market and the pup was still there. She bought him out of her pay that she had received that day. The style for furs at that time was a large cape type fur for the neck and a large barrel shape muff for the hands. Gladys carried the pup nestled against her and her large muff. Although it took twenty minutes to walk home, the pup was nice and warm when she arrived. Her sister greeted them cheerily and took the bundle into the kitchen for his supper. The intelligent eyes responded immediately to his chosen name: Mac.

II

George Hannaford phoned Charles at home to give him the news immediately. The council had accepted their bid for the plastering contract of the new Hamilton Public Library.

"Charles, is that you? They accepted our bid. We have the contract for the downtown library!" George had a difficult time keeping the excitement out of his voice.

"That's great news. Can you get the crew that was working for Ted to join us? It's going to be a big job. Do we have any timelines yet?" Charles was always thinking and planning ahead. With Alfred and Robert gone, he and Cousin George were the business partners. His brother Arthur was becoming more limited in what he could do physically, and Charles felt at times he tried to do too much with his heart condition. Frank was a good worker, but he hadn't been the same since his son's death.

"Louisa would like to have you and Lavinia for a meal on Sunday. My brother Arthur is returning home to England next week so we wanted a visit before he left. What time does your church service finish? Ivy and Norman have Sunday School in the afternoon, but they will be back by four o'clock." George waited for an answer.

"Five o'clock would be a good time. I'll tell Lavinia. She will want to bring something, I'm sure, so I'll see if I can get her to call Lou." Charles' hesitancy was not for himself, but for his wife whose relationship with her sister was becoming a little strained for no reason apparent to him. He would like to see his cousin Arthur once more before he returned to England.

"Do you think we should advertize for workmen in the paper?" asked George.

"Let's wait until we have that contract signed and can find out what the timeline will be." The men rang off, both looking forward to this huge new project.

At the laying of the cornerstone, his Honour, Colonel J. M. Gibson, the lieutenant governor of Ontario, was presented with an engraved trowel, on August 23, 1911. The shell of the building had been up before the winter. The roof was on and they could start their plastering as soon as a boiler was installed. Without the heat, the plaster would never set properly. The main entrance way was a spacious courtyard where a person could look up into the second floor reading rooms and book shelves. Beams subdivided the ceilings into sections about ten feet by ten feet, and there were dozens of these on each floor. Around the inside of each beam just below the ceiling were evenly spaced blocks of plaster. Around each of the central pillars, plaster Corinthian tops were added. In addition to twelve regular crew, twelve more men were hired to labour, bringing pails of silver sand, bags of plaster of Paris and lime up the stairs. They set up scaffolding, took it down, cleaned out moulds, pails and swept floors. The plasterers mixed plaster in pails for pouring into moulds, or in wooden troughs for the base coats. Lath scratchers were needed for the ceilings, trowels for the walls, cutting tools for the trimming. In a well-coordinated effort the men completed the work to schedule.

Gladys listened to the excited talk at the table in the evenings. She was so pleased, and impressed by her father's work.

"Has this been the most difficult job you ever did?" she asked her father.

"Well, the co-ordinating of all the men has been the most challenging of anything. We've had to work around other tradesmen who are not quite finished.

"Will we be invited to the opening, do you think, Father?"

Charles looked at Gladys' hopeful expression and was happy to be able to answer in the affirmative. She was always so enthusiastic about everything in life, never sitting back and letting things pass.

III

"The men need to assemble for a picture. The photographer will be coming tomorrow morning before we start the final clean up," George told Charles. Charles would inform the men when they arrived.

"Did he say where he wants us?" asked Charles.

"He said the foyer, but I told him there would be better light on the second floor in the corner where the big windows are facing east. The men should wear their work clothes. We can wear our suits, if that's alright. Might as well have the bosses stand out a little," laughed George.

Charles was pleased with the work the men had done. Some, like the young Jack Bailey would continue to work for Hannaford Brothers. Others would return to former jobs. They had worked hard to get it done in a matter of months. In some ways, it was the most significant work they had ever done. It certainly was the largest.

IV

Lavinia greeted her husband at the door.

"How does Arthur seem today?" inquired Charles.

"Your mother has been with him most of the day. She sits and reads the paper to him. He just hates to have to lie around, but he is getting more tired with everything he does."

By the beginning of July, Arthur was bedridden. His mother continued to read to him. Lavinia tried to make appetizing tidbits for him to eat, but he remained quite lethargic, picked at his food, and was sleeping much of the time. July twenty-first his heart stopped. Elizabeth Ann bent her head over him from where she sat and wept, unable to keep the tears from flowing this time. This was her fifth child she would see buried. Only Charles remained, and thankfully his two girls. Thanking the Lord Robert had not lived to see Arthur's decline and death, Elizabeth Ann finally wiped her eyes and went into the kitchen to inform the others.

The funeral was held two days later in the afternoon at 232 Robinson Street. The Reverend H. Mc Diamid officiated at the house and accompanied the family to the Hamilton Cemetery on York. George and his brother Alfred, Frank and his half-brother Bill, all Hannaford's, George Pope, cousin, and Charles Eden, friend, carried the coffin to its final resting place at the Hannaford grave site where sister, brothers and father had already been buried.

PART FOUR

Bailey
FAMILY

twenty-two

John Bailey = Margaret Harris
(1799 -)   (1816 -)

| John | Sarah | **Thomas = Ann Jones** | Richard | Samuel | Harriet | Emmanuel |
| (1837 -) | | **(1841 -) (1845 -)** | | | (1856-) | |

Bailey residence, The Bryn, Hyssington, Montgomeryshire.

JOHN STRODE QUICKLY OUT OF THE TALL STONE GATE OF THE BRYN, HYSSINGTON, swinging to the right along the roadway towards the north fields where he knew his son John would be hard at work drawing and pegging down the hedgerows. John, the father, was angered by the old man Owain Price's remark about the Baileys being "English yer know." It made no difference to him that Baileys had been recruited by the Earl of Powys to help stabilize the Welsh borderlands in the 1200s, and his family had owned land since the 1700's, farming the rough, rocky soil, improving things as well as any of the best of them all in these isolated, rural hills. John felt as Welsh as any of his neighbours.

The other news that had vexed him to no end was from his son Thomas in Liverpool saying he had married Ann Jones. John had warned Thomas about making hasty decisions and sewing wild oats, but the deed was complete, and his compulsive, cheery son was now married to a young woman whom they knew nothing about, except that she was young, and passionate.

John was thankful it wasn't his oldest son that had left, to whom the main farm would one day be passed. His only concern was that young John, now twenty-eight, had shown no interest in any woman, young or old, since the passing of his childhood sweetheart nearly eight years ago. For a few years now, John had lived at Runice, in an area called The Marsh, having Sarah his younger sister do for him, and with brother Samuel who had had enough schooling. Perhaps John would be like himself and marry later in his thirties, a woman sixteen years his junior, or like John's own father John who married his wife Sarah later in life. His son John was the third generation of John Baileys to be born in Montgomeryshire, Wales.

The village of Hyssington was in the peculiar position of being in Montgomeryshire, but having Bishop's Castle to the southeast, Mucklewick Hill to the east, the Shipeley Hill to the north, Chirbury to the northwest and Churchstoke to the west, all in Shropshire. These were the Welsh Marshes, dotted with decaying castles from the English lords who had tried to tame the Welsh in the Middle Ages, and loops of lands' borderlines shifted along the hills and rivers over the centuries back and forth between English Shropshire and Welsh Montgomeryshire.

II

Young John was bent over the hedge row, expertly notching branches to be drawn down to ground level. His father guessed this to be an old hedgerow by the number of varieties. Bushes of holly, hawthorn, and hazel were mixed in with blackthorn and elder. Sparrows flitted in and out of the hedge. John made note of some bramble bushes which would need to be cut out. After the fall's work was complete, the job of laying the hedges was started by John and his son, and they continued into the later months of winter when the snow would start to accumulate. Now they began this chore since the harvest was complete, the animals chosen for slaughter had been preserved, and some others sold.

"Did you see the rooks' nest in the trees at Romney's Road?"

"I did indeed," answered young John in reply to his father. Never a man of many words, John nodded to his father in greeting.

"That young brother of yours has gone and got married to Ann Jones," announced John the father, eyeing his son carefully for a reaction.

"Thomas is a fool," was the single phrase John spoke. He knew little of Ann except she had smiled flirtatiously with him at their one meeting, and was still only twenty-years-old at the present. Young John speculated they had run off to relatives in Liverpool to be married, after Thomas finished his contract farming, and now he would be working in the big industrial city which he would hate after a few years. More than likely a young 'un was already well on the way.

"Are Richard and Samuel coming to help before noon?" asked young John.

"They'll be bringing the noon meal with them, no doubt. Your sister Harriet is looking after Emmanuel who seems to be a bit fussy this morning. Your mother was baking some fresh bread when I left her," replied John senior.

John thought gratefully of his wife, remembering the busy days more than twenty years ago. He had been the sole executor of his father's will, and had also taken in his younger brother. He had had to mortgage the farm in 1835 just before marrying to purchase a field at Runnis Gate. He very much appreciated his wife's help, her youthful vigour and her endearing smile. Beauty or being in love had little to do with his choice, and she was his helpmate without whom he would be a lonely man. Would that his sons choose as wisely.

III

Thomas was anxious to get bedded in Bishop's Castle before the sunset. Tomorrow would be nearly a four mile walk to Pentre Willey where he had rented a farm. They would have to carry a few belongings and their daughter Margaret, who at just over a year, could hardly be expected to cover the distance.

"Thank God we managed to get the connection in Lydham Station for the new train to Bishop's Castle. There would be no place there, but a barn in which to sleep! I forgot how isolated we are here," Ann stated, emphasizing the isolated. Thomas knew she would miss some things about the busy city, but he hated his job in Liverpool, disliked the crowds, the smells and when he found Ann in the neighbourhood public house sitting with Margaret on her knee, both chomping happily on crunchy fish which they could ill afford, he had made the decision. A mug of beer had sat half consumed on the thick plank table, a clear statement of Ann's independent nature.

After a late arrival in Bishop's Castle, and a very short sleep, Thomas, Ann and Margaret set off with bread and cheese first thing in the morning, the sun behind them.

"Let's rest here please, Tom. I'm so weary after the late night last night."

"If we just head a ways up the road heading north from Bishop's Moat, we can climb up the hill following the stream that starts at Leton Hill and get as many drinks from fresh Welsh water as we need." Within minutes, Thomas pointed to the east.

"You can see the Crugim Hill Race Course, just over there, but we turn here and follow this path along the stream to Pentre Willey where I can find out about our farm." After another hour of clamouring over rocks and slippery terrain, they finally reached the track to the farm.

"If I knew how hard that was going to be, I would'ave went along the road beside Caer-din!" Thomas exclaimed. Ann, looking somewhat pekid, was just getting to the lane. Thomas, put his arm around her waist, and smiled into her face. He still yearned for her as much as the day he married her.

"Never mind, love. We'll soon be there."

Two dogs yapped as they came in the muddy lane of the farm. There were two barns, both needing repair. The hedgerows hadn't been laid in years, and Thomas was beginning to wonder if there would be too much work for him. Fortunately the house looked to be a good size, and so there might be the hope of having a proper roof over their heads.

Thomas looked somewhat grim when returning from the house. They would need to stay in the lean-to until the present tenant farmer's family got moved.

"They planned on staying at least another week to help us get started with the set up. I'm not sure what state the cattle and sheep are in, but the lean-to might be cleaner than the house. Bring Maggie along while we look inside the lean-to."

"I expect they think we will cook outdoors, and we will, won't we Maggie. It will be just like camping out," spoke Ann cheerily.

The lean-to was not too poorly furnished. On the hard earth-packed floor was a cow hide over which a gray mattress of straw was spread. Three or four rough woollen blankets were neatly stacked on top. In the corner was a tripod holding a large metal cauldron for cooking. Perhaps this was the summer kitchen, when the extra heat from the fire was unwanted in the main house. Fortunately, this was early May and nights were still cool.

"I can't wait to take Maggie for a walk along the roadway and look at the wildflowers. The daffodils are done now and the crab apple trees nearly finished, but the bluebells are out and wild roses and daisies will come soon. That was one thing I missed about Wales. The flowers. Not that there weren't a few lovely gardens in Liverpool, but very formal and artificial, if you ask me."

"The garden is out back of the sheep shed. I hope the garden got more care than the buildings have. I'm not sure how much time you'll have to go walking." Thomas was somewhat glum, but tried to put on a more cheerful face for Ann's sake. Hard work would fix most of it.

Sheep of all sizes were milling around the fences. Ann took Maggie to the field gate to look at the lambs and ewes. She had not forgotten the sound of bleating sheep, high-pitched mews from the lambs wanting to be fed, bold, low-pitched bleats from the older ewes and everything in between. It was a natural choir, spreading to the far corners of the fields. So green were most of the fields, Ann had to squeeze little Maggie with the joy of being in the countryside again. She might miss the shops and friends, but not the busy roads with carriages bustling to and fro everywhere. The smells from the gutters had not been so pleasant either.

twenty-three

Thomas Bailey Family: Pentre Willey, Montgomeryshire: 1868

John Bailey = Margaret Harris
_____|_____(con't. below)
| | | |
Sarah = George Mountford **Thomas Bailey = Ann Jones** Richard   Samuel

(con't. from above)_____
                              | | |
                          Harriet Emmanuel John

| | | |
Elizabeth Mary   Margaret **Alfred Richard**

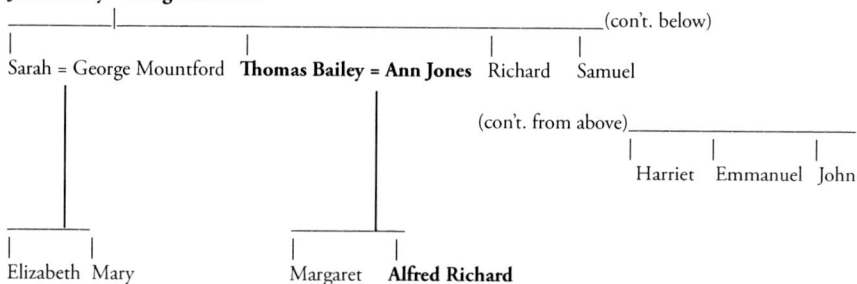

Primitive Methodist church Hyssington, Montgomeryshire.

NOVEMBER HAD BEEN WET AND COLD. THE DROVERS HAD PASSED ALONG THE Kerry Ridgeway with their herds of cattle going all the way to London Town along the Great North Road, their faithful dogs trotting alongside the herd. Drovers made nightly stops at inns along the route where they would pay in advance, for food which their dogs would be fed when returning the exact route of the trip down to London Town, stopping at each inn where their masters had paid for a meal and resting spot for them. Cattle could be rested at the fourteenth-century tollgate at the Angel before completing the last leg of their journey to Smithfield. Numerous pens and sheds still remained along the road despite the huge new Royal Agricultural Hall built in Islington in 1862.

Once the cattle were sold, the feisty dogs of the drovers would return home to their farms. Tucked into a pouch attached to the dogs' collars were messages to family that all was well. After resting up and dropping a few shillings at local public houses, the drovers would return on foot to their homes in Wales and western Shropshire. Some preferred to make the trip to the new industrial city of Birmingham, a freeman's market place.

"Maggie! Stay out of the pigs' slop pail. Why don't you go and see if your pa has some treat for you? Mam will be in as soon as she finishes hanging up these clothes." Ann stretched her aching back. The baby wouldn't be born until January, but she already felt uncomfortable. Thank goodness they had been able to settle into the house as soon as the previous family had left. Ann felt the loneliness of the uninhabited valley especially as her pregnancy progressed. After looking up at darkening clouds, Ann wondered if it was worth hanging all these things outside, or whether she should just stoke up a fire in the lean-to and hang them in there to dry.

II

Alfred Richard Bailey was born ten days after Christmas. His father was so pleased that both his children were very robust. It had been a good move to return to their own countryside. Thomas felt it would be the right time to visit with his parents at the Bryn. It was cold, but not too much snow had collected this winter.

"Margaret, did you see your new baby brother?" Thomas took Maggie's hand and brought her to the side of the bed where Ann lay now with Alfred. Her solemn blue eyes widened as Ann tipped the baby towards her so she could see his little face though he was now swaddled in two blankets.

"Oh. Da baby is red." Maggie's statements were usually succinct, and as far as she was concerned that was all there was to say. It would be two years before she could lead him around the yard, and along the track to the meadow, stopping to look at flowers and lambs on the way. For now, her small cotton-covered ball proved more interesting.

III

The trek up to The Bryn in Hyssington to visit Thomas' parents seemed longer than the four and a half miles Thomas had estimated. Ann began stoutly enough, breathing in the brisk February air deeply. Alfred was so well bundled, Ann had kept checking to see his baby breaths came out as tiny puffs of condensation in the small opening of the blankets. She was surprised she felt as well as she did through the farms at Pentre-ewn and Upper Aston right up to the top of the Montgomery road. In the valley of the Camwad River, the pathway was wet, the river high, almost overflowing its banks. Now Ann was beginning to tire. They could spot Broadway Hall where they would turn west in a slight detour before heading northeast at Ivy House.

"Thomas! You must slow down. Maggie is in tears with trying to keep up and Alfred is getting heavy." To herself Ann added, "And never mind me. I can manage." Thomas, somewhat impatient to arrive in time for a noon dinner, picked Maggie up in his arms and strode uphill towards Hyssington. Now Ann took her time.

"There you are, Auntie Ann," exclaimed eight-year-old Harriet. "We've bin waiting all morning for ya." Six-year-old Emmanuel shyly peeked from behind Harriet's shoulders. He was tall for his age, and nearly matched Harriet in height. He had none of her confidence just yet with people he considered strangers.

"Richard! Good to see you." Thomas and Ann greeted all of Thomas' siblings with exuberance, even John, who gave little indication that he was pleased to see any of them, other than with a slight nod of the head.

"Samuel, go and call your father in from the west shed. We can eat shortly now. Oh, I'm so happy to see you all. Let me see little Alfred. Oh my, he's pink. He must be toasty all bundled up like that." Margaret happily took baby Alfred from her daughter-in-law's hands, and leaned down to give her granddaughter Maggie a hug.

"He's red. He's really red." Margaret laughed and beckoned a young woman by the name of Beatrice over to be introduced. Thomas looked at Richard and his eyebrows shot up in high arches over his blue eyes when Richard gave a one-sided smile and flicked his head in her direction.

"Sarah, how are you? My, you must be on small portions. Is George not feeding you?" teased Thomas with a wink at his older sister, at the same time pumping his brother-in-law's hand in greeting. Before Thomas left Hyssington, George Mountford, who was ten years his senior, had seemed like a confirmed bachelor. He lived at Bryngnot with his unmarried brother, sister, and mother. At sixty-eight she was still farming thirty acres with her children's help, and George was the village maltster. Thomas knew that Sarah and George's sister had been friends, but he never guessed that Sarah had any feelings for George, so it was a surprise for him she had married George. Their two- and three year-old girls were very quiet.

"Pa! It's good to see you," Thomas continued with glad greetings for his father. They hadn't seen each other since before Thomas' marriage. He's aged, thought Thomas, observing his father's slightly stooped shoulders and more deeply weathered wrinkles. Although it was only four years, there was a big difference. Thomas felt his father had always driven himself, moving from one major project to another, always improving the farm, the stone walls, the stock. Thomas knew he might have stayed and helped out, but there were four brothers who would grow into helping around the farm as his father slowed down.

"This is Ann, Pa." Thomas brought his wife closer to him in an affectionate hug, encouraging her with a smile.

"Tis' a pleasure, sir, to meet you at last," uncharacteristically lowering her head in a moment of shyness.

"Oh, it's so good to see all of you here," sighed Margaret looking around at her children, the first time they had all been gathered for a meal in at least five years. She had been down with Thomas' youngest brother and sister to Pentre-Willey twice for a visit with Thomas, Ann and Maggie, but now here were her seven seated around the solid oak plank which served as a table.

"John, Sarah, Thomas, Richard, Samuel, Harriet, and Emmanuel," rhymed off Margaret, nodding her blessing on each one of her children, tears of joy welling up to the lower rims of her eyes. Her husband John harrumphed at the far end of the table.

"Ah, Ma, don't be sad," consoled Harriet, who taking her mother's hand began to stroke it.

Besides roasted lamb done to a turn, winter vegetables from the garden and straw pit were heaped in large bowls on the table. Butter, honey, and loaves of bread were passed around. The adults helped themselves to jugs of cider and malt, and served generous glasses of fresh warm milk to the children. Ann was enjoying the malt, and thought since she was nursing an extra mug wouldn't hurt her. She felt her cheeks flush hotly when her brother-in-law John glowered his disapproval as she reached for her third mug. She quickly changed her arm to reach towards the milk. Fine for the men to have three without question.

"How are things over in the valley?" John asked Thomas.

"Things are doing well. I want to expand the herd, and am planting a mixed grass in the spring. There are some new ideas out there about how much pasture land it takes to feed cattle with grain feed on the side."

"Grain is expensive," interrupted John.

"Yes, but the return is good," replied Thomas.

"Father, would you like to try my bread pudding? I made it myself," Sarah proudly announced. She did much of the cooking for John, and frequently helped her mother. There were always extra hands to feed with three farms to run.

"Thomas and I hope to get a wagon fixed soon. Edwards has been promising to get the parts ready. Then all we need is another horse and we can make it to Bishop's Castle for market on Fridays with no problem." Ann didn't realize Thomas had already been making progress in that direction, and hoped to have the wagon ready early next month. For the time being, they all walked everywhere and it kept them healthy. Most of the visitors departed that evening, but at first light Thomas, Ann, and the children would make the trek home down the valley.

IV

THOMAS BAILEY FAMILY: PENTRE WILLEY, MONTGOMERYSHIRE: 1878

The apple blossoms and hedgerows delighted the eye, and the smell of the blooms filled the air. Thomas looked happily down at his rosy wife and newest addition, baby John. There had to be a John in the family, and he was not about to break with tradition. Margaret, Alfred, and Mary Harriet tried playing cat's in the cradle with string rescued from a parcel. Margaret, or Miss Maggie as she was called in times of favour, was easily frustrated when learning new things and Thomas wished she had not brought it along. He wondered that the children couldn't just enjoy looking at the colourful spring countryside and enjoy it without so much chatter. Ann was bringing butter and eggs to market. He was looking for a few new lambs for the stock, but later today would enjoy meeting with cousins and friends.

"I don't think we can ever count on living at The Bryn, Ann. John seems determined to keep the farm in his name, though he needs my help and Richard's at haying time. I think we should consider moving to town in a year or two. What do you say?" asked Thomas, knowing full well that Ann was itching to get into town and make a few friends.

"Oh, Tom, that would be wonderful. You know I've wanted to get to Bishop's Castle for some time now. Will your brother expect you to be in Hyssington every day? It would mean so much if we didn't have to make that trip every day. I wish we could send the children to a real school."

"I'm using the chance to supply the town with chickens, geese, and hens. I'm going to need Margaret and Alf's help. Mary, John, and Edwin will all go to school for a time." He could sense a slight disappointment in the drop of her shoulders. He knew with the downturn in farming, that they would all have to work hard just to feed the family, and some would choose other paths. Alfred had the work ethic of his grandfather, and himself for that matter. There was nothing else for it.

twenty-four

THOMAS BEGAN DEALING IN POULTRY AND GAME AND BUTCHERING WHEN THEY moved to the house between a shoemaker and Jenkins Yard. Both Thomas and Ann became familiar in the congregation of the Primitive Methodist Church down the road. Nearby public houses were frequented by a different social circle, and Thomas and Ann never made appearances there, but strove to keep up with their religious circle of friends. Thomas often spent long days and short nights at Bryn House during busy seasons, returning to town as often as he could. Then, on Saturday evenings they washed up in preparation for Sunday services.

II

Ann felt the low ceilings cramped the two main-floor rooms of their Bishop Castle's lodgings, especially in inclement weather. Margaret was such a help, but was asked to assist her father on most days. Ann knew she liked to help her Grandma Margaret too, especially since Grandpa John had died. Four years ago John senior had passed on after suffering a painful illness for ten days. Once the death duty was paid, there was precious little left for their part of the family. They still missed his vibrant presence.

Ann called to her daughter. "Maggie, would ya help me string this rope between the chairs before ya go downstairs, so we can at least get our Thomas' things dry. Oh, he goes through nappies so fast that I can't keep up with them." They strung the ropes between the pair of humped-ladder back, elbow chairs so the clothing might drape in front of the small fireplace. The two Bishop's Castle style chairs of green ash would serve to support the ropes.

"See ya later, Ma," Margaret called as she headed towards the yard where the most recent flocks were being kept until her father butchered them.

"Thank ya so much, Maggie. Now don't let that Mountford fellow give you any trouble when he comes to the door. He needs a good smack at the side of the head for the way he talks to ya!" Maggie blushed from her neck to cheeks instantly, but only laughed.

"Oh, and remind yer pa that ye'll be needing to look after yer brother and the shop here when I go to market tomorrow, it being Friday." Ann settled between the arms of a chair holding the laundry, and prepared to nurse Thomas.

Young Edwin had started school this year and Mary and John were also attending the big red brick *National School*, so Ann was alone with baby Thomas, only nine months old when the census taker came around Bishop's Castle in the district of Clun in 1881. Thomas was a good sleeper so she had been downstairs resting her feet in the main room for a few minutes of quiet time and a swig or two from the bottle kept in her deep apron pocket, when she was called to the door to answer the record-taker's questions. She was becoming annoyed with the dark-haired, bespectacled man's repeatedly asking, "Are you sure?' He must be hard of hearing. She wasn't slurring her words, surely.

III

Ann enjoyed a good lengthy stroll some afternoons with Thomas sitting upright in a new perambulator. They usually rounded the corner onto Church Street where right next to each other two carpenters lived with their unmarried children. She glanced towards the Church of England, then at the Six Bells where Samuel Bright, his wife and nine children ran a thriving business. She decided today she would walk up toward The Castle.

"Hello, Ann. Look at that boy Thomas! Doesn't he look like his father?" called Margaret Pugh from the door of the public house her son operated. Although a little gruff, Ann knew her well enough to know that a hard life had toughened her only on the outside. It didn't hurt to be friendly with the neighbours. Ann felt it her outwardly Christian duty to accept publicans, the same as any other business people and tried not to feel superior or inferior as the case might be.

Ann and baby Thomas passed a number of private houses, which she knew to be occupied by masons, servants and general labourers. The next residence was the lodge house keeper and his wife, Richard and Harriet Cross. It was a respectable establishment, catering mainly to widowers with young children or unmarried domestics.

Claudine Taylor, the bank manager's wife, gave a brisk nod as she entered the front door of their dwelling, dressed in full gown, a light, short-waisted jacket with gathers at the center back which emphasized a good sized bustle of glossy striped fabric. Claudine considered herself a class above the Bailey family. Ann sighed, thinking of her own plain woollen dress, but looked over at Thomas' bobbing head and smiled. She had the man she wanted and the children she loved. Ann turned in at the next shop with Thomas in her arms.

"Good day to ya, Elizabeth and Margaret," Ann greeted the grocer and her shop assistant. "Have you any raisins? I'll get a pound of that dried fruit, too. I want to make a *bara brith*, the Welsh fruitcake my mother used to make." Ann placed these beside young Thomas as she pushed off up the street. She passed the Independent and Wesleyan chapels and the chemist's shop. Next door was her friend Mary Harris who was the local wine and spirits merchant. Already widowed at forty-six, Mary and her two sons sold wine from the vaults as well as farmed enough land to employ three men. Ann thought of stopping in to see if Mary was taking a break, but decided that she would like to walk further up Church Street to see if her brother-in-law might repair the heel on her shoe.

Charlotte Powis came towards her, head down.

"Hello, Charlotte," greeted Ann.

"Oh, hello, Ann Bailey. I didn't see you coming. How are the children? I see young Thomas here is doing well." Charlotte placed the letters she was carrying in her left hand so that she might tickle Thomas under the chin.

"Anything for me today?" Ann asked none too hopefully. She rarely received news from relatives, but just on the off chance, she thought she might ask the mail carrier.

"No, I'm afraid not. Mrs. Bright got one from Shrewsbury, though.

Ann went on by the shoemaker, William Robinson's private house, and nodded to Elizabeth Lloyd who was sitting near enough the window of the draper's shop to have light for her delicate millenary creations. She was very gifted, and Ann thought she could have made a name for herself in the city, even London, had she not been hopeful of Harry Leager's attention with whom she worked. At the china shop, Ann slowed to look at the attractive setting displayed in the bay window. Of course she had no need for fancy china, but it was always lovely to look.

At the Castle Hotel Sarah Nelson greeted her from the doorway as Ann entered the garden with Thomas in her arms.

"Hello, Ann."

"How are things with you, Sarah?" They had only recently taken over the Castle Hotel and Public House, and Sarah found it busy even with three or four employed helpers. Her eight-month-old daughter Agnes cooed from an outdoor bench seat.

"Oh aren't you just so sweet, and look at those rosy cheeks," gushed Ann. She hoped to have another girl soon. Three boys in a row were enough. Ann drew the conversation around to the activities of the church, hoping that Sarah might join them at chapel. Ann had been contemplating organizing a tea to raise funds for the church and thought Sarah would meet new people and make more friends outside of her own family if she participated in some of the activities.

An hour later, Ann and a sleeping Thomas headed back down the hill. To the right up Welsh Street were Edwin and Sarah Beddoes' The Black Lion, John and Richard Thomas, shoemakers, Mr. John Lane physician and surgeon, and Edward Jones, shoemaker. She heard the train whistle as it crossed the roadway before passing into the town's station, just a few blocks over to her left. She cut through Market Square so she could go under the house on crutches, a building with such a large overhang that wooden posts supported the upper level. It allowed her to miss sight of the gloomy jail in the vaults of the Town Hall. She allowed gravity to hurry her down the steep hill toward home. Past Edwin Lewis' public house, William Pugh's tailor shop, past houses where she knew shoemakers, ironmongers, and grocers lived.

Then she came to Thomas' brother's house. Samuel worked as a boot and shoemaker. He, his wife Eliza, and three children were situated in a private house of their own in Bishop's Castle. Samuel was one of the Bailey family who had no interest in farming. Because there were now several shoemakers in town, and a dozen apprentices, there had been some discussion about moving to a town with more of a market for fine, buttoned up shoes as well as heavy-soled work boots. She put the brake on the perambulator and stepped inside the main floor shop to attend to her much needed repair. Long skirts did have their advantages when it came to the expense of shoes.

When she exited, Ann couldn't see the one-handed clock on St. John's Church at the end of the street, but she could hear the fifteen-minute bell ringing the quarter hour past. She wanted to get into the house before the children returned from school, and besides, Thomas would have soaked every layer of clothing and nappies on which he was sleeping. Face flushed with hurrying, she pushed open the door and pulled the perambulator up the step into the narrow hall.

The clothes draped in front of the fireplace were still damp as Ann had not been there to feed more coal into the fire. She looked at the worn knobs of the chair backs. She thought of Eliza's fine, side-buttoned boots, and Claudine's flowing gown, but Ann preferred fine furniture. Her desire was to own at least two Clun chairs, their gentle curves and lovely trio of spindles joining two cross pieces in polished wood gleaming in the sunlight. There was a third spindle across the top of the back, and some she had seen, had double spindles between the legs of the chair.

"Ma, we're home," yelled Edwin the moment he entered the door.

"Sh, shush. Thomas is sleeping," scolded Ann. Thomas chose to wake at that moment, but Ann didn't turn her attention away from Edwin.

"How did you get that?" she asked, examining the blue and yellow swelling around Edwin's puffy eye.

"Will Edwards."

"And why did Will Edwards, your friend, blacken your eye?" asked Ann crossly.

"'Cause I said his parents was dull, calling 'is brother Edward Edwards."

"Well, maybe you just deserved that. If I get a report from Miss Pope about your behaviour again, you might end up in the Union Workhouse, so just you mind. There's already eighty people there to keep you company. You better take that jacket off so's I can mend it. Mary, take Ned out the back to wash up." Young John stood watching wide-eyed, slate and book under his arm. Ann pulled her gentle son towards her.

"Ah, come here and give us a *cwtch*."

twenty-five

Thomas Bailey = Ann Jones

Margaret	**Alfred = Elizabeth**		Mary	John	Edwin	Thomas	William	Lillian	Gladys
(1866-)	(1868-)	(1866 -)	(1870 -)	(1873 -)	(1876 -)	(1881 -)	(1882-)	(1885-)	(1887 -)

THE HOUSE ON WELSH STREET IN BISHOP'S CASTLE WAS IN A STATE OF anticipation. Thomas stroked his chin vigorously while awaiting the birth of his tenth child.

"Father, any news?" asked Edwin coming into the room warm-red and dusty from his farm work at the Bryn.

"Nothing yet. How did that carriage repair go this afternoon?"

"Oh fine. Sharp was there trying to give instructions, but John ignored him. Is Mary up there?" Edwin asked, pointing up the steps to the birthing room. His father nodded. Mary and the nursing sister he had hired were both in attendance. Last time the local mid-wife was not what Thomas would consider efficient or sterile in her work. Movement from upstairs indicated the men would not have long to wait. Thomas hoped the birth would happen before the younger children got home from school. He didn't want a lot of noise distracting him from trying to decipher the sounds emanating from above.

"Where's little Gladys Annie?" asked Edward about his year-old sister.

"Next door with Mrs. Pugh. She's going to stay for the evening and maybe for the night, depending on how things go here. Mary will have her hands full so I don't think we can expect her to make our tea. How about you cut some bread and put the water on now so it's ready when the scholars come home?"

Within an hour, moments after the younger children arrived home, Margaret hurried down the stairs red-faced and perspiring.

"It's a girl, Pa. Elizabeth Jane. She's doing fine, and now Mrs. Roberts wants a cuppa. Did you get your tea yet?

"Yes, thank ya, Maggie. Well, well. Our tenth. I guess we should be thanking the good Lord she's a healthy one, and not be complaining it's not a brother to help out, eh, lads?"

II

Thomas' brother John was lonely. It was his own fault he knew. No wife, no children, his parents both passed on. Even his youngest brother Emmanuel, always such a help, had gone and married. Ever since, he had felt a sadness hovering over him. Years before, his sister and husband George Mountford had gone back over to Churchstoke where George was born. When Sarah died, she had left George with eight children. John missed the quiet camaraderie of the maltster. Then Tom's children had been moving all over creation. Even his brother Richard, whom he had relied on as family contact, was farming Runnis Gate at Shelve, a few miles to the north and infrequently visited.

"John, there you are. I thought we could talk about the land you want to sell to the church. Wilcox promised to come about five so he could have a look at the layout. George Jones and Will Davies are lined up to help with the circuit preaching. This will make thirteen places on the circuit. You're not opposed to having the quarterly meetings printed up are you? There is some talk that two pence is too much for a copy, but it eliminates any confusion, and the congregations want to know how they are keeping up with their share of contributions. It just isn't right that the Church of England gets our tithes and leaves us the expense of keeping up our own buildings and keeping our preachers. They sit too comfortably in their dioceses if you ask me."

When Samuel Lister finished his address, John spoke but a few words.

"It's the Lord's work I want to hear being preached, printed quarterlies or no." The two men moved up the hill to the corner lot on the west side of the road where a small stone church would be constructed on property which John Bailey was about to sell for ten pounds. There was enough interest in having a Hyssington church building, rather than making the trip to the Bishop's Castle Primitive Methodist Church building.

John thought of the massive yews that shaded the grave markers of family and friends up the road at St. Etheldreda's Church of England graveyard. His father, his sister, and now just last November, his mother, Margaret he helped bury there. He had stood on that hillside looking over green hills, hedgerows winding down valleys and up slopes. There was no green like it; no fresh air, no mists settling in low parts could compare to these hills where his family had lived, farmed, worked, died, and were buried. Wilcox was in sight now, and John would have to make conversation or be made to feel uncomfortable in the silence he so craved.

III

Bailey Family: Hyssington, Montgomeryshire: 1890s

"I don't see why Samuel had to move all the way north of Shrewsbury to Wem," complained John about their brother to Thomas. They were in the middle of separating some sheep ready for lambing and could have used an extra hand.

"There was no work for another shoemaker. None for the drapers either. I can understand why Samuel wanted to move his family even if 'tis all the way to Wem. He's got seven young ones to feed."

Thomas understood their brother Samuel's situation far better than John who had never married. He and Ann had had ten children themselves. John was just feeling the extra workload now that their youngest brother and his wife were out at Lower Tasker in Hyssington Marsh. Emmanuel had his own farm to work and family to care for now.

"Look at my Alfred Richard as far away as Manchester. We just have to accept that things aren't the same anymore. People have to find work, and mining has been going down the vent for some time now." Thomas glanced over at his brother John to see if he had picked up on the joke, but it was lost on the person Thomas thought of as his too serious, glum brother.

"Fine thing that wife of yours goin' off to Manchester by herself," retorted John.

"She wanted to see her first grandchild. Here she is three months old and I haven't seen wee Maggie myself. Maybe I'll go to Manchester too one of these days if the trains keep running from Bishop's Castle. Seems they're always in money troubles. I can't sees what with bringing in goods and taking out cattle they can't make a go of the line."

Thomas had moved the family into smaller lodgings on Welsh Street. He and Ann had mourned the death of their youngest child, Elizabeth Jane, who had died not yet a year old in 1889. That same spring Alfred took his bride Elizabeth Hotchkiss with him to Manchester where he had been working. Then Thomas and Ann's eighteen year-old son John had been hired as a preacher for the Methodist circuit north of Birmingham at Castle Gresley. Thomas was so pleased John had felt the call, but he felt John spent too much of his time in book learning. His and Ann's oldest daughter Margaret was still at home at twenty-five, but he didn't think for long. She had been seen speaking to the insurance adjuster, George Bowen, after service on a Tuesday or Sunday. Lillian and Gladys were still young enough to be needing care at home, and now young Edwin was getting anxious to work out. He needed a close watch since Thomas had found him in the Boar's Head engaging in a bare-knuckle fist fight which the publican had moved outside. Edwin had been a bit of a scrapper since he started school, and now he didn't mind imbibing the odd malt or two as well. No wonder Ann had wanted to get away for a few weeks until things quieted down.

IV

In Manchester, Alfred looked at his mother, who after placing Maggie in her basket, had nodded to sleep with an empty cup in her hand. He took it from her gently, trying not to wake her because he knew she would be irritable. Elizabeth, his wife, and Mary his sister should be home from shopping for the daily groceries very shortly then he would prepare for work at the noisy railway yard. He hated working in the filth and dusty air, but at least he wasn't underground in a mine. Underground meant more money, but to him it wasn't worth it. He hoped for something better in the future for his family, and that would probably mean a move out of Britain.

There were men on the streets looking for work. The orphanages were full. Daily he saw groups of people with all their belongings standing on rail platforms ready to head out from ports for Canada, the United States of America, New Zealand, and Australia. He had seen lines of young children escorted by severe looking matrons, headed off to the Liverpool docks ready for transport. He felt a heavy sadness at their little frightened heads turning side to side, seemingly searching the crowds to the left and the right hoping for rescue. The older ones joked, pushing each other with their elbows and nervously laughing, looking on their journey to a new country as an adventure.

Alfred's in-laws were very different from his own family. There was little communication once they moved to Manchester. Elizabeth's father had married a woman with young illegitimate children in 1866. This gave Elizabeth two half-siblings, and then a full brother was born two years after her. By age fourteen, Elizabeth had worked for her Aunt Sarah and Uncle Francis Marston at the Priestweston Red Lion Inn as a domestic. Her father had moved back to Churchstoke when her mother died. She was heartbroken when he took William with him. In fact, he had taken Amos and Emma with him as well. Amos was now working in the lead mine at Churchstoke, helping to support the family. She shuddered, thinking how glad she was to have been away from dark-eyed, staring Amos.

Before his marriage, Elizabeth's father, Richard Hotchkiss had lived in Hyssington, and so had known the Bailey family before Elizabeth married Alfred. She knew Alfred was set against some members of his own family drinking so much, so she had no fear of him squandering his pay. When they moved to Manchester, Alfred had joined the Odd Fellows, and made sure they found a chapel to attend.

"Well, here we are," laughed Liz. Mary and Elizabeth brought the packages into the eating area of the back room. Alfred's sister, Mary was staying with them so she could train as a nurse.

"Has the young lady been asleep the whole time?" asked Elizabeth of her daughter.

"No, Mother was talking to her and rocking her until she fell asleep," responded Alfred.

"Until who fell asleep? Maggie or your mother?" quipped Elizabeth. Alfred sighed, knowing Elizabeth had every right to criticize his mother's drinking behaviour. It was a "mother's ruin" that made her so jolly at times, but it also made her a demon behind a horse-drawn cart, and cross with the world. He and his family would not touch alcohol, which made him ask Elizabeth, "Are we going to that temperance meeting at the Odd Fellows Hall Thursday evening?"

"If Mary can stay to look after Maggie, I will. When is your mother going home?"

"That I can't say, but I imagine Father will expect her soon. By the way, here is a letter come from Montgomeryshire. Your brother I presume," as he handed a penny post letter to her on his way out.

Elizabeth sat herself down to rest her feet and read her brother's letter from Broadway Mill in Churchstoke. He lived with the miller and his family, working as the carter to transport the flour to surrounding villages, farms and bakeries. She missed Will, and wondered if her and Alfred's life went according to plan, whether he would join them by moving to Canada.

twenty-six

"ANN, STOP FUSSING. WE NEED TO GET INTO THE COACH RIGHT AWAY." THOMAS' voice was gruff, cutting in its sharpness. Ann was fussing with her youngest daughters Lillian and Gladys' collars because she needed something to do. Both young girls were in tears, and kept their hankies in their hands. Ann knew Thomas was trying to control his emotions, as was she, because out of all their children, they couldn't understand why their son John had been the one taken from life on this earth. He was twenty-three. His most recent appointment had been to the Primitive Methodist Church in Chadsmoor. They had been so proud of his abilities, of his passion for preaching. She had been just thinking how fortunate she was that Margaret, her oldest daughter had just safely delivered a third child, when they got the heart-breaking news from Chadsmoor.

"There now, you two. Stop your sniffling. Your eyes are all red. Let's get into the coach. Richard is waiting," and Ann led them out the front door down the step into the bright, very warm day in July. They had a long journey to the Cannock Cemetery. Alfred was meeting them there as Elizabeth was too close to delivering their third child to make the journey. Oh, Ann thought, were there clouds and thunder to keep us company. The train was stuffy, and Ann felt offended by the cheerful chatter among younger people on an outing. Couldn't they see the family was suffering? The traditional black garments should have been a clue.

Alfred was waiting at the cemetery gate, his suit jacket too warm and too tight for the hot day. He was intensely saddened by his younger brother's death. John was one of Alfred's favourite brothers: quiet, unassuming, yet with a passion for God that Alfred admired. Quite a number of John's congregational members were in attendance. He had been well-liked as a preacher. Some came over to the family to offer sympathy. Most of the family kept their eyes downcast. Their black clothing seemed to be steaming, wet tears and perspiration evaporated as clumps of earth hit the pine box deep in its grave.

Words of the preacher floated across the heat waves. "Ashes to ashes... dust to dust..."

II

Ann was returning from a trip into Manchester, after meeting Alfred and Elizabeth's third child. She had needed a rest after her accident last month, when the wheel came flying off the carriage as she rounded the corner at Church Street. How embarrassing. She was somewhat woozy after the fall, or perhaps she had been woozy beforehand, but she didn't argue about being assisted into the Six Bells for a beverage to help her recover from the shock. Thomas would hardly be sympathetic. She was just relieved that no-one had been with her as she took the carriage at full tilt from the market down the hill, whipping the horse from a near standing position, hair flying in the wind despite her respectable hat being carefully pinned in place before she left her place in the market stall.

"Well, how does our young grandson John look? "inquired Thomas, as he helped Anne off the train platform on her return from the big city of Manchester.

"I've been waiting here a quarter of an hour," she chastised him, at the same time gripping his arm tightly. "Our Maggie is a fine big girl now. John, or Jack as they are calling him, and I think it suits him, is a fine young lad. He's small for his age, but then Alf is somewhat thin, and he's very talkative for a boy. He's taken to talking to his baby sister, Annie." Ann was delighted that Alfred and Elizabeth had named the baby born August ninth, 1895 after her. "The three are lovely children. Alf and Liz are taking them well in hand. No shenanigans with them." They took the wagon up to Hyssington for the remainder of the day. Young Ned was going to look after the shop, and Thomas wanted to get in some fresh poultry.

III

Alfred told them at work he would need to be taking the twenty-fifth of June off for his sister's funeral. In an old, worn carpet bag he placed his suit jacket, the same one he had worn not many months ago last year for his brother John's funeral. Five-year-old Maggie watched her father with big eyes, waiting for his usual lifting of her high in the air and a big squeezy hug on the flight down. She always squealed in glee, but was disappointed when her father only gave her a pat on the head, and then went over to her mother who was trying to calm a crying Annie. Maggie didn't feel anything was right. Something had changed yesterday when they told her that her Aunt Margaret Ann had died of a "ce-re-bral hem-mor-age". Why did people die? Did this mean she would never see her again? What about George and her little cousins Will, Gladys, and James? What would they do without their mam?

IV

The usual procedure was for Thomas to go up to The Bryn House in Hyssington and help his brother John with the animals on a Monday. Sometimes Gladys and Lillian came with him to help clean and cook in their uncle's kitchen. Today was different. Ann had wanted to accompany her husband.

"In here, Thomas," called John weakly from the bedroom.

"What, not up yet?" but his question was stopped short the moment Thomas saw the beads of perspiration on John's forehead.

"You better see if anyone is around at the malt house, Ann, to fetch the doctor," directed Thomas. John would never have allowed them to summon the doctor had he been well, but at the moment he was too ill to protest.

"How long have you been like this?" asked Thomas.

"All night," moaned John. His fevered face, contorted by pain, was blotchy red and white at the same time. He held his stomach. Thomas was concerned.

"You just might have to take a few days and rest up. I'll look after the animals," offered Thomas. He would stay and Ann could perhaps look after the shop. Although their attitude toward each other had softened over the years, Thomas didn't think Ann would want to be alone with John so sick.

"Ann, is that you?" called Thomas down the stairwell after her return.

"I'm about to make a pot of tea," replied Ann. "See if John wants a slice of bread and butter or some soup."

John just shook his head, refusing anything to eat. He might try the tea he thought, but he just couldn't understand what was wrong. His gut had been acting up lately, but nothing that he could think of that would give him this pain. He tried hard to breathe shallowly, to keep from disturbing his abdomen and causing more pain.

"I'm just going to look after the animals, John. Ann will be up in a minute with some tea. See if you can't drink some. Strong black tea and lots of sugar. That should help some." John nodded and closed his eyes.

Ann was shocked to see the beaded sweat pouring from John's forehead even more profusely. She could tell he was in too much pain for the toast, but perhaps he would drink some tea. At that moment, Dr. Puckle came in the backdoor downstairs.

"We got a patient up there?" he called.

"Right this way, Doctor. My, you was fast!" Ann waved him up the narrow stairs into the bedroom to the left. "In here, Doctor."

Dr. Jones frowned when he read the thermometer. He poked around John's abdomen and groin, eliciting groans of discomfort from John. He shook his head.

"How long has he been like this?" he asked. Ann shrugged her shoulders. Something had prompted her to accompany Thomas today and now she knew why. He was going to need gentle care by the looks of it.

"Will he recover, Doctor?" Ann asked quietly.

The doctor closed his bag and shrugged just slightly.

"I believe it's *peritonitis*. I'll give you this white powder if he's in much pain. I'll be by this way tomorrow and we'll see how he is." The doctor left Ann on the landing listening to John's groans. She wondered if she should tell him about the morphine powder or not. The situation did not look promising.

Thomas came in while Ann was cutting some bread and buttering it. She was glad she had made a loaf to bring with her, even though John was not likely to eat any of it. His fever was worse and he was vomiting.

"Tom, do you know what *peritonitis* is?" His tired look became one of concern.

"I know it's not good. I believe George Mountford's father died of it. I think I'll get up to Runnis Marsh to see if Emmanuel can help with the animals. I may be a while. There's some cloud coming in and I think we'll have rain this afternoon before I'm back. Keep an eye on him," Thomas said as he nodded his leave. He wondered if this would be the last of the Baileys at The Bryn House. Once John passed, God willing he wouldn't just yet, The Bryn House would come under new ownership, and their long-time, family dwelling would be lost to strangers.

"Of course, I will. I may try to give him some of the white powder if he's awake." Ann went up the stairs to see about changing the bedding. John had perspired so much the sheets were soaking. Now there was a mess to clean up by the basin she had strategically placed by the bedside. She rolled him to one side, he groaning, she grunting. She was able to pull the sheets from beneath him and place a new one down before rolling him onto his other side. In this way she changed the bedding, and then tried to get some of the white powder mixed with cool tea into John's mouth. It dribbled down the creases of his chin, but she was mostly successful. She gave a glance at his quivering body on the bed, saddened to see him suffer so, and, regretting earlier resentments, headed down the stairs to the outdoor scrubbing tub with the bedding. She wasn't long before returning upstairs.

"John, do you think you might like something to drink? I've got the kettle on." Ann stood still at the foot of the bed. He was dead she was sure, so still and clammy looking. She reached to shake his arm, but knew he had gone to meet his Maker. She listened in vain for his breathing, and then went downstairs to await Thomas who would be on his return by now, on the evening of the twenty-fourth of June 1898.

twenty-seven

BISHOP'S CASTLE, SHROPSHIRE: 1901-19

Thomas Bailey = Ann Jones

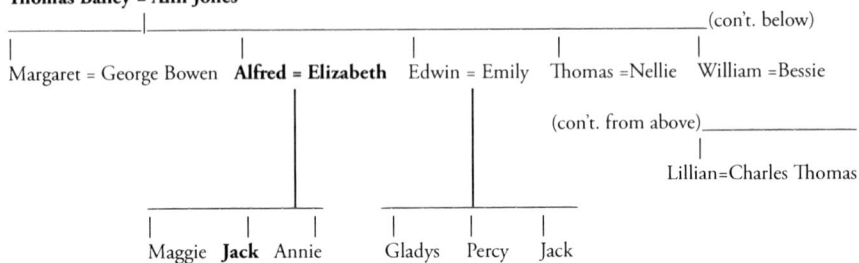

```
        |                                                                    (con't. below)
|                     |              |              |            |
Margaret = George Bowen   Alfred = Elizabeth   Edwin = Emily   Thomas = Nellie   William = Bessie

                                                       (con't. from above)_____
                                                                 |
                                                       Lillian = Charles Thomas

      |      |      |          |       |      |
   Maggie  Jack  Annie      Gladys  Percy   Jack
```

Edwin (Ned) Bailey holding son, Jack.

ANN'S CARRIAGE CAME WILDLY DOWN THE CASTLE GREEN ON HER RETURN TO Bishop's Castle from Hyssington where she had been housekeeping for her husband and son Thomas. She never knew why the horse couldn't control itself better, when it knew the route was so steep. She threw off her bonnet at the door, and was stunned to see her nearly three-year old granddaughter with a little bundle of her clothing tucked under her arm.

"Gram, Daddy come get me." After making this statement, Little Glad stood holding her thirteen-year-old Aunt Gladys' hand and looked with uncertainty at her grandmother.

"Well, we could have had more notice. When did this come about, Gladys?" Ann asked of her daughter.

"We got a wire this morning that Edwin was coming to get Little Glad now that Emily is better and little John is fit and healthy."

Tears clouded Ann's vision as she bent down to draw her petite granddaughter towards her. The fresh country air had not done much to rejuvenate Gladys' tiny frame. Ann understood her son Edwin and his wife Emily would want their young daughter to be with them, especially since her health had not drastically improved with fresh town air, as she had so hoped. But, oh, she would miss her sweet face.

"When does Edwin arrive?" she asked of Gladys, the elder.

"The noon train. Will's gone with his mail cart to meet it before he goes back to the job." Gladys looked sadly at her niece whom she had grown to love in the weeks she had been with them in Bishop's Castle. Now all she had to look forward to was laundry, cleaning and tidying up after her mother and youngest brother Will. At least her sister Lillian had a domestic position and was getting some wages.

Edwin arrived to mixed emotions springing from his sister, mother, and daughter. His mother had become cross, and Edwin could smell her gin breath. Ann did not want to give up Little Glad. His sister Gladys looked stricken with sadness, while still trying to comfort Little Glad who had become frightened at the turmoil which her pre-departure had caused.

"Well, Mother, we must be off to get that return train. Have you got your things, Glad?" asked her father. His sister nodded on behalf of her niece, tears coursing down her cheeks. She gave her a final hug, and flung herself around to go into the kitchen. Ann was quiet. She suddenly had had a feeling that this would be the last time she would see her granddaughter.

A few weeks later, Ann and Thomas heard the news of their granddaughter's death. Little Glad had succumbed to scarlet fever and died on the thirtieth of December at her parents' home in Birmingham.

II

The years 1905 and 1906 were a whirlwind of activity. Thomas tried to sort out the order of events. He wanted a last visit with Alfred and his family before they left for Canada.

"Can ya be sensible and invite them here, woman? I'm sure they want to see all the family," begged Thomas.

"What family? Who's still here in Bishop's Castle, hey, who? It only makes sense that we go up there or we may not see them before sailing. What's the date?" Ann asked.

"Their passage is booked on the vessel *Vancouver*, and they leave from Liverpool the twenty-six of April. I guess we could wave them off, but I want a proper visit too."

They did wave them off. Thomas and Ann stretched their arms tall and vigorously waved, hoping their son could see them among the thousands. Edwin, his sisters, young Percy, and Tom were there to see their brother and family off, looking somewhat envious, but knowing too, this would probably be the last time any of them would see Alfred and his little family. They waved red handkerchiefs trying to attract the family leaning on the railings of the 3400-tonne *Vancouver*. Thirteen-year-old Maggie looked so lady-like. Jack, full of eleven-year-old excitement, waved and cheered so loudly that his younger sister Annie covered her ears. Alfred remained stoic, but Elizabeth beside him wiped her eyes and blew her nose into Alfred's handkerchief. Thomas, Ann and the girls stood on the dock, until the ship moved forward, white sides gleaming from brilliant sunlight. Green water churned beneath its stern where the rudders kicked up bubbling foam.

What would it be like to be leaving everyone you knew behind, to go into a strange, wild country of mountains and snow, and flat prairies where you can see no one for miles? Ann thought to herself. They had seen the posters; they had heard the reports of many friends' families who wanted what they said was a better life for their children. Canada was the land of opportunity, they said.

"Well, shall we go on home?" asked Thomas of his four adult children. Ann needed little prompting. She regretted not having something special to give to Alfred and her grandchildren. Something to remind them of home. There was not even a family Bible or tatted hankies which she could pass on. She tucked away the red hankie she had been waving, wishing that the familiar weight of a bottle in the deep pocket of her apron was there, but her Sunday dress was not outfitted with such a thing. The waves of the steamer were flattening out now and the puffing stacks blurring in the undistinguishable distance. She lifted her head and turned to follow the remaining family.

III

Will was the first to let his parents know about his plans to get married. He had hinted at it during the harvest time when he returned to Hyssington from West Bromwich, Staffordshire to help his father. It was a quick stop in at his parents' lodgings to let them know that come the New Year of 1905, he and Bessie Blount would be tying the knot. Will was not unhappy to be in the city. He remembered the early days of his career as a mail cart driver. The mail had to get through from Bishop's Castle to Craven Arms and back in a cart that was open to all kinds of weather. He shivered thinking of it.

Young Thomas let them know after the fact when in the fall of 1906, he and Nellie Tabbener signed the marriage register. He ran a butchering business in West Bromwich, which made him a good living, or would have, had he not spent so much time in the locals. Thomas had worked with his father raising poultry, and had assisted his grandfather and uncle at lambing and sheep shearing times. Will and he still made trips to Bishop's Castle to help at busy times on the farm. Young Thomas knew a good butchering animal when he saw one. West Bromwich to the northwest of Birmingham was a big part of the industrial expansion of the previous century, and it continued to grow, fed by grocers and butchers such as Thomas.

Edwin's announcement of going to Canada was somewhat easier for his parents to accept than the move of Alfred. From the reports Liz wrote from their home in Hamilton, Ontario, the move sounded beneficial. Their children were all to be in school until fourteen years of age when they finished what Canadians called elementary school. By that time they had learned to read and write well, and in fact Jack had shown a great proficiency in his writing and talked of being a writer some day, unless he followed his Reverend Uncle John's path in the ministry.

Now Thomas and Ann sat in their quarters at 27 Church Street trying to sound brave at losing another son and his family to emigration.

"They haven't been happy since Little Glad was taken," testified Ann, "especially Emily. She took it very hard. Maybe it's the best thing for them. A new start."

"It's an awful long way to go to lose yer troubles," argued Thomas. "What's Edwin goin' to do in Ontario? He won't take to farmin' in that winter weather."

"Where's the tin types they sent before they left?"

"They aren't called tin types anymore. These are photographs. Here."

Ann took the two small photos and studied them closely. There was Emily holding three-year-old Percy's hand, and six-year-old John leaned against his mother's side, her arm protectively over his shoulder. There was a shrub behind them and a shuttered window of a brick building which must be their house.

"Young Percy must have been squirming around. His face is blurry, but oh, isn't that a nice big collar he has. Emily is smiling. She must be looking forward to moving."

"Maybe the picture was took before she found out they was emigrating," speculated Thomas gruffly.

"She's let John's hair grow and look at those curls. Percy is dark and his is straight. Those short bangs down the front suit him. I think he looks like you must have," said Ann, glancing at her husband who was puffing on a pipe. He was preparing himself for retirement, and had taken to trying to decipher the price of commodities in the newspapers. Neither his sight nor his reading was that good.

"Where did you say they were going in Ontario? Cheltenham? They want to go to a new country, but they sure like being reminded of home. Most of the place names I hear about, except Toronto, are from back home here in the old country, like they have a London, Cambridge, Dundas, Ancaster, Binbrook, Durham, and then counties like Oxford, Kent, 'n Essex. Isn't that funny?"

The *Ionian* left her berth on the seventeenth of May in 1906, carrying a thousand passengers in steerage, second class, and first class. Edwin, Emily and their two boys were among many headed to Ontario and the new western provinces via Montreal. During the three week journey some of these people became friends; some were homesick, some seasick. A few, mostly men and young boys, thought they were heading on the best adventure ever.

Thomas and Ann soon began receiving news of new grandchildren. William Arthur was born to William and Bessie, followed by Eleanor Kathleen born to Thomas and Nell, all in West Bromwich, near Birmingham. Lillian announced she was marrying Charles Thomas and a year later John Thomas was born. Thomas senior thought humorously they should have named him after himself, but of course he already had the surname Thomas. He was proud to comment within three years that his sons Edwin, Thomas, and William had all named a son after him.

IV

"Ann, the census man is here. Can you answer his questions so's I can get back to the shop?" Thomas continued out the door as he put his jacket on, leaving the door open for the census taker to peer into the narrow hall. Ann emerged from the sitting room, tidying her hair. When it came to the question "Where were you born?" Ann thought of her birth place: Llandyssil, Montgomeryshire. She hardly knew the place, they had stayed there so short a time. Her father moved them frequently, looking for employment, and so all of her siblings had been born in different villages. Now that none of her children remained at home, it was quiet. Even the two boarders did not lighten the heavy silence of the rooms.

PART FIVE

Bailey and Hannaford

FAMILIES

twenty-eight

ALFRED CONSIDERED HIMSELF A SUPERINTENDENT OF THE HAMILTON STEEL Works. It was really a custodial position, checking the floors for debris, the dials on the furnaces, the gates that should be closed, or open. Jobs were not as plentiful as the stories depicted on posters. Elizabeth had written home that he was the superintendent, and was pleased with such a position. His brother Edwin, known as Ned and young son Percy were visiting from the small community north of Toronto called Cheltenham where they had been hired to farm.

A friend had given Alfred a copy of the *Hamilton Spectator Carnival Souvenir* of 1903. There were at least six pages of businesses listed with details. Under "STEEL WORKS" he found his company.

"The Hamilton Steel and Iron Company Limited. Pig Iron, iron and steel bars, bands, nails, washers, forgings, etc. Capital invested $2,000,000; 850 hands." It was beyond Alfred's comprehension that such an amount of money had been invested in a single company.

"Percy, how would you like to see the big steel plant where I work? How about it Ned? Would you like to come down to the plant for a bit of a tour?" Alfred asked his brother before he had a chance to head down to the local bar. It wasn't a local pub, the hub of the social community of working class families, as there had been in England. There was what they called a bar, and the men of Italian and Irish nationalities and the Conservatives would go down after work and drink heavily, cause a ruckus and be pushed out onto the street swearing and hollering. Alfred never went into a bar and he didn't drink alcohol. He had seen what it did to some family members and neighbours, and now he could see a pattern with Ned. Alfred and his family would never drink after signing the Temperance pledge.

Alfred noticed too that his brother and son had not tried in the least to temper their accents or vocabulary. He and Elizabeth had made sure that the children made every effort to lose any sign of their English accents as soon as they were able. They wanted their family to be seen as Canadians, not immigrants. They made a point of sharing the 'Canadianisms' they had learned each day, with the rest of the family. It became almost a game.

"Come on, Percy, bring your da and we'll go down to the factory." Ned nodded his head at the hissing results of cooling steel rods, both square and round. He had worked in a factory so he knew what to expect. Seven-year-old Percy looked impressed.

"You coming to church with us on Sunday, Ned?" Alfred Richard asked his brother.

"Nah, we'll be getting back tonight. Nellie is anxious about getting the final packing done before too long. We'll be taking the 'Harvester Excursion' along with hundreds of others I suppose. That soft-hearted Nellie wants to take Mrs. Heath with us out west from Cheltenham. I told her leave well enough alone. We don't need a former Bernardo orphan from the slums of England to burden us. We already got plenty of trouble, don't we Percy?" Ned cuffed his son affectionately.

II

It was two months before news came that everyone in Ned's family had finally arrived in the west and that they would be homesteading to the northwest of Saskatoon. The tracks in the prairie land crossed just to the south of their land. Because Percy got scarlet fever, Ned had had to go on by himself in order to collect the furniture which had gone ahead of them. Emily and Percy were quarantined for two weeks while Mrs. Heath took young Jack into the store to stay with her. After the quarantine was lifted, Emily, Percy, Jack, and Mrs. Heath were all on the wooden train, the 'Harvester Excursion' with all the workers from Ontario who were looking for short term work at a dollar a day. Emily had somehow found the five dollars for Mrs. Heath to go with them.

The first project was to build a waterproof, warm building to live in. Since there were few trees, most homesteaders started with the thick rooted grasses which covered the prairies. Still a young lad, Jack helped pile the sod for the 'soddy', but even with both he and Mrs. Heath heaving them up, they had trouble getting the top pieces.

"Jack, get a move on with those pieces! You're not keeping up," shouted his pa getting close to the building site with a fresh sled of sod he had cut. The sod was cut in pieces of about 3'x 1 ½ ' and was at least 12" thick. To prevent crumbling, all the pieces cut in a day had to be laid the same day, like bricks, one row on top of the other in a staggered pattern until the walls were about 8' high. Cutting with a sharp 'cutting plough' was just as hard work as laying the sod, but faster.

"We can't get it up. It's too heavy!" complained Jack.

"I'll show you too heavy," and Ned prepared to give his son a sound beating, but was stopped by Mrs. Heath.

"You hit that boy and I'll hit you on the side of the head with a shovel!" she exclaimed, raising the shovel in her hands. Ned backed off, and just huffed. He took her scolding, but wasn't happy.

"Come, on, you two. I'll give ya a hand. Jack, you climb up top there." Lumber was used for the top and bottom of windows and above the door. The roof of the Baileys' soddy would have a wooden framework to hold more pieces of sod. It provided a small, but well-insulated cheap cabin for the homesteaders. They would stucco it in the future to prevent too much erosion.

Once the soddy was built, Jack and Mrs. Heath would cut wood on the weekends with a two handled saw. During the week Mrs. Heath worked in a hotel. Emily and young Jack spent much of their time in the tent preparing the food. Emily became quite creative with a cook pot and small fire in a pit. They had to be very cautious with a fire as wind blew day and night.

III

Back in Hamilton, Jack and Annie went as far as possible in school before they went out to work at sixteen, but Maggie was sent out to work at fourteen, without regrets. She was more interested in homemaking than in schooling, though Elizabeth was adamant that they could afford to keep them in school as long as possible. Both Jack and Annie were taking some high school courses at night. Elizabeth took a job as a clerk to help with mortgage payments. R.G. Dunn was a large mercantile on Hughson Street South, which paid fair wages. Their new home at 423 Jackson Street was ready for them to move into in 1909. Alfred had been working as a labourer after he and several of the others at the steel plant had been let go. "Reorganizing" they said. 'More like poor management,' thought Alfred. He continued to look for more permanent work, but there was not much growth at the moment. Things in the family seemed to remain in a steady routine until November of 1910.

"Maggie, are you sure about this?" Elizabeth asked her oldest daughter.

"There's no rush, you know, Mag. You're only nineteen. You've only been working for a few years. You might like more time to see the world," suggested her father. "He will expect certain things you know," warned Alfred. He had no idea that Maggie was already 'in the family way'.

"Oh, Pa, of course I know he will, but he's so kind, and quiet. He's not pressuring me at all. I know what I want, and I want to marry Alf. And not just because of his name either," quipped Maggie with a teasing smile. Alfred looked at his oldest daughter full of fresh hope and not much younger than himself when he married Elizabeth. Alfred Miller had already spoken to him asking permission to marry Maggie.

"Well, he is a steady fellow with a good job in electrics and has saved almost enough for an automobile. I hope he plans on buying a house before he does that though." Alfred paused, looking at his daughter's flushed cheeks, and expectant hope in her eyes.

"Oh, go on with you then. Go and relieve the poor fellow of his worry. I suppose you'll want to marry before the New Year. And if you want to move in here, it would help with the mortgage payments."

"Oh, thank you, Pa. Yes, definitely before the New Year -- before Christmas. Then we can have a little time together without having to lose too much time from work. How does the twenty-first of December fit with your plans?" Her mother nodded, but Maggie barely heard their answer before she turned to hurry into the den where she had seated Alf while he waited for her to discuss his proposal with her parents. He was a good ten years older than the slim girl he hoped to marry, but he had worked hard and was trying to save his money. He didn't drink, and that he knew was important to Alfred Richard, rather Nick, as he was called by the family. For now he would be Mr. Bailey to Alfred Miller, as was customary. Although Alfred was Anglican, he hoped that the difference in their religion was not going to be a problem. By next Christmas he hoped to move to their own home with his bride. For the time being, they would all share the residence on Jackson Street West.

IV

Jack was preparing to read Thomas Peacock's *Maid Marian* for school, when he suddenly felt fevered and nauseated. His mother came in hurrying quickly in response to his calls, but was too late to get a bucket to catch Jack's dinner which was forcing its way out. She knew he had quite a fever just by his flushed face.

"Maggie, can you get a wet washcloth, the pail and a rag. We have some cleaning up to do. This has hit your brother very sudden like."

By morning Elizabeth had decided she should take Jack to the doctor, or see if he could make a house call. Annie was sent off down the street to find out from a neighbour who might be available.

The verdict was typhoid. Where would he have found that horrid disease? Canada was where they said the water was so pure and clean, a person could drink out of the streams almost anywhere, so they had said. It was four months before Jack felt well enough to wander around the house and look after himself totally, although he had enjoyed some time studying, and reading.

twenty-nine

"WELL, LIZ," ALFRED EXCLAIMED AS HE ENTERED THE KITCHEN ONE EVENING before dinner. "I got myself a job. One I think will stick." A renewed building surge was beginning to expand and employed many that had had little or no work in the past year or so.

"Well, where is it and what is it? Are they paying a fair wage? Is it contract work, or is this more permanent?" Elizabeth stood at the sink with soapy water washing potatoes, still a staple in her family, while she fired off these questions like a drill sergeant.

"You know the big building on James Street down by the market place they've been renovating? It's just opened up as a department store and they were looking for clerks. They've got great big show windows opening on the street where you can see the market. It was a good business move if you ask me. That Mr. Wheelan is quite the boss man."

II

The Hamilton Times was offering him a little work, but Jack wanted more. Dictionary constantly beside him, he read and he wrote every spare minute. He had been able to attend three years of high school, but his desire didn't stop there. He took classes whenever the time and money allowed, and he knew his writing had improved. Sometimes he felt so close to the Lord, he felt his calling might be as a preacher, but always the excitement of the newspaper office drew him back into thinking he really wanted to be a reporter. A chance to do a front-page item would set him on the path.

"I read Henry Ford is planning to start up a moving assembly line for making cars," interrupted Jack. "I'd like to see that!"

"I heard at the Lodge that the Hannaford Brothers are looking for some extra temporary help while they plaster the Hamilton Public Library," responded Alfred to his young son. "I'm surprised it's taken so long to get this far. I thought the cornerstone had been laid back in August of 1911."

Jack knew his father was trying to be helpful. Jobs were not very easy to get with so many of the new immigrants from all over Europe now coming to Canada and this part of Southern Ontario. Jack went to 232 Robinson Street.

"George, there's a young man by the name of Jack Bailey that wants to apply for work as a plasterer."

"Looks a little slight, if you ask me," George Hannaford commented quietly to his first cousin, Charles. They were both looking out into the workyard through the partially open shed door. A hatless, sandy-brown haired young man stood digging his boot into the dirt while looking around him. His observant eyes hesitated over certain piles of lumber, frames, and pails as he stood his full five foot-eight height.

"He's from the old country," offered Charles. They were keen to employ new immigrants from their homeland of England.

"Well, let's try him out. I know we need to hire someone since... since your brother Arthur has been unable to work, and since Frank left." George could see the lips tighten within Charles' thick moustache, so he walked over to the door and called out.

"You're on, Jack. Be here at 6:20 tomorrow morning to help load up. We'll be expecting you."

The big job was to get the Hamilton Public Library ceilings completed by the March deadline. All the sub-contractors were in place and except for some sombre observances over Arthur's death, there was an air of anticipation and excitement.

Jack returned home quite chipper with this new, temporary job to tide him over until he could get fulltime work.

"Annie, can you read me this letter from the Mountfords in Shropshire? Maybe you can make sense of it," Alfred asked his daughter.

"Thank the Lord the children have more reading and writing skills than we was given," remarked Elizabeth.

Annie read the rather elaborate script of the handwritten letter.

"The Mountfords are moving to Canada, and they are sending Edward and Pryce over first to get a farm up north of here. Who are the Mountfords? Do we know them?"

"They were neighbours near Hyssington and Bishop's Castle. You would never have met them, although come to think of it, Edward came to visit in Manchester once when he was looking for work before he started mining at Minsterly," replied Elizabeth. "What does it say about when they are coming? Do they need a place to stay?" Alfred and Elizabeth knew how difficult it was moving into a strange country.

"No, it says the two boys are headed up to Shelburne, wherever that is, and they already have an offer on land there. Edward and Pryce have to register the claim. It's odd, but I thought everyone wanted to go west to farm like cousins Ned and Emily," contemplated Annie.

"Well, I think it's none too soon for them to be making the move. The miners had a poor go of it in Wales, I can tell you that. Farming weren't any easy way of life either," Alfred commented knowingly.

It was just a few months later when they received a telegram informing them of the untimely death of Pryce, aged nineteen. Their evening meal was quiet that night.

"Poor Eleanor and Ed. They haven't even arrived in Canada yet. They can't even bury their poor son. What Edward must be feeling about losing his brother like that!" exclaimed Elizabeth.

"Well, I imagine he had Pryce buried local. It was an aneurysm that got him sudden like. They maybe will have a service after the family gets here. How many other children do they have?" inquired Alfred.

"Oh, about six, or seven. I lost count after Arthur. Suzanna is your age, Jack," Elizabeth said, looking straight at her son.

Jack frowned and shrugged his shoulders. His mind was on his work at the newspaper. He was hoping to get past writing the obituaries without having to go in for collecting advertizing. He wrote constantly, when he wasn't reading. Sometime he would like to be asked to speak to groups at one of the smaller Methodists churches in an evening service. For now, attending the Christian Men's Club each Sunday afternoon at three was a real joy.

II

"I'll be fine in a moment, thanks," Jack reassuringly told his father, Alfred. He had just started to work with his father in the yard when he had an accident.

"Are you sure?" asked Alfred, unconvinced. The lad was pale, and Alfred thought he had heard something snap. "I wonder if you didn't crack a rib as you landed. You twisted around too fast to catch that piece of lumber. You should have let it fall," he said, glancing back at the rogue piece which had unbalanced Jack causing him to fall.

Jack was still sprawled on the pile of lumber, unevenly stacked, ready for the fencing project they were to about to begin. He breathed shallowly for a minute, and then picked himself up. He was in a great deal of pain; however, Jack was not about to let his fall stop him from work. Not only did his father need – no, expect Jack's help, but also he was not about to let his wounded pride stop him, though at the moment his rib cage hurt like blazes. It was some days before he could lift a full pail or more than one piece of lumber. It was going to be a challenge to work at the library, lifting and fetching.

thirty

HANNAFORDS MEET BAILEYS: HAMILTON, ONTARIO: 1913

Charles and George Hannaford and their crew for plastering the Hamilton Library.

Robert and Elizabeth Hannaford.

GLADYS WAS VERY EXCITED. UPON HER FATHER'S RECOMMENDATION, SHE TOOK out a 25-cent Sick and Funeral Benefit Certificate with the Royal Templars of Temperance. She studied the purple sections the office clerk had typed: *Miss Gladys Lavinia Hannaford*, a member of *Sovereign* Council, No. 9, located at *Hamilton, Ont.* She signed under the Financial Secretary's signature on the seventh of February 1913. Now she was an adult.

"Father, did you know that this will cover fifty dollars funeral benefit. That would be some funeral!"

"Gladys, usually that benefit goes to the family, not just for the cost of the funeral. Sorry to disappoint you, but there won't be a parade on such a sad occasion," corrected her father. He watched her face comprehend the reality of such an occasion, but she quickly smiled and opened up the tri-folded paper.

"At least I would receive $3.00 per week if I were unable to work. That's almost as much pay as I get now!" She refolded the document and took it away for safe keeping. Her father shook his head at her vitality. Where did she get her spontaneous vim? They had felt so fortunate to have her survive scarlet fever at four years of age. Her eardrum burst, causing a hole in it, but since then, one would never know that she suffered a significant hearing loss because of it.

Gladys was thrilled because she preferred working over going to school. She became efficient in her typing, her figures, and general bookkeeping. Her father had let the company know she was available when he was in ordering the plaster and plasterer's hair for his business. Freemans just had a position open up at the Barton Street branch and had expanded their coal, coke, and wood business to include builders' supplies such as mortar, Portland cement, clay, gravel, and bricks, among other things. Gladys knew a great deal about the materials having listened to father, uncle, and grandfather, discuss business so frequently.

II

Jack Bailey became uncomfortably tense for no apparent reason when Charles Hannaford, his employer, first asked him to go into the house at 232 Robinson Street to see how Gladys was getting along with the coffee making. The men were loading scaffolding and forms.

"Your father wondered how the coffee was coming along," Jack said quietly to the young girl he knew to be Gladys, Charles' daughter.

"It's coming just fine. I'm nearly done the grinding. Myrtle has the kettle on. Myrt, they want the coffee. I'm finished grinding," Gladys hollered to her sister. She smiled broadly at the young man in the doorway.

"Are you Jack?" she asked.

"That would be me. Jack Bailey. I'm one of the new workers," answered Jack.

"You must be from the old country, aren't you, although you don't have much of an accent?" inquired Gladys, swishing her skirts noisily as she turned from the counter.

"Glad, you could have got...oh! I didn't see you there," interrupted Myrtle. "I need to get my hair done before I go to work. Couldn't you make the coffee, please?" Myrtle pleaded with her sister.

"I have just as much to do... oh! All right, you go on." Gladys smiled again at Jack and at that moment Jack's heart began to pound just at the sight of this vibrant young woman.

Walking to work that day, Gladys studied the hem of her skirt in the glass windows of the store fronts. It was a little longer than she liked. She was pleased with the fullness of it, but not the length. When she had made it, she really could only judge the hem length by her other skirts, but the trend was just a little shorter. She would fix it at noon.

"Hello, Bill. Good morning, Mr. Freeman," nodded Gladys in greeting the men at the office. They had a busy day lined up with payroll due in a day, and a whole group of small orders for coal, wood, and building supplies for which bookkeeping took a great deal of time. Gladys enjoyed the busy routine and camaraderie of the office staff. During their break, the girls in the office chatted about the upcoming picnic and excursion to Balmy Beach. They had an interest in the suffragettes who paraded, picketed, bombed, or threw themselves in front of Lord Asquith's automobile and were sent to jail, in aid of getting the women's vote. They all would like the vote, but it seemed to them the English women were extreme in their approach.

"Men have all the luck though. They can ask you for a date, but we can't ask them. They control the money, and hand it out in dribs and drabs, complaining all the while. I even have to hand over my entire pay every week to my father, and then he gives me back a whole fifty cents as if he had earned it," complained Helen.

"That's the way it is in my house, only it's me ma that hands me the fifty cents. Pa wouldn't think that I might need a little something sometime," agreed Alice. Gladys kept quiet about that point. At her home, she just assumed she was to hand over her pay to her mother for housekeeping. She thought maybe her father was softer than most men when it came to dealing with his wife. Gladys wasn't going to argue. Her mother had told her to keep a dollar back every week and not to be asking too often for extras. Gladys was careful with money because her grandparents had taught her a few things about not squandering money. There were too many who had little or nothing, and Gladys suspected that her grandparents had been in that position before they came to Canada.

Most of the violent activity surrounding suffragettes and politics was going on in England and once their boss joined them, the conversation would turn to the aggressive behaviour of the German or Russian armies.

At noon Gladys walked swiftly home for her dinner.

"Mother, I'm just going to hem this skirt," and before her mother had time to argue, Gladys had gone up the stairs to the sewing machine, threaded the needle and was preparing to turn up the hem the width of the original hem. Gladys wanted to do this in a hurry, and so pulled the hem up from the back of her skirt and began. When she had gone as far around as the material would allow, she stood part way up, swung the skirt around on her waist, and proceeded as far along again as she could. In this manner she had the skirt hemmed without taking it off, and was downstairs ready for her dinner in short order.

"Did you change your mind then? I thought I heard the machine going fast enough to take the hind quarters off a rocking horse! What were you doing?" asked Lavinia, Gladys's mother.

"I did the hem. I just did it while it was still on, and just kept swinging it around as I went," Gladys smugly informed her mother.

"Well, I never..!" exclaimed her mother, mouth agape. Her daughter's impulsive behaviour was so far from her own contemplative nature, and her quiet mannered husband's, Lavinia wondered where Gladys got her spunk. She failed to remember her own father giving her the nickname of 'Topsy' with good reason.

II

After a few mornings of Charles nodding him into the house, Jack began asking if he should get the coffee, and then it became a routine that Jack would go into the back doorway of the kitchen and watch Gladys make the coffee and pour it into the new thermoses. Myrtle withdrew her services the minute she saw Jack. Although a handsome young man, she had other responsibilities and thought that her presence might interfere somehow, as he appeared to be rather shy and bashful. She was still within hearing distance anyway.

"How did your father learn his trade, Gladys?" Jack tried to ask questions that would get Gladys talking, and then he could just listen and happily watch her radiant face during animated conversation.

"Oh, my grandfather and his brothers were plasterers in Torquay where they grew up. That's in Devon, you know. They don't get snow like we do, and there are palm trees you know. Grandpa and Uncle Alf started their own business when they came to Canada." Jack appreciated the fact the brothers had worked hard and done very well for themselves, and now their sons and nephew were carrying on with the business.

"Didn't your uncle have another son that was a plasterer?" Jack had checked the listings for the past three years in the *Might's and Vernon's Business Directories* in the old library, and had found a Frank Hannaford.

"My cousin Frank didn't really like being in the business, and he's gone back to being a traveling salesman. Bill likes it though. He wants to carry on in his father's footsteps. He's a smart businessman. One day cousin Norman will be old enough to work for the business too. That's George's son, my dad's cousin."

thirty-one

ONE EVENING AT 423 JACKSON STREET, JACK ASKED HIS SISTER ANNIE FOR SOME paper.

"Are you using this little notebook, Annie? I need some paper to write on."

"Oh, sure," she readily agreed, "I don't need that little scribbler. Here let me take out the shorthand exercises. You won't want them. What do you want it for, anyway?"

"Oh, just some writing. Maybe some poems," offered Jack.

"Poems? There's a nice little poem in tonight's paper -- something about the Titanic survivors."

"Oh, I don't want to copy poems. I intend to write my own. I want to be a really good writer someday you know," Jack stated with conviction.

"But poems?" asked Annie.

"Well, writing is writing, and the more practice I get the better. Here, let me get one and you can tell me what you think. I wrote it on Christmas eve." Upon returning to her room, Jack proceeded to read:

"<u>Morning Meditation</u>

Oh! For a life of gayness and mirth
With no thought, but that of pleasure.
To travel idly around this earth,
In luxury and leisure.
To partake of all which the world has best.
And enjoy it in peace and rest.
Always travelling while having life and health.
And a superabundance of wealth.
But as I mused, there came the thought,
What if these should fail?
When face to face with Him, thou art brought;
What would they avail?

Let us then, forgetting self
Seeking such fellow man to help
And living in a broader sphere,
Find pleasure thus, in living here.   24/12/13"

"Oh, that's good, Jack. I like it. You've got all the right rhythms and rhymes."

"Well, maybe the last bit needs changes," and Jack penciled some in.

"How's this? 'So let us then, forgetting self,/Seeking some fellow man to help'?" Jack hadn't intended asking his younger sister for approval, but with his older sister Maggie married and busy with a husband and child, he wanted someone with a sympathetic ear who could still listen objectively. Not so sympathetic that he would share his next inspirations with her, but for a few things he could test out his writing and his speaking voice. He intended presenting a speech for the Temperance Society next month, and he could use Annie for practice.

"Thanks, Annie," Jack said, waving the notebook in his hand on his way into his room.

Jack, sitting at his desk which faced the window, took out his ink pot and pen, opened Annie's thin note book which had been stamped, MISS BAILEY, and began writing.

Love is like an earthquake,
Which causes much unrest.
But though inflicting heartache,
Is a not unwelcome guest.   31/12/13

The following morning Jack met with disappointment as he entered the kitchen to see Myrtle grinding the coffee. She looked up at him with a pleasant glance, not quite a smile, her dark head of waves and poufs pinned in a manner reminding him of his sister, Annie. That evening he wrote in his little notebook.

Love is like a bubble
And when it breaks
Removes much trouble,
and relieves heartaches.   1/1/14

II

Jack had been using the Underwood typewriter at the newspaper office where he worked as a junior reporter on Saturdays. He had spent the day filing and tidying up, and as there was no Sunday paper, things in the office were quiet enough that he could type up his speech, making a purple carbon copy. When not busy with work, Jack could hardly keep focussed on anything except his love of a young woman, and the writing of poetry helped allay his restlessness.

His little notebook was the last thing to which he turned in an evening, usually after a full work day, and perhaps an hour or two spent with Gladys, his sister Annie, and some of Gladys' Hannaford cousins. Myrtle was likely to hang about if she were not out with her other working friends. Images filled his mind as he quickly wrote "The Lighthouse".

"At a point upon our rock-bound shore,

Where the dreadful breakers roar,"... As usual the first two lines came easily, were the sum of his initial inspiration, and the rest would either follow quickly, or every word or phrase could be a struggle. After the first eight lines of this January evening's creation, he changed the metre.

Out on those waves tempest tossed
There comes a ship which seems hopelessly lost
Her captain seems frantic, her mate almost mad
Each man of the crew was unusually sad.

The sea had been rough, her port she must reach,
She is steering straight for that treacherous beach
But as o'er the sea falls the darkness of night
There comes from the lighthouse, that beam so bright.
No longer doubtful of the way to go,
Her captain knows now where deep waters flow.
Past that bar, now covered with foam
He enters the harbour, the sailor is home.

Jack carried on, slipping the message in at the end: "but stay one moment, and ask yourself why, The light oft seems so dim in you and I."

On another evening he chided himself for being so frivolous as to spend free moments trying to express his pent up emotions, then another verse would appear in his little notebook:

Oh, waste not precious, golden time
In idly making words to rhyme,
But fill each line with helpful thought
Of joy, and love, or comfort brought.

Jack wondered at times if he would make a decent preacher. Was God calling him to improve himself and his writing skills so that he might lead people to the Lord? He scrawled yet another verse as it came to him:

Let each day have its own appointed task,
When from the dawn light removes the mask.
And hour by hour throughout the day.
Seek someone to lead, into the narrow way.

On a cold February evening, Jack was invited into the Hannafords' home by a smiling Myrtle as was becoming routine.

"Jack's here, Glad. Aren't you ready yet?" she'd ask in a teasing tone, knowing Gladys was doing her best to get her waves under control and her ears partly covered while maintaining a stylish pompadour.

"Good evening, my dear," greeted Jack as they headed for the cosy den where Charles had his office desk. The door always remained open, but the room usually provided some privacy.

"Oh, Jack, you look very dapper tonight. Are you going somewhere special?" Gladys would nudge him affectionately. She always brought in some kind of mending or hand work. Tonight she was carrying a new little bundle with instructions for tatting. She hoped someday to make a runner, but to start, it was enough just to do a very small doily.

"I was thinking about the future. What would you think if I trained as a preacher?"

He hoped she would approve. He wanted her by his side and that was his daily prayer.

"Say not, that I have no gift
Some poor, forsaken man to lift
To a higher, nobler, better plane,
Than is found in pleasure's crowded lane."

He quoted her the verse he had written the night before.

"Oh, I thought you wanted to be a writer. The life of a preacher is very hard," explained Gladys, thinking about how difficult it might be to be a preacher's wife.

"No less difficult a career than that of a writer," mused Jack. He had seen the reporters at the newspaper scrambling and sometimes so tired that they could hardly focus on anything but putting the story they were following into correct format.

"I hope that you will be agreeable to whatever direction the Lord leads me," he asked, his eyes shining with that honest idealism so powerful in his youthful enthusiasm.

III

Annie was very excited and talked so quickly that her mother hardly understood her.

"Oh. I've got the job. They offered it to me, right there on the spot. Oh, mother, you should see the inside of the building. It's the Federal Life building on Delaware, you know the one that takes up the whole of a city block. They have elevators and marble floors, and brass railings; that's where his office is!"

"Whose office?" asked a bewildered Elizabeth.

"Mr. Hugh Murray's office. He is an insurance agent, and I'm going to be his stenographer." Annie was thrilled with the prospect. It was a good job for a nineteen-year-old, but she had done well in her final examinations, and when they tested her at the office, she had done equally as well, not allowing her nervous stomach to hamper her skills one bit.

thirty-two

JACK ENTERED THE ROYAL TEMPLAR HALL ON THE CORNER OF KING AND Catherine Streets, minutes before he was to speak. His prepared speech in his hand, he pulled open the heavy oak door on Friday evening to face the Sovereign Council during the silver medal Oratory contest.

"Mr. Chairman and Friends, I would like this evening, for a short time, to speak to you about Intemperance. By this word, I mean the use for beverage purposes, of alcoholic liquors; for while a man may be immoderate in many other ways, he is not usually spoken of as intemperate, unless he is addicted to excessive use of intoxicating liquors. Intemperance is the result of an unbridled appetite, which, if allowed to hold sway will not cease its destructive work until death relieves the victim. Numerous and sad are the cases of blighted lives which are brought to our notice continually. Scarcely a day passes without hearing of someone who has fallen beneath the touch of this demon Drink. An evil, not a necessary evil, and yet a licensed evil, it is allowed to work its havoc in our Country, our homes and among those we love best. None are safe against the attacks of this cunning, wily traffic. Some of us it is true, never have tasted it, and God helping us never will, but who knows when, in a moment of temptation, a weaker brother may not fall."

Jack carried on, clearly articulating, knowing his case to be true and heartfelt. As he continued his speech, he thought of the stories of his grandmother, the foul smell on her breath during her visits to Manchester, and the disappointment and hurt experienced by his father.

"What is more heart-rending than to see a home where the Mother is addicted to the habit of drinking...? While the women here do not frequent the bar-rooms as in the Old Country, one needs but to watch the stores where liquor is sold in order to comprehend the enormity of the destruction that is going on in our midst. We have but to notice the 'booze wagon' of the liquor store and see how it is carrying destruction where the bar-room cannot reach. Away with the bar-room, yes away with the bar-room indeed; but away,

away, with the shop license too, should be our cry." Jack felt the adrenalin rush through his veins, throbbing at his temples causing him to grow warm. He continued.

'Total Prohibition' is the cry of some. Stop making the stuff and nobody will drink it they say. I would to God that we could; and yet others say the time is not at present, and friends, it never will be until we make it so. Rome was not built in a day. The British Navy as we see it to-day, is the work of years, the result of co-operation of the strength and integrity of a mighty people." Jack gestured emphatically, and caught a drip of perspiration from his forehead.

"Therefore let us remember that we are fighting in a righteous cause and against a powerful foe; for the enemy is entrenched behind years of preparation and with great financial means as ammunition. Political graft and corruption is an ally and what cunning and deceptive methods they employ in their endeavours to baffle us and frustrate our plans. But if we would defeat this enemy, we must send ironclad against ironclad, we must equip with heavy armament and quick firing guns, made of the most sanguine hope; firing – righteousness and justice and having for gunners, those who love the cause and are true."

Jack felt his use of the figurative language of war was appropriate to the times. Armament building in Europe was creating tension across Europe, and he wanted the audience to feel inspired by this picture of fighting a great battle, a battle that had been within his family back in Shropshire.

"We may not all be able to get into the firing line and yet, there are many ways in which we all may help. We may not all be able to stand on the public platform and express our views upon this matter, but we can at least talk with those with whom we come in daily contact. We may not all be able to render large financial assistance but we can, at least, give the 'widow's mite'. Above all, we can all use vote or influence on election day that will ensure the election to our City Council, Provincial, and Dominion Legislatives, those who are most favourable to the cause of Temperance."

As he gazed intently over the audience and council, predominantly Methodist Liberals, Jack concluded.

"Here sons could grow up amid clean environments and become such a race of hardy Christian manhood, possessing clean morals, sturdy physique and a reputation for integrity and thrift that would become the envy and admiration of the civilized world. Oh may that day not be far distant when Canada shall assert herself and set a pattern for other nations, to follow." He concluded his final paragraph, and breathing heavily, took his seat to a loud, but controlled applause.

Percy Lewis and Peter Sterling, fellow contestants, broke their own applause to slap Jack on the back as he sat down.

Dr. Emory, Dominion Secretary of the Royal Templars, gave a few remarks, and after the musical program by Miss Daisy Tarvis and the Sovereign council brass quartet, Miss Nellie Pyke, according to the news report, "one of Hamilton's coming elocutionists, gave a recitation." Jack read the results of his victory the next day in *The Hamilton Spectator*, giving a nod of satisfaction.

II

"Jack, you really must have delivered that speech with might," remarked Annie after reading the review in the evening paper. Looking up, she saw that Jack had yet another brown paper package under his arm and was headed up the stairs.

"What have you got there? Another book?" she asked with a frown. "What are you going to do with all those books you already have on your shelf? You must spend a fortune on books!"

"Worth every penny they are, and I read them more than once." The package under his arm became almost electrifying, so important was it. Jack feared his sister would ask what books were in it, and this he had no intention of mentioning. He bounded up the stairs before further comment could be made. Alone in his room he unwrapped the package. The plain-brown-bound *The Writing Expert* was set aside to reveal a much smaller, pale-blue-bound book *A Moment's Thought on LOVE*. Inside the front cover Jack wrote:

Let fate do her worst
there are relics of joy,
Bright dreams of the past
which she cannot destroy
Which come in the night-time
of sorrow and care,
And bring back the feature
which joy used to wear:-
Long, long be my heart with
such memories filled,--
Like the vase in which
roses have once been distilled.
You may break, you may

shatter the vase, if you will
But the scent of the roses
Will hang round it still.

He wondered how to sign it. Should he sign it at all? What would happen if Gladys' mother or father saw the book? Or worse still, her sister Myrtle? He simply drew a line and thumbed through the pages. There were poems and short pieces of prose by Lord Houghton, John Doone, Emerson, Kingsley, George Elliot, and Plato.

On Saturday afternoon, a cold, brisk January day, Jack called on Gladys as he said he would. She greeted him with a spontaneous smile, but held back any indication that the happiness was because of his presence. He was sure that she was interested in him, but she didn't always demonstrate it. She was young and interested in everything. Her infectious laugh and buoyant demeanour lightened his mood and sent him home to his desk. Here, he would try to pour forth his feelings about love, words he dare not yet say.

You may laugh if you will
At the love-sick swain
But you had better keep still,
For e're long you may be the same.   1/2/14

thirty-three

HE THOUGHT OF HIS SISTER ANNIE, SOMEWHAT IN AWE OF HIS MOOD, BUT STILL too young, he thought, to appreciate the depth for which Gladys had overtaken his feelings. At least she didn't jab in the ribs, and smirk the way Myrtle did with her sister, Gladys, although they were a friendly threesome. The walk between Baileys on Jackson Street and Hannafords on Robinson Street was a short, ten-block hike, shorter if one went through the bowling green. Annie had started to accompany him. She and Gladys, both office girls and the same age were becoming good friends. Jack would hurry home after an evening with the bright star of his sweetheart shining like a beacon. If things did not go well, he was near to despondent. Then he would slowly go to his room and open his little orange notebook to the next empty page and pencil in a verse:

"This too, is the story, so sad, yet true.

And it may be accounted to me or to you.

Just a smile of scorn, instead of delight

May upon many a life place its own tainted blight.   2/1/14"

His love of Gladys was second only to the love he had for his Lord. His father and mother had thought he should have a practical trade – like plastering, but Jack liked speaking and on some occasions delivered a message at Zion Methodist, or another local church. He sometimes thought of his uncle, the Reverend John Bailey who had been a hired preacher at eighteen, but whose life was cut short at age twenty-three. At these times he would feel a zeal for God's love that he wished to share with everyone, but especially Gladys. She remained less zealous than he, but never belittled him for his faith. At other times he felt the only thing he wanted to do was write, whether a lecture, a poem, or an article for the pulpit. He enjoyed studying the English language, its nuances, the tremendous vocabulary with which he could express the thoughts of his heart and mind.

"To-night I wanted to be just with you, Gladys," smiled Jack as they strolled in chilly spring evening air. They followed the path in the park to where lights were coming from a newly installed bandstand.

"Do you think dancing is against God's will?" queried Gladys, thinking of the office girls' talk of dances and big band music, thinking too of some new tunes which she and Ethel were trying to learn from listening to the radio.

"I don't think it's a very godly activity, no. There are so many other things that we can do with our energy." Pulling her around to face him, he looked earnestly into her eyes. If eyes could be flashing, Gladys' were. She could feel his warmth, but had been duly warned by mother and older sister of the passions of young men. She intended to put him off for some time yet, if she could, although before summer's end she might just have to allow him a kiss. She anticipated the future, but drew herself back and grasped his hand while stepping back onto the path. No caresses yet.

Later as Jack trod up the stairs, he could hear a poem starting in his mind: "You say that you feel it would not be right/For him in his arms to hold you tight." He thought of her dancing eyes, never mind the unholy thought of her dancing body, or her innocent question tonight. She loved him he was sure, so why deny him so much as a kiss?

He wrote. His passions filled the lines. By verse four he expressed some frustration:

"Do without it! Why yes, if I really must.
But life might seem brighter for this little trust.
Though if to refuse it, you still deem it best,
Then may God give me patience, is my one request.
Do you think that the Father who looks down from above,
On His children with always that same dear love,
Would forbid it!? Nay! But rather would his richest blessing impart
To see such response from your noble, true heart."

II

In January Jack had read of England's Prime Minister's declaration that the arms buildup in Western Europe was 'organized insanity.' Then some of the senior trade union officials who were trying to get miners to strike in their South African mines were deported back to England. In February, *The Hamilton Spectator* reported Ulster's opposition to Home Rule for Ireland. Men were preparing for civil war. In March, Germany's Kaiser Wilhelm II fuelled further war speculation with building up more arms. Jack asked himself, "Cannot the world live in peace?"

Gladys would sit close, she would hold his hand, and she would turn and look at him lovingly. At last she allowed Jack to kiss her full on the lips. His heart raced, his palms grew sweaty, despite his aching hip. He loved Gladys. He wanted her for his wife, and dreamed of married bliss. At times his rheumatism would act up, causing pain, and crankiness. He always regretted those moments, but Gladys forgave him, and understood his discomfort. Her own father suffered with such pain as did her grandmother. Gladys' mother Elizabeth Ann would often sit with her knitting by the stove in an evening, warming her aching bones.

Jack became so smitten with Gladys as his own one true love, that he had a difficult time sleeping. One night in April he got out of bed and took up his pencil:

That Dear Sweetheart of Mine
As I sit at evening, with my darling, all alone,
And look upon that face, the dearest I have known,
I let my fancy wander, until from Future's iron grasp,
A worthy place I've torn, for the hand which now I clasp.

The verses flowed, as one comforting image after another gave him the release his passions desired. Oh, love was grand.

And now as we sit together, my heart with joy is filled.
To picture you, my Queen, in the castles that I build,
When I shall be a preacher and the message tell so true,
To dear ones who are waiting, and I'll owe it all to you.

He carried on finishing the nine verse poem before dawn, and lying back for a short reprieve. Things would be wonderful once he and Gladys were married. He was twenty-one, a good age for a man to be married, but he would need to work on his career as a Methodist minister and begin to save more money so they could at least afford a little flat, or rather apartment, as they called it in Canada.

thirty-four

GLADYS HAPPENED TO GO THROUGH THE FRONT HALLWAY ON HER RETURN TO work after dinner at noon. She was regretting having eaten the turnips and felt more comfortable standing. The blue envelope, already opened, letter beside it, beckoned her. Though not addressed to her, she read it curiously.

34 High St.
Prescott, Lancashire
May 22nd, 1914

My dear Louie & Topsy,

I daresay you will be surprised to hear from me after so long a time, but better late than never perhaps you have heard from Dave I believe that we are thinking of going to Canada so I put off writing until I was pretty sure of the time we were likely to go. My eldest son has got a very good position in the Canada Wire and Cable Co. Toronto and all being well we shall be leaving England somewhere about August next so you are only 40 miles off (so I am told) am looking forward to seeing you both. I was at Jeanie's a fortnight ago and she gave me your letter to read and showed me the book of views you sent. I have two other sons, they are both married and they will be coming out as well though not perhaps all together but my daughter will be going with myself & son and his little boy, who lost his mother when he was born out in Russia so I have brought him up.

I have heard now and then from Dave how you were doing but not many particulars. He told me you (Topsy) had never been well since you went out. I can't seem to call you anything else, yet I should like to have a letter from you when you can spare time but I will write again when I hear from you, and tell you when we are starting for certain. Jeannie was very pleased to hear from you and seemed pleased that we were going to be near to you both. She seems in very poor health and quite broken down after looking after Robert for so long it does not seem 24 years since you went away, though so many things have happened since then. I daresay Dave has told you that Samuel had left me many years ago. I do not know if he is dead or alive and what is more I do not care. He never was much good as you know. I have lost sight of Tom for some time, but am trying to find him, as I would like to see him before I go away. Well I must draw to a close now hoping you are both quite well, and will hear from you soon. With very best love

From your affectionate sister

Sarah Money

Gladys was stunned with all the news.

"Mother," she called as she turned back toward the kitchen. "You never said Aunt Sarah had written. When did you get this letter? Do you think we can go to Toronto to visit them? We could stay with Ellen or Carrie and her husband. What's her son's name and why was his son born in Russia?"

Lavinia sighed. She had been "Topsy" since she was a very young child. The youngest of six, she had been a lively youngster, always full of energy, and curiosity. She had not been very lively since the move to Canada. The cold chilled her to her bones, even with the warm fur mufflers which Charles insisted she have.

"I see you read the letter, then. Addressed to you was it?" she questioned Gladys, eyebrows raised.

"Well, no, but I figured if it was addressed to both you and Louie, you wouldn't mind me reading it," Gladys, with downcast eyes, answered a little more quietly. Her mother's pursed lips overrode the slight hint of a smile.

"Albert, Sarah's son was working in Moscow when his son was born. Basil is his name I believe, if you look at the back of the picture of your Aunt Sarah and her grandson she sent. Poor Margaret, his mother. She died about a month after his birth. She was unlikely able to get proper treatment. Conditions in Russia are not very sanitary even now."

Her mother's look of sorrowful remembrances turned away Gladys' next question about Samuel. Where was he? Was he the one she remembered hearing about running off with someone half his age? There were things she would like to know, but her mother was unlikely to be very forthcoming with more information. Maybe she could correspond with her uncle David. He might tell her more.

thirty-five

THE WORLD WAS STUNNED WHEN THE NEWS WAS RELEASED: THE *EMPRESS OF Ireland* had been sunk. Over thirty Hamiltonians had lost their lives on that liner along with thousands of others. On Sunday, June the 7th, crowds began to gather in Dundurn Park mid-afternoon for a memorial service. It was estimated there were 15,000 in attendance. The thirteenth Battalion Band played Mendelssohn's Funeral March, according to *The Spectator*'s report. Feelings were mixed, but strong. Some wanted to turn any war away from the Canadian side of the Atlantic and others wanted to get over to Europe and put an end to the political chaos, the apparent aggression, especially after the sinking of the *Empress of Ireland*.

II

Jack was in Brantford. A group was there training for the Army Medical Corps. They were mainly young men such as him with minor health issues, or men considered too old to be in combat. If it came to him going overseas, which Jack doubted, although his medical record indicated he was healthy enough to go, they would be there to pick up the wounded and bring them to safety. There were nurses and stretcher bearers of all ages going to France and Britain to help in the military hospitals. Large estate homes were being taken over all the time for military convalescent homes. Right now he liked the change to a small town like Brantford, but felt unsettled in some ways. He was happy to be able to communicate in a written format with Gladys, and hoped she would appreciate a little humour.

78 Richmond St.
Brantford
June 24, 1914

Dear Gladys,

It is with fear and trembling that I am attempting to write this, my first letter to you. As I have nothing to say I will be as long as possible. I am enjoying good health so far (and hope you are in the best of health and spirits too.)

It is now about nine o'clock and since supper I have been out on the veranda. I am getting plenty of rest (and hope you are too). I have an enormous appetite, (and hope you have too). I am working, but not very hard (and hope you are too). In fact I have plenty of everything except <u>you</u> and that I could wish for (and hope you do too).

I think that I will be down on Saturday, and would like to know if you care for that, if not let me know. If I am going to (which I believe I ought to) I will be compelled to come down on Monday, so may as well come home for the week end, obtain stimulus for the passion that alone can make men stand and win; and also say good bye for good-night for last Sunday night.

He signed off for the night and hoped Gladys would respond in kind.

Gladys came into the dim hall at noon and saw the letter on the side board in plain view. Well, her parents, grandmother, and sister would have something to think about. She resolved not to reveal its contents. Quickly she headed to the front veranda with it and studied the post mark: Brantford Jun 25 11 AM 1914, ONT. The red two-cent King George stamp was cancelled out with "Brantford OLD HOME WEEK AUG 9-14." She was relishing everything about the letter: the way he put the words on the page, his penmanship, his touch of humour. When she finished reading it, she carefully folded it back up, replaced it in the envelope and went to her room to look for a safe place to keep this, her first letter from her dear Jack.

Jack caught up on his newspaper reading the following weekend. The headlines of last Saturday July 4 read: "ROYAL DEAD ARE LAID TO REST. Artsteman, Austria, July 4 - The bodies of the assassinated Archduke and consort..." Jack went on to read the article beside it. "SQUABBLE OVER TREE TRIMMING. Parks and Works Department refuse to do it. - And the Hydro Board is Going to Stand Pat." This held little interest for him.

On another page he checked his favourite column: *Knotty Points*. The first question was, "Is it legal for parties to place poison in such a manner that it will destroy their neighbours' chickens? Subscriber. No, it is not. - Ed." Jack laughed. Someone, likely a woman, was trying to let a neighbour know that she knew what was going on, but was too afraid to confront the neighbour with it directly. Jack then sat down to do what he really wanted to do: write to Gladys.

78 Richmond St., Brantford

July 7th, 1914

Dear Gladys,

Having said that I would write on Tuesday night, and "being a man of my word", I must now take upon myself the (irksome duty) of penning this epistle.

With this introduction (which you know how to take) I will proceed. The weather here for the last two days has just been glorious, & if it is the same at the Beach you should have enjoyed yourselves, if not I hope you enjoyed your-self anyway, and will continue to do so for the rest of your holiday.

I hope that the mosquitoes are not bothering you much now, and if I might give some medical advice, I would say take Health Salts as I believe it is the water that is causing thee trouble. (I was <u>raised</u> in quite a number of places Monday morning) & since coming here I have not been bothered although the mosquitoes bite here just the same, so I think it is the water.

There is one thing I like in writing. It is a difficult thing to quarrel and so I can speak (out of the fullness of the heart) without danger of any <u>slapping</u> etc., not that you ever indulge in such liberties, but that there is no immediate likelihood of you doing so. Still the "wounds of a friend are faithful but the kisses of an enemy are deceitful". Needless to say I would like to have both from a friend.

I suppose Mrs Church Aunt Susie has gone home, if not kindly remember me to her and also to our little friends, Muriel and Dorothy, not forgetting any others who might care. If you are not coming up to town for Sunday and I am to come down you had better let me know what provisions I am to bring, whether (potatoes or cabbage) as it has been very cheap living for one during the past two weekends.

I do not think there is much more that I can say, always remembering that words cannot express some feelings, so I think I will close expressing the desire to be near one whom I again commit to the care of One who is able to save to the uttermost; and hoping that absence makes the heart grow fonder of your unworthy yet

Loving Jack X

S.W.A.K.

(Signed)

As you wander at eve, o'er that sandy beach,
And hear the lessons those wild waves teach
I would ask you to listen for the beat of a heart
That should awaken yours, though miles apart.

P. S. Tell Annie that I will try to write her Wed. or Thursday.

thirty-six

HAMILTON, ONTARIO: SUMMER AND FALL OF 1914

Gladys and Jack.

Annie Bailey and Gladys Hannaford.

The peaceful routine evenings of being together was reduced to weekends with Gladys and Jack, sometimes accompanied by sisters, or friends. Gladys' parents had rented a beach house for the summer months, which they had done in previous summers. If the weather was hot, there were times on the bay or Burlington Beach swimming and rowing. After his course, Jack continued his work as a plasterer, part-time newspaper writing, and poetry. Thursday July 9th's *Hamilton Spectator* had an item about the new two dollar bill which was considered very artistic in design. The framed figures of king and queen faced a decorative number two and the corners each had a number two with other designs. The pale green made a lovely background for the bold black printing of Dominion of Canada. Friday's paper had an item that pleased Jack immensely: "NO BOOZE FOR CITY EMPLOYEES." He glanced over the list of students who had passed Departmental Exams. He recognized few names as it had been some time since he was out of school, but he was rather shocked to find that only 61 percent of them had been successful.

II

"So, Myrtle, what does your father say about the czar now that he's mobilized more than a million troops?" asked George Mountford, who was visiting from his family farm near Shelburne.

"He's wondering what the plans are. He thinks it's a direct result of Austrian troops invading Serbia, and the Russians coming to the aid of their Serbian allies," was her knowledgeable reply.

"Well, I'm glad that Britain is so strong. They are definitely superior, and together with the Allies, are a formidable foe. I would think the German armies would turn on their heels and run," Annie said.

"Gladys, let's take the row boat out. It's such a pleasant day. We can still talk, if you like," suggested Jack.

"Oh, you just want her to yourself," teased Myrtle, pleased for her sister, yet at the same time a little envious as she had no serious beau.

After pushing off from the dock, Gladys asked Jack in all seriousness, "Do you think there will be trouble in Europe, enough to cause a great war?" Jack looked at her earnest eyes, and pondered.

"There is bound to be trouble. All a person reads in the papers is about which countries are mobilizing troops, and which countries threaten to invade. The militia in Canada has had fewer than four thousand in it for years, but they are building it up. If Britain goes to war, then Canada will certainly follow to support her." He watched the small waves ripple with each dip of the oar, spreading outwardly for a long time after.

"Well, I hope there isn't. If there is, it should be over in a hurry, don't you think, Jack?"

"It might not go as quickly as people hope. Who knows how much preparation Germany has already done? I know Annie and plenty of others think that the military can be licked into shape in no time, and the war ended in a hurry, but, I'm not so sure," Jack responded contemplatively.

"Then there's the business of the sinking of the *Empress of Ireland*. The paper said the collier ship Storsand is being blamed for the terrible loss of life and the sinking of the steamer, although there was a terrible fog. More than a thousand people were lost in the St. Lawrence River. We don't need a war to cause death and destruction. It happens enough accidentally," Ethel said.

Gladys interrupted, wanting to change the topic.

"There was a picture of the thousand voice choir that is performing at the Armouries a few days next week. I hope Myrtle and Ethel and I can go. Mother says it will be too crowded for her. I'm sorry you won't be around to go with us. Do you think Annie will want to go?"

"Oh, very likely."

Later that evening Jack tried to express his new mood. All the talk of war among family and friends had sobered him. He asked himself, would I want to fight, and kill people? They most likely wouldn't take him with his vision. He had worn glasses for years. He wasn't a strong build, and he suffered on occasion with rheumatism. He wondered what a war would mean to his and Gladys' relationship. Would she expect him to join up, get in a uniform, and fight? Is this what God had intended for him and all the other young men including his friends? He read late into the night. Rudyard Kipling was a favourite author. His thoughts transferred into poetry.

> Were all the sky one vast white page,
> And every tree a flowing pen
> From all the seas to drain their ink
> And could you them command, to write
> While from the earth all wisdom drew
> To tell you why I seem so changed–
> I fear they just would write

In one great word across the page
That only time can changes bring,
For time hath changed us from a babe
To full grown men and women
Hath made us sick, and well again
And made us angered then subdued
All passion till like quiet lambs
We seek the gentle things and kinds,
'Til time that makes us to forget
And also brings us memories
Some bright and good, some drab and ill,
But all which had a part
In that great past where we may dwell
Till Time again doth move us on.

This Time doth change not one, but all,
And each may see the other.
Yet never has the gift been given
To see our other self.
So Time brings changes all around
Though sometimes we fail to see it.
And while a change we sometimes see–
It's course is altered, yet no man
Can stop that river flowing,
Just so with time when're it seeks,
to check the course of Love
It may divert it many way
But stop it! Ah, it cannot.
So worry not o'er trifling change
'Tis but another way of Love.   Aug 2/14

Two days later, Britain declared war on Germany.

II

Jack had read Bleyer's *Newspaper Writing and Editing* from cover to cover, but a few days later returned to "Chapter IV: Structure and Style in News Stories." It would be many years before he could think of writing features but there was no harm in his being prepared. His editor was impressed with his work and promised more work in the future, depending on the war draft. He told Jack he would surely be called up and might be allowed to work as an observer.

Jack read, "The first essential of good copy is legibility. Typewritten copy, double or triple spaced is always preferred." Jack's thoughts wandered to where he could borrow a typewriter on which to practise. This might mean scouring the second-hand shops and surplus stores on a regular basis. With this thought lodged in his mind, he went on to read more of the news in *The Hamilton Herald* and *The Spectator*. How different in style were news stories of war to the poems he heard in his head. Bombastic military leaders, over-confident politicians who were sure they had the answers for a quick end to the war, and zealous youth all thought it was time a war put the European aggressors in their place. Posters stirred up patriotic pride, whereas his passionate poems were on the honourable side of love, not in the hateful vein of killing other humans.

III

"Gladys, I didn't know you knew how to knit!" exclaimed Ellen. She was home on a break, having been away training as a nurse.

"I feel it fills in a long evening, especially now it's too cold to go many places. Everyone at the office is making socks and scarves. I'm really just learning, so I'm sticking with scarves until I get the hang of four needles for socks. Don't the women in your office knit for the boys overseas?"

"Oh, yes, everyone is knitting that can knit, and sometimes we take things down to the canteen before the boys are sent off. Oh, the soldiers look so handsome in their uniforms, but I say, some look too young to be holding a rifle."

"They say things are going to get worse in Europe. Britain is suffering heavy losses, but how could they stay out of it after the Germans invaded Belgium?" asked Gladys.

Ethel and Gladys still enjoyed sitting down at the piano, playing old songs like "It's a Long Way to Tipperary" by Jack Judge, "The Girl I Left Behind," or "The Maple Leaf Forever," but now they heard new songs on the radio and learned them by listening, although sometimes they splurged on new sheet music. Gordon V. Thompson had come out with "Remember Nurse Cavell," and to Gladys' delight, "When Jack Comes Back." She figured Jack would sign up sometime soon. Every eligible young man was in a hurry to sign up. They barrelled out "It's Jolly Good Luck to Johnnie Cannuck", " Good Luck to the Boys of the Allies", and "Oh, the man who's dressed in Khaki is the man who fights the foe..." They were full of romantic images of the handsome soldiers marching out to battle. It was much harder to imagine any of these boys raising a rifle to kill, or being fatally wounded.

All summer Gladys had read headlines about war: "CROWNING FOLLY OF THE CRAZY GERMAN EMPEROR. ITALY DEFIES KAISER. BELGIANS WAGING MIGHTY WARFARE AGAINST GERMANY." On August 7th the headlines had been about the Canadians in the firing line on the continent. Now a new contingent of 18,000 men was to be deployed immediately to Europe. On August 11th, one week after the declaration of war, the entire front page was war news. There were further columns on the inside of the paper. August eighteenth's *Spectator* announced: "Canada's Duty Is to Assist Motherland." It made Gladys' head spin.

thirty-seven

Back: Alfred Bailey, Charles and Lavinia Hannaford, Annie and Elizabeth Bailey.
Front: Mrytle, Harold, and Gladys.

THE UNOFFICIAL TRUCE IN THE TRENCHES ALONG THE WESTERN FRONT LASTED for a few hours on Christmas Day when there was good will toward mankind. There was soccer, singing, and gifts exchanged by enemy troops in No Man's Land. After that, war continued. There was not to be an early end after all, as some had predicted. In February, German U-Boats were moving in for the kill in the Dardenelles. The British Empire and its allies moved to defend the Suez Canal against the Turks, thus losing much needed troops for the attack on Gallipoli. In the same month, one thousand suffragettes made their way over to France to do war work with the wounded. In March, King George V offered to abstain from alcohol as an example to the munitions workers. By the first of April at least 33,000 women had signed up for war work in Britain. They operated railways, they worked in offices, and they ran the farms. They began working in factories and in mines. Many joined the Women's Land Army.

II

In February, Jack's twenty-second birthday had passed with no more than good wishes from his parents and a quick peck on the cheek from his sister Annie who discreetly handed him a small parcel; probably the lovely pair of hand-knit socks she had been working on for the past two months. He hoped each sock was approximately the same size. They would be very useful, he mused, as he looked out at the stormy February weather. A good day for sitting by the wood stove in the Hannafords' kitchen, if Gladys allowed, although the old armchair in the den was cosy with the two of them seated side by side. He sighed. Work first.

"Jack, did Mother tell you that Edward Mountford married on the third of March?" asked Annie.

"He did! Was it that young Maggie Lee? I hope he didn't marry her just to avoid going to war," Jack joked. He knew they were not taking married men off to war if they could help it, and farmers were essential to food production for the nation and for overseas.

On the Hannaford side, Percy Hannaford married Ida on the sixth of March, even though he was signing up for the army. His cousin Charles couldn't understand it and openly expressed his views.

"Why would a young man get himself married just before he goes off to that deadly war on the continent? There's terrible carnage going on. They say conditions in the trenches are unimaginable. Food is rancid, their feet are always wet, and this winter has killed thousands. She'll have nothing but worry and heartbreak," Charles commented to his wife, Lavinia at the breakfast table.

"Would you have left me waiting to see if you came back from war without marrying me first?" she questioned him. His moustache flickered in amusement. Lavinia always had an answer, or a question which made him stop and ponder. Gladys took note. Maybe having a husband in constant danger of being shot or suffering from cold or terrible food would not be so romantic. She wouldn't want Jack to be off in France or Belgium in those conditions. Maybe the Canadian troops had better conditions, but she didn't think so. She'd ask him the next time.

III

Immediately Jack knew something was wrong. The quiet of the house alone was enough to alert him, but Gladys' tear-stained face and puffy red eyes confirmed something of importance. This was April 7th, 1915: no significant anniversary or news story came to his mind.

"What is it, Gladys?" he asked tenderly, removing his hat and stepping into the dim hall.

"It's Grandma, Grandma Hannaford. She's... gone. Oh, Jack, I don't know what I'll do without her. She was always here when I needed her. She might have appeared to be gruff, but she suffered a lot of heartaches. She talked with me so often when I needed to figure things out, or when everyone else was too busy."

Jack simply held onto both arms and let Gladys sniffle and wipe her tears with her embroidered hankie. He had never been close to either of his parents' parents, so he was not entirely able to empathise with Gladys' sense of loss.

"She went back to England two years ago you know. I'm so glad she was able to go. She didn't want to go very much after my grandfather, Robert, died, but her brother Will insisted she go with him and the couple he lives with. Oh, Uncle Will is really going to miss her, too. He used to come and visit regularly from over on Cannon Street." Gladys continued with her reminiscences, and Jack listened, stroking her hand occasionally.

"Oh, you are such a comfort, Jack." He smiled at her with that bashful, loving look he was wont to give her at every meeting.

IV

The next day Jack scanned through *The Spectator* searching for Elizabeth Hannaford's death notice. The funeral would be on Saturday the tenth at 3:30 p.m. Gladys would be busy until then, but he would attend the funeral and interment at the Hamilton Cemetery.

"Mother," Jack asked his mother, "where are you and father going to be buried? Have you given any thought to it?"

"What, do you think we will soon be underground? Your father and I have actually discussed it, but we haven't any decisions made? What made you ask?"

"Oh, Gladys' grandmother died yesterday."

"I'm sorry to hear that. She was well up in years I suppose," commented Elizabeth.

"It says here seventy-years-old and seventeen days. They had a special cake for her seventieth birthday, but just with family. Maybe she wasn't well even then."

Jack continued to scan the newspaper. Elizabeth enjoyed listening to her son read in his clear voice. He could make a fine preacher one day.

"There's a sale on men's hats here. Tomorrow they are fifty-nine cents and you could get 'The best guaranteed kid gloves in all Canada' today for only a dollar, or how about an egg beater for fifteen cents or a two-gallon bucket for nine cents? Actually that's a good price, Mother."

"Is there any news from England, son?"

"A Cork Steamer Escaped - Manchester, England, April 7 – The captain of the cork Steamer Ouse reported on his arrival here from Rotterdam to-day that for the fifteen miles east of Galloper lightship two German hydroplanes hurled eleven bombs at his vessel. The Ouse escaped by taking a zigzag course until the Germans exhausted their bomb supply." Jack noticed the serious look of contemplation upon his mother's face, knowing that her brother and all his father's family faced war at close hand. Everyday there was danger. When he talked of signing up, her face had paled. "You are our only son," she had simply stated. Jack tried to lighten her mood.

"Now here, Mother, is something you should take note of: 'DOUGHNUTS SHOULD NOT BE EATEN. The simple little doughnut is hard to digest and has been known to cause serious trouble. But if you must eat them take ONE SPOONFUL of buckthorn bark, glycerine, etc., as mixed in Adler-i-ka,'" Jack read, enunciating each syllable with such ridiculous pauses and in such a tone that his mother was laughing and wiping tears from her face with her apron before he could finish.

"'And all sour stomach, gas, and constipation is relieved AT ONCE. This mixture is so POWERFUL and cleanses bowels so thorough that ONE bottle has relieved mild cases of appendicitis.' I wonder what two bottles would do to you?" joked Jack.

thirty-eight

ON APRIL 22, GERMANS WEARING MASKS BROKE THROUGH FOUR MILES OF Allied troops spraying chlorine tear gas, blinding and maiming the troops. The yellow-green cloud came drifting over the hill towards the Allied troops, instantly causing choking attacks. There was confusion on both sides, and eventually the Allies regained the front line lost in the second battle of Ypres. In May, the Austrians bombed Venice in response to the Italians' declaration of war -- on the Allied side. Since the Italians had originally been part of the Triple Alliance of Germany, it was a surprise that they had switched sides to join the Allies.

It seemed a constant push from every direction to sign up for active duty to fight the war. On Monday July 5th, one headline on the first page of *The Hamilton Spectator* read: "Activity at Armouries – 400 men required without delay." Two days later it read: "Captain Huggins makes Appeal for Recruits." Private Albert Jarman, a Hamilton soldier, was pictured. He had been killed in action. On Monday, July 12th, the startling headline was another reminder that everyone should do his or her duty: "S.O.S. Remember the Lusitania's Message –Send Out Soldiers". The tragedy of the sinking of this passenger liner by a German U-boat off the coast of Ireland, and the loss of many British and American lives had been on everyone's lips for days.

Gladys asked about his signing up a few times and it hurt him more each time.

"I'm sorry, Jack," she'd apologize. "I thought you wanted to sign up. You know how important soldiers are right now. You would look very dashing in a uniform." Gladys just didn't stop to think that Jack might be right in his being ineligible.

Finally, Jack went to the Armouries to see if they would take him for active duty, without his mother or father's knowledge. Not that he needed their permission, but he was doubtful that he would even be given a chance after a medical examination. He wore glasses, after all, he had a protruding rib which affected his ability to hike a long distance, and he had rheumatism. He waited in line. There were young men that were too young. There were men obviously too old. And there was him. With his glasses. The major at the desk took one look at

Jack as he stepped forward from the line, and shook his head. "Sorry chappy. It just won't do to have a soldier on the front line with glasses."

"Are there other contingents I might try? What about the medical corps? Or war correspondents?"

"Sorry. We need fighting men at the moment. Check in the New Year if we haven't beaten the bloody Jerries by then."

II

Jack was happy to have a job plastering, as temporary as he thought it might be. There were more SITUATIONS WANTED than HELP WANTED. He continued to see Gladys at 232 Robinson Street each morning and most evenings, and he continued to write his poetry. This night of the nineteenth of July in 1915, he began "The Journey". He fondly thought of the warm evenings that he and Gladys shared. After the four stanza poem, he began a new page: *Night-time Reveries*. Nights were the hardest time to turn off his mind and give his body a rest, and so began his nightly diary for nearly two months during the summer of 1915.

> We sometimes feel embittered
> by Fate's oppressive hand.
> Denying us the pleasure in which we delight
> But may our prayer this even be
> as at Thy throne we stand
> God Bless us all and keep us
> throughout the coming night. 19/7/15 (Longing and waiting)

The next evening the bracketed note read "violent upheaval all around". On the twenty-first his note stated the "bonfire trouble still simmering, but G & I A R." He had developed a series of initials to record in short form when he and Gladys were all right with each other. On the twenty-second it was a "Wet night, power off, some play *Pit* on veranda. G & G outs G & I A R". His inspired poem reminded him of his real journey in life:

> Another day has passed away
> And now we stop and ponder
> If we but had things just our way.
> Would anyone be fonder.
> Of us, for what we could have done

In kindly word, or thought, or deed
From early dawn till setting sun.
To fill some lonely brother's need.

thirty-nine

SOME DAYS WERE PLAIN PLEASURES SUCH AS WALKING TO THE POST OFFICE. AT times he and Gladys would walk slowly by some wealthy business family's estate or mansion. 'Wesanford,' the residence of Mrs. Sanford on Jackson Street, was frequently under their scrutiny. The stone mansion's central door was approached by a concrete walkway. Above the main front door was a double door leading onto a small balcony. On either side of the door were the typical bay windows of the period, but above the second story were two steeply peaked and ornate dormers with a tower of sorts between them which rose to the lofty heights of a fourth floor. On the left hand side was the spacious glass conservatory, behind which another circular extension was hardly seen from the roadside.

The E. Fisher residence on James Street South was another grand Victorian mansion, somewhat more modest, and the C. T. Grantham home on Stinson Street which, with its mansard roof and wide three-sided veranda , the grand three-storied building was slightly diminished in apparent size. The Aberdeen Avenue home of W.J. Copp, *Pinehurst* on Jackson Street West, home of W. Southam, and *Elmhurst* of J.C. Person on Hughson Street were other homes of note.

Gladys and Jack more often visited the many natural places of beauty along the edge of the city at the base of the Niagara escarpment. It was always called "The Mountain," and attractive waterfalls fell over the limestone layers with lively freshness during the spring months. Chedoke Waterfall was a beauty in particular. Many hiked up trails, sometimes picnicking near the grounds of the sanatorium on the mountaintop. Gladys was always very content to walk along slowly when she was with Jack. At other times she moved quickly, always doing something. She didn't waste time. If she was sitting, her hands were busy; if she was walking to a particular place she didn't stroll, she hurried.

Jack spoke at Barton Street Methodist Church on July 25th. His energy was spent after such an occasion, but his mind and heart were filled with the love that could change the world around him. The remainder of Sunday was one of quiet reflection.

Through this day Thy love hath brought me
Guiding, keeping, leading on.
And I pray that I may see Thee
Till my life's work here is done.

II

Many days were spent at the Hannafords' rented cottage at Burlington Beach. The train was handy and inexpensive to get within blocks of it. On the twenty-seventh of the month Evelyn and Myrtle arrived, joining Jack and Gladys, Charles and Lavinia.

The next day was a fine one for bathing in the lake. The lightweight wool swimming costumes went to just above everyone's knees. Some were striped, some plain, most were dark, and all were modest. The weather was so warm and summer-like a number of the Hannaford cousins came, some with family. Carrie, Andrew, and Ellen arrived. Time was spent on the beach drying or sunning. The H. L. Bastien row boat, built in Hamilton, was most often frequented by Jack and Gladys, but others took their turns whenever the lake was calm and inviting.

Health, and strength and a peaceful mind
Pleasure this day Thou did'st help me to find.
For all Thy goodness I'll praise Thy name.
And seek to serve Thee, and not seek fame.

Jack penciled these words on the 29th: "Oscar and two of his friends joined the family. Cousin Gertie said farewell after her two day holiday". They all attended the Burlington Baptist Church on August 1st, but Jack had trouble keeping all the dynamics of friends, family, and his sweetheart straight, and as a result became out of sorts, and Gladys became standoffish. His temper simmered, and he regretted some of his words, though he did not know what he said to offend Gladys so much.

If I could now just one and all,
My wounding words this night recall,
I'd gladly do it, count it gain
To save a loved one so much pain.

By evening, after some quiet time alone with Gladys, Jack felt things had sorted themselves out. The weather was so hot and humid, that Carrie, her husband Andy Simpson, and some of their cousins and friends arrived. Charles was quiet and easy going, but Lavinia never seemed to stop. Myrtle and Gladys tried to make sure their mother had an afternoon rest, and were happy to help around the cottage, but often Lavinia just wanted to be alone, and that had happened so infrequently since her marriage, that she took every opportunity to work alone preparing food for whomever showed up. As they all contributed something, there was plenty at meals. The hot weather drew the young people to the beach and they enjoyed every aspect of Lake Ontario at the Burlington Beach. On August 2nd Jack wrote:

> Surely this day with quietness fraught
> A blessing of peace to my heart has brought
> How blessed the Future if each single day
> Could only be spent in the same pleasant way.

The young took every advantage of these blissful, warm sunny days. On the ninth Ethel, Carrie, Myrtle, Miss Riley, and Jack were out for a row. Annie had remained at home. There were bonfires some evenings, picnics on Sundays, walks downtown, bathing, rowing and sunning. Just a word or a glance from Gladys could still his anxious heart, after a word or thoughtless gesture from others would try his patience. They saw each other daily, sometimes just for an hour in the evening when Gladys would be crocheting.

> O how often we could gladden
> some poor lonely aching heart
> Yet so oft we're apt to sadden
> By some careless, cutting dart.

Jack wrote this during his evening review of the day. Sometimes love was just painful, and he felt his only solace lay in his thoughts of the Lord. He had few plastering jobs to do these days. George and Charles had enough skilled help and labourers with a longer time in the company so that he and others had not been often called when the job at the Hamilton Public Library had been finished. Building was slow this summer, but war efforts picked up momentum. No day went by without some report of war in the papers.

forty

ON THE 26 OF AUGUST JACK WENT UP TO THE TORONTO, HAMILTON, BUFFALO Railway office, but found no job available. Jack was beginning to feel that his and Gladys' relationship was at a stalemate. He did not seem to be making any headway with her: "Have you ever had a longing, that would almost drive you mad? For some passing fleeting trivial/Which just then would make you glad?" She was content enough to be with him, but just as happy to be off with her sister Myrtle, or Ethel or other friends from the office. This day he went with Ethel to take pictures in Burlington. Having some skill with a camera was a new requirement for most newspapers.

On the 15th of August, Jack spoke at Zion. He was happy to see Gladys waiting for him, and he took her home where they talked in the familiar armchair of the den, reassuring Jack that things were all right between them. Most of his late evening and night hours were spent thinking or writing of "Love". He re-read his nine verse poem of the eighth of the month. The last two verses he liked best:

Some men scoff and sneer, and chaff
Others at us mildly laugh
When with joy we gladly fall
Vanquished, give to Love our all.
Yet with pride, I will confess it
though no doubt that you can guess it
I am willing all to give,
Just to let this Soul-Love, live.

Some would say that he was besotted, and perhaps he was, but the heavenly Father was never far from his mind: "Often when our passions rise/ High as heavens clouded skies/ From amidst the racking riot/ Comes Thy deep and soothing quiet," he wrote in conclusion to the day of the fifteenth in August.

Jack tried reviewing his father's 1903 copy of *The Hamilton Spectator's Carnival Souvenir* booklet to help stimulate ideas for employment. There was everything from boot, brick, broom, and biscuit manufacturers, to paint, paper box, piano, pickle, pottery, and pump manufacturers. He should surely find some other type of employment to fill in time, but more women were being hired than men. Some had begun to stare at him when he walked the streets, thinking probably that he was of an age that should be in the armed forces, and accusingly curious about why he was not. Most had no idea that wearing glasses disqualified him.

With headlines such as "Captain Huggins makes Appeal for Recruits," everyone's patriotism swelled. If the death toll kept up in the Western Front, they might soon accept a man with Jack's deficiencies. He thought of the men like George Mountford, Riley, Mel Silk, Percy Hannaford, others from the office, or relatives in Britain who might never return from the battlefields.

The next evening Jack wrote out the poem which had been gestating all day in his head. The little orange notebook was becoming full, but there was still plenty of space for him to record his dreams and desires.

O, I love a girl; she is Queen of my heart,
In fact, of my life, she's the much greater part;
I miss her, I want her, I think she wants me: -
To think I'll soon see her, just fills me with glee.

Sometimes she's so shy, yet Love makes her bold.
She's given unto me a heart pure as gold,
To cherish and keep, watch over and love,
Till the dawn of the morning when we go above.

Her eyes tell their story, the blush on her cheek
Is a picture that I would go far to seek.
Her voice like some angels seems to inspire
To be noble and kind and reach some plane higher.

Oh no, she's not perfect, there never was yet
A woman so flawless there was naught to regret;
If such were the case, man would not dare
Ever to ask her his own life to share.

But though this be so, I know nonetheless,
That she is the one I desire to possess,
I've compared her with others; it's been to their loss,
For she's Queen of my heart, of my life she's the "Boss".   16/8/15

In the August 18th *Hamilton Spectator* there was news from the front: "Under Heavy Gun and Rifle Fire Allied Troops Move Forward", and "Eastern Front and Gallipoli Peninsula Are Scenes of Some Very Stubborn Engagements." The war was stretching out longer than most people expected. Things were complicated in Europe. It had not ended by Christmas 1914. Jack couldn't understand all this firing lethal weapons at each other. It reminded him of the Israelites 'smoting' their enemies, the Amorites, the Philistines and others in the Old Testament. It seemed far removed from the Christ's loving advice to turn the other cheek.

forty-one

THROUGHOUT SEPTEMBER JACK MET WITH GLADYS FREQUENTLY. FALL SLOWLY passed into winter. Troops in Europe had experienced horrors of war on all sides. The sale of Stonehenge for 6600 pounds sterling barely made the papers. Some people were pushing for conscription in Canada. Jack spoke at a number of different churches on Sunday evenings. He wrote obituaries and advertisements for the *Hamilton Herald* on occasion. Gladys's birthday on Halloween was celebrated modestly with a small cake at the family evening meal. Myrtle gave her a small parcel containing more of the beige crochet cotton with which to make her planned tablecloth. Annie and Jack came over after the dinner hour and their gift was accompanied by a poem Gladys put with all her other correspondence from Jack and others. His, she especially treasured.

Birthday Greetings
I can see as I sit and ponder,
on this bright and cheerful day
The face of a friend that I know
whose smile has a winsome way
Of imparting sunshine and gladness
and help to those cast down,
A face that seldom, if ever, wears
ought that resemble a frown.

Tis the face of a lovely maiden,
today in her twenty-first year;
Your face is the one that I speak

For as sunshine comes in at the window,
or as rivers from little springs start
so your face but reflects the beauty
and pureness of your heart.

And this is my wish on your
birthday, the best I think of any;
I wish you good health and prosperity,
returns of the day – Ah! Many,
But I wish that your heart's
thoughts be noble, your life be so true and sweet
That at all times you may be
worthy the Saviour's glad smile to meet.   Jack   31/10/15

Gladys particularly like the first two verses. She hoped that Jack didn't think she had any ignoble thoughts. She wanted to be worthy, and yet she felt a little afraid of being too perfect in his eyes. Would she be a disappointment to him? Was he too conscientious, too ideal for her? She enjoyed laughter and celebration. She enjoyed the company of many young men and women, and she enjoyed the freedom to choose to skate, or picnic, or go riding whenever there were such activities.

II

Jack was surprised to see a *Hills Sight Seeing Auto* holding half a dozen people round the corner near James Street where he was walking. He hadn't seen it around for a while, and although it was at first popular, Jack thought perhaps it had not been able to make a go of it. He was headed toward Robert Street where the Armouries had their drill hall. Several regiments were housed here during peace time. The 13th Regiment was the military band which for years had beaten the Toronto Corps in Crown competitions. The Fourth Field Battalion, formed in 1855, had conducted a salute to the Prince of Wales during his 1860 visit. It came to be known as a "crack infantry Corps of the Canadian Militia" according to *Spectator* reports. In later years the 91st Regiment was formed, then in 1900 Number Seven Corps became the Bearer Company. Members would attend camp military camp to become initiated.

Since extensive renovations in 1908, the Armouries had included a bowling alley, a shooting gallery which was technically a small rifle range, and a running track. Jack wanted to stay fit, just in case he should be called up to be a stretcher bearer with Number Seven. He felt with his small stature, agility and speed would be important if ever rescuing wounded soldiers. There were quite a number there this particular evening, and Jack felt comforted by the fact that many were like himself, just not quite the perfect athletic specimens the military sent to war.

forty-two

IN JANUARY OF 1916, JACK'S INFLUENZA TOOK A TURN FOR THE WORSE. His rheumatism added pain and he ended up at home recovering for a few days without word from Gladys. This was one time that he wished they had the phone line to their house, but his father remained disinterested. At last a letter arrived and he was able to answer it with an attempt at humour, to cover up his loneliness.

Jan. 9/16

Dear Gladys,

Just a line to let you know how much I appreciated your lovely letter (if words could tell) It was more good to me than all the medicine I had. I am pleased to hear that you are getting better, but sorry that Mother is sick, and also Myrtle not being well will make it harder. The tone of your letter was like a tonic and I have had near to hand and read it often and it would almost seem needless for me to say how much I long for you.

Now dear, you must excuse scribble and these rambling remarks as I have just got up and feel a little bit dizzy. It would not be right if I did not say something in our language, but...

I cannot write in rhyme
Just at this present time,
But I must say,
That all the day
and all the long night through
I long and pray for you.

Your loving Jack

Jack had not known that Gladys, Myrtle and Lavinia had all been sick and that was the reason, of course, that there had been no news sooner. His own father and mother had had some illness, but he seemed to have taken the worst of it. Annie had escaped it for this year.

When next they met, both were still feeling out of sorts and an argument ensued. They worked at sorting it out; Jack never liked to leave things unsettled with his Gladys, but it was with longing and heartache of some sort that influenced his nightly poem.

Father of the weary, and Saviour of the lost,
Who but Thee can help us, when we're tempest-tossed?
Who can soothe our sorrow -- who our sins forgive?
None but Thee, our Saviour, by whose love we live.

We are always certain, if we come to Thee,
Of the Father's pardon, grace so full and free.
So tonight I come Lord, asking Thou wilt be
Merciful to me Lord, sinner though I be.

Thou dost know my thoughts, Lord, nothing can I hide.
Keep Thy Holy Spirit ever near my side.
Guiding and directing thoughts, ideals high,
Through temptations' pathway, as the days go by.

Pardon my transgressions, many as they are,
Some just little trifles, others that might mar
Life, and make it sad Lord, for an aching heart,
But Thy Spirit doth Lord, wisdom then impart.   Jan 1916

Daily, Jack was in search of work. Sometimes he would call in at the *Hamilton Times* hoping for a few hours' work, checking copy, writing obituaries. There hadn't been much. So much of the news came from wire services or correspondents in Europe now. There were daily reports on the status of troops, about Hamilton soldiers who had been killed in action. At times he wished he could be on the front himself.

Between stretches of work, Jack spent more time writing. His poetry had become increasingly wistful, believing that Gladys was not as much in love with him as he was with her. The spring air in April, the dampness of the greening grass, and the smell of lilacs only encouraged his mournful tune: "To-night I am sad and lonely, /in a wilderness I tread," or "As the night gives shelter from troubles, /that constantly through the day". On the twelfth of April an acrostic poem appeared penciled in the little orange notebook:

Great is the passion of man for a maid,
Like oaks in the forest by strong winds swayed,
A force all around, unseen yet strong,
Drives all before it, takes all along,
Yields for direction to no hand but God,
Symbol of power, His Son the waves trod.

Man, in the tempest often quakes with fear.
Yet God doth in due time the pathway make clear.

Learning more fully each day to trust
On God for his guidance, it follows he must,
Venture through danger, yet know it's alright,
Enter at daybreak, come safe out at night.

Jack prayed for a settling of his heart, feeling that Gladys had more control over him than he had control of his own feelings. He just didn't feel he could continue to wait much longer.

forty-three

"Well, George Mountford! This is a surprise. What are you doing here? I thought you had signed up." Jack could hear his mother greet their family friend from Shelburne, all the way up the stairs. The two families had known each other in the old country, and were distantly related somehow. Jack pushed back his chair where he had been writing, putting in time before heading to the Hannaford's.

"George. Good to see you old man. How are you? You signed up, haven't you?" asked Jack, running his eyes up and down George's uniform which seemed plain, but his shoulders and arms of farming strength could be seen bulging in places.

"Yup. Fourteenth of February," was George's response. Annie came somewhat quietly around the corner from the kitchen. She wondered if she would see George in uniform, and was not disappointed.

"Hello, George," she brightly greeted him.

"Hello, Annie," said George, adding a nod of his head her way. They were all still standing in the narrow hall entrance when Jack mentioned that he would be heading out to see Gladys.

"I was going tonight, as well, remember, Jack? Why don't we bring George along? Myrt and Ethel will be there, and perhaps Carrie and Andy. It would be fun," Annie concluded as she started putting on scarf, coat, hat, boots and muff. Canadian winters still chilled her.

Gladys greeted them all at the door, as she quickly escorted them in before further gusts of snowy wind could enter as well. Her smile brightened when she saw the young man in uniform. Oh, he looked handsome with his dark hair, and brown eyes.

"So who are you signed up with?" asked Gladys after they had all settled in the living room drinking some hot cocoa.

"164th Battalion."

"Are you going overseas, do you know?" asked Annie. She would offer to write to him, send him news of home, and help keep his spirits up. Many of her girlfriends were writing to men overseas. Just men friends and acquaintances they were. There were such horrible stories of the conditions on the front that the girls back home felt it their duty to keep some sort of normality going, so they wrote letters.

"Far as I know, we go west to train, then overseas," was George's response. The enemy would never get secrets out of him through careless talk.

"Annie and Gladys want to write to you, and so do I," piped in Myrtle. "Would you like us to write?"

"I didn't get much school. I don't write so good."

"Oh, we don't mind. You don't have to write a whole lot. Just let us know that you are alive and well," encouraged Myrtle who seemed to know quite a bit about the situation. Gladys suspected that she was already writing to at least one young man in the forces. George took the moment that Annie and Jack were fetching their winter gear which was drying behind the kitchen wood-stove, to speak to Gladys.

"I'd like it if you wrote to me too, Gladys. I'll try to write back. I don't know when I'll get shipped over to Europe." Gladys nodded, somewhat surprised by the special request. He looked so young, younger than his nineteen years.

II

Jack slipped into the Hannaford kitchen where Myrtle and Annie were playing Solo Whisk, a game of cards from Britain which Annie preferred to the game of bridge.

"I'm on my way home now, Annie. Are you alright to come along later on your own?" he asked his sister.

"Oh, surely, I am," Annie responded, somewhat defensively. She turned to question his leaving so soon after arriving, but was stopped by the downcast demeanour of his face and shoulders. "I'll see you later at home."

Jack was already in his room with the light out when Annie returned that evening, but she didn't give it much thought. In the middle of the night Jack lit a candle rather than turning on the bare overhead light bulb. Every part of him ached as he wrote in the dim flickering light:

To My Lost Love
She is not here, that love of mine
And though I miss her and repine
I cannot find her, perchance she strays
Along some rough and stony ways.

I cannot say what path she chose,
I only know that I did lose
Her from my sight, and it may be,
That nevermore her face I'll see.

She was so pure, and true, and kind –
Such other on this earth I shall not find.
And how I loved her, tender, sweet
Such pleasure 'twas for us to meet.

She was my life, my hope, and my joy.
With here 'twas bliss without alloy.
My cloud by day, and fire by night,
For her I strove to do the right.

No flash of fire shone in her eye,
She would not in a passion fly.
Nor from her lips passed words of scorn
For in her heart kind thoughts were born.

She was to me a perfect plan
Of all that any mortal man
could hope for in this world of strife
To wed, and call his darling wife.
You ask me did a quarrel part
This treasure from my hungry heart
What was her name, how did she go?
With fleeting wings or footsteps slow?

'Twas not in anger we did sever
Cords I thought that would forever
Hold us close through life's dread fears,
Bind us firm in Death's cold years.

Not like lightning did she wander
But through years as I did ponder

Slowly as the fall of night
Drifted she from out of sight.

Simply her name, 'twas just ideal
And now I know she was not real
And though she pleased me a boy,
She'll n'er return to give me joy.   21/4/16

Four days later Jack closed his little orange notebook for the last time for many years. He had just filled the final page with a short poem entitled "Farewell" and felt such sadness, perhaps more than the few days beforehand. It was as though a chapter of his life was finished, but he didn't want it to be.

forty-four

IN THE LATTER PART OF MARCH, GLADYS AND ANNIE CONSPIRED TO HAVE A surprise anniversary party for Alfred and Elizabeth Bailey. Their twenty-fifth anniversary had passed almost unnoticed. They hadn't really said anything to their children with the war effort being at the forefront. This year Annie was determined to prepare special food and entertainment, and Gladys insisted that they have it at Robinson Street so they could truly make it a surprise. Ethel was to be home for some of the musical entertainment, and then the girls were excited when Harold Forrest, George, and two friends of Jack were on leave and also able to attend.

Jack felt most uncomfortable and had to plead with Annie not to make him recite any poems. His heart was just not in it. He had felt pressure to attend the party for his parents' sake, of course, but did not have much pleasure in watching Gladys' animated talk with the other young men. His parents were partly aware of his pain, and being shy, private persons were quite bashful being the centre of attention. Ethel got out her camera, capturing everyone in a picture to remember the occasion, but Jack kept his eye from the camera, watching Gladys glumly, as she carried on without a second glance at him. He never knew how she was avoiding even a glimpse of him, for fear she would burst into tears.

II

Gladys was never quite sure what had precipitated the separation between Jack and her. She didn't feel comfortable with the fact that it just seemed to happen. He had been so passionate, so much her beau for the past two years, she didn't think they would ever part. Why had she tried to loosen the bonds? No, she wasn't ready for marriage. Jack would have married her in a flash, but never asked with the war on, without him having steady work. She had regretted the break from the moment it happened, because she knew deep down that stubbornness was at the root of the dissention.

She had just changed jobs herself. Balfour, Smye and Company on Duke Street had hired her at a better salary than she had had at Freeman's. She had liked the work at Freeman's, but felt this was a step up in the secretary's world and to work for wholesale grocers who supplied tea, coffee, sugar, and all manner of goods was so much cleaner and interesting than building supplies with grey, red, and brown mortars. She had to practice her shorthand because it was one of the requirements of the job.

III

Gladys received her first mail from George Mountford in the middle of June. It wasn't a letter exactly. The title of the souvenir folder was "Broncho Busters Wild West Cowboy" with a sketch in shades of brown of a blanketed horse rearing up trying to throw his cowboy rider in Western attire, off his back. She wouldn't have known it was from George except by the handwriting: Miss Gladys Hannaford/ Hamilton Ont. /232 Robinson St. Below was "The Stampede" Winnipeg printed in brown. Inside were twenty-two coloured sketches of rides, cowgirls, and horsemen. She spent a great deal of time studying the pictures, wondering if George had wanted to say anything, but just couldn't find the words. Jack would have had no trouble with what to say. He always had words, beautifully put together. She didn't mention that she had received this to either Annie or Jack, not wanting to cause any misunderstanding. Annie had received something similar from George with a short note scribbled on it which she described in detail to Gladys, so Gladys took it to mean that she could think of George as a friend.

IV

"Mother, listen to this." Jack proceeded to read the front page news article about how telephones were going to be made available for private patients in hospitals. His mother knew what Jack was leading to.

"Your father will not have a telephone. We can't afford one. Now if both you and Annie were bringing in a full wage, we might be able to join the modern world. Myself, I don't see a need, but it won't be happening just yet," Elizabeth said, cutting off Jack's hope of the modern contraption being added to the kitchen wall. He often left early in the morning in hopes of being sent by *The Hamilton Times* to cover a news story. It did not happen often. He thought how much time it might save him if he could go directly to the police station, the court house, or the scene of an accident. Jack was spending more time at the League of the Christian Men's Club. Friday evenings were spent at the Royal Templar's' Hall at the corner of King and Catherine.

Months of war passed; a war that was increasingly felt in Canada as more troops faced the front only to be slaughtered. Jack and Annie's sister Maggie and her husband now had three children and had just recently moved out of the Bailey home into their own. Little five year-old Alf was a strong, busy lad; two year-old Maggie was having a tough time of it. She was born a 'blue' baby, and needed special care. They had to keep her calm and sometimes she went to stay with her grandparents so that she could rest and be quiet to keep her heart beating at a steady pace. Baby Dorothy was third. Sometimes Jack and Annie would go over and visit. Sundays were family days and then all the Miller family would appear for dinner at Jackson Street. Annie and Gladys continued to see each other. There was no reason for them not to be friends. Gladys continued to enter the elocution challenges held at the Templars' Hall. She won a silver medal, but she still greatly admired Jack's speaking ability and gold medal wins. They avoided contact during these events, the hurt too fresh.

The scare of infant paralysis had closed Sunday schools all over the city during the month of August and September. It later was named polio, but the out breaks in the first half of the 20th century appeared to have attacked young children, even infants. Kindergarten classes had not yet been given the go ahead to resume before October seventh. There had been only one fresh case of infant paralysis during that first week in October, but three cases of chickenpox, nine cases of diphtheria, two cases of scarlet fever, three cases of mumps, five cases of whooping cough, and twelve cases of measles. For a city the size of Hamilton, Medical Health Officer Roberts felt things were under control.

Periodically a letter would arrive from England explaining about the shortages of foodstuffs, the rations. Since November of 1914 in Britain, income tax had been doubled to help pay for the war effort, and some things were impossible to get. So far, all Bailey relatives that had enlisted were safe. Of course the Berlin Olympic Games scheduled for 1916, had been cancelled in February of 1915. They heard from Aunt Emily out in Saskatchewan that there had been a census taken. Emily ran a store now near the farm in Eagle Creek, and things were tough, but going well. She was so thankful none of her boys were old enough to sign up.

"Jack, you missed your chance with Suzanna Mountford." Jack scowled in response to his father's joking. "She went and married that Alfred South whom Eleanor mentioned in her earlier letter." Jack just looked at his father.

"I suppose George will want to come to the big city. We'll have to take him out to the creek for some skating. He certainly enjoyed it last time," Jack said thoughtfully, thinking of handsome, dark-haired uniformed George, the centre of attention with Gladys, Annie and Myrtle.

"He'd be the eldest boy at home now," mused Jack, thinking of the war.

forty-five

JACK WALKED INTO THE *HAMILTON TIMES* OFFICE AND KATHLEEN, THE BOSS'S stenographer, smiled and waved him over.

"The boss wants to see you, Jack. Just knock on the door and go on in," nodding her head in the direction of the glass door of the editor in chief. She stopped her typing briefly to answer the phone.

"Jack! Good to see you." Jack looked to the wooden armchair facing the large mahogany, paper-strewn surface of the editor, and positioned himself to sit down.

"No point in sitting down, lad. See that empty desk at the far end of that row," pointing through the window with an oversized index finger. "It's yours. You can sign papers with Kathleen later. Care for a celebratory drink?" Seeing Jack's face pale noticeably, he laughed. "One of those, eh? Well, good. Better that way. You can start by covering Bishop Clark's address at Christ Church Cathedral tomorrow. Got trolley fare to get out there?" he asked reaching into his pocket.

"Oh, yes, sir. That won't be necessary. And thank you!" He was so excited that he almost tripped when his toe caught the cuff of his pants.

"Oh, by the way Jack, you're on for the advertisements with Ed for today."

Jack wasn't long to get settled at the desk, organizing it in the fashion that suited him. His predecessor Frank had signed up for the armed forces, and left quickly in order to visit family at Stoney Creek before training. Jack tested the typewriter.

Jack looked at the list and slips of scrawled notes Ed had given him. A new Dr. Lewis would be, apparently, Hamilton's first osteopath. "Treats all diseases." There were only three pieces of real estate for sale. Not much for the City of Hamilton. Under 'Rooms to Let' one address was Gore, the other Victoria. Not much there either. He was feeling better now than he had since writing his as yet, unanswered note to Gladys on her birthday. It was a poem really, and the only one he had written in months. It was one last attempt to have her return to him, and then he would leave her alone. He had been quite frank, telling her he loved her and "I may make a pledge with you/ To love you- and to ask-/ If you will love me too." Since there was no answer, he would accept that as a no, although it wouldn't change his feelings for her, no, not in a million years.

Jack looked over the headlines of their competitor's Monday paper, February 5th, first edition. "Female Labour in GREAT BRITAIN NOW 3,231,000". My heavens, thought Jack. Who's left at home? Who looks after the children? Two more front page articles caught his attention. "Prepare for the return of Soldiers - BORDEN AGREES". Really? Would they be returning anytime soon? Now here was something: "Moved to Montreal, Quebec Labatt's Wines and Liquors - Mail Order Department" and below was a half page ad. Ha, just like that evil industry to plan a way around Prohibition. There are some who cannot seem to do without. If they only knew of the harm they are doing to their families and their morals, he thought. He took a quick glance at the glass windows of his boss' office.

II

Gladys was enjoying her new position at Belfours and Smye. The other staff was friendly and helpful. Orders went out to small town stores all over Ontario. She realized how fortunate they were in Canada that most foods were still readily available. When would this war be over? She and her friends often gathered to knit during the evening. Some shared news received from overseas, others waited anxiously to hear from brothers, friends, husbands and fathers. She had seen a few young widows in black, thinking how sad it was. She didn't know anyone personally who had lost anyone yet, and was thankful her father was too old to go to war, Harold, her sister's beau was not overseas, and that Jack, well, she had heard from Annie that Jack was in the Medical Corps, but not on active service yet. She was pleased he had finally got on as a reporter at *The Hamilton Daily Times*. She knew he would be good. When she occasionally looked at a newspaper, she couldn't figure out which items he might have written. Unless it was from a wire service, there was no mention of who wrote what.

She was looking forward to skating on Saturday night. The weather had been bitterly cold. It wouldn't be quite the same without the young men; only Ethel, Irene, Myrtle, Annie and she would be going, but they would have fun, she thought, smiling to herself, glad to have friends and just to be alive, enjoying life. Her father had taught both Myrtle and Gladys to drive the Model-T which he had purchased. His wife had no interest in driving it, and looked on with concern whenever four or five of the young ladies and gentlemen piled in to go driving just for pleasure. Gladys was thrilled with the feeling of independence it gave her, although she still loved the horses which pulled the carriage, and could often be seen taking them treats and leading them around for exercise. Her mother hoped the automobile would be put away for the winter, and then perhaps they would all lose interest in it.

III

"Jack, get this to the Press Room for Rodney right away," Ed shouted at Jack, causing him to jump with a start. Recovering quickly, he was reaching for the page while already heading between the rows of desks towards the typesetting room. His eyes scanned the Times Special Wire report from Washington on this the fifth of February: "WILSON, STILL HOPEFUL, MAKES READY FOR WAR/ U.S President Appeals to Congress to Clear Decks for Action. /Believes Other Neutrals, Acting With Him, Will Force Peace." This was to be below the double-leaded, 120-point headline: "UNITED STATES GRIMLY PREPARING FOR WAR". In much smaller print, likely only an eight point body, were domestic complaints about the Tilbury Gas Company and city pipes bursting. Both issues were arising because of extreme cold. Jack's adrenalin coursed through his tired body. Tonight he would sleep.

Two days later, Jack looked over the final edition of Wednesday, February 7th's paper: "STARVATION FOR AUSTRIA" indicated that Austria had used up foods harvested in its own country and since the frost was impeding the potato supply, the German government would be shipping in supplies from Romania in March. What will the people be eating in the meantime? wondered Jack. The headline "JEWISH RELIEF - Call to all Classes to Aid the Sufferers" caught Jack's attention. He read with interest that Jew was fighting against Jew "While from one point of view they are all Jews, from another they are Englishmen, Frenchmen, Russian, and Italians." He read with concentration about fighting for ideals: "It is to determine whether liberty or order, whether militarism of commercialism, whether autocracy of democracy shall determine the course of the world's history during the next century or so...in other words each of the chief nations at war in Europe regards itself as the chosen race, carrying on the divine mission...British ideals largely coincide with [the Jews'] own and thus his soul cleaves to England in no artificial attachment, but in truth has become his substitute for the lost, and not yet recovered Zion." How would his co-worker Jacob regard this idea?

"Jack, get these typed up and organize them. Shortest to longest under the Editorial Notes column," called Jack's boss waving a scrawled sheet in Jack's direction. Even as Jack was headed over, Kathleen was calling to the editor to answer his phone. Someone with urgent news was on the line.

Jack settled at his typewriter. He counted the words in the shortest three and chose the starting one; "Are we ready for fourth war loan now?" He enjoyed his editor's writing and wit. "Eat less and work harder is now the order of the day." True, much food was being sent to the troops, by all countries. In Europe, even Germany, people were starving or dying from disease easily spread because of malnutrition. There were late crops of turnips, and these might save some from starving. Oh, and here was an interesting bit: "There is said to be much unrest in Germany. The Russian Revolution is agitating the people. The Kaiser may well fear an upheaval among his own people."

Next, Jack lined up THE FUNNY SIDE under the boxed heading. "Take No Chances. Ethel–How many times do you make a young man propose before you say yes? Muriel–If you have to make him propose, you better say yes the first time." He liked that one. When the final edition on Monday, March 26th came out, he checked the page containing his work. The Music and Drama column caught his attention. The music to "Robin Hood" hummed away in his mind as he read: "O, promise me that someday you and I/ Will take our love together to some sky;" Jack sighed and shook his head. Enough! "The Million Dollar Doll" was the attraction at the Grand Theatre next Friday and Saturday. Jack looked forward to the day when he might get free tickets to do the press reports on musical and theatre. Wouldn't that be wonderful! Being paid to do what you enjoyed the most, well, almost the most, briefly thinking of a cosy armchair in a den. He felt like that arm chair – relegated to the garage.

forty-six

GLADYS EXCITEDLY OPENED A LETTER ADDRESSED TO HER. SHE THOUGHT PERHAPS George's handwriting was improving somewhat. He probably had written more during the war than in the previous seven or eight years.

Dear Gladys

Just at last I thought I would write you a few lines as I said to Myrtle in the last letter I wrote to her that I was going to write to you so this is Sunday and no place to go so I will write now if I can think of any news to tell you for we are in the back woods of Sussex and don't hear of very much new but we always find a little new once in a while. Well we are having some of the best weather we want to have but it is too hot for anything this last few weeks. Well I guess it will be a lot like summer over there now as it would be very nice in the old City of Hamilton. I would like to be back for a while but we are a long way from there now, but I hope there's a day coming when I get back there but we have a great risk to run some of these days when we go out to France but I don't know when that day going over there is but as far as we know we will going over in three or four weeks time but we are not quite sure but I will let you know when we do go out. So you know.

Well I guess you will have some time now going around in the car as I would like to have a ride in now as we are in the lonesome place I ever was in but we can put up with for a while if we get out safe and get back as good as we was when we left but I won't forget the day we left there for I don't think I got dry yet after that good weather but I never got a cold one good thing but we sure had a dandy good trip all the way over but I don't like living in this country after living in a country like Canada. Well remember me to all of them now as I am as happy as a lark but I don't like this country now.

I would like to be back for another skate but I guess I'll not get back for a while but I hope to get back for next winter if this war was over by then but it might not be. Say will you please send me one of your photos if you have one there as it seems a long time since I see you so if I had one I could look at it any time. Well I don't know of very much new to tell you now as there's not very much to tell you now but if you write I will find time to write you. So I will close for now hope you are all well. I remain as ever G F Mountford.

#663420

Pte Geo F Mountford

No 3 Company

MJH Pilk is well. I am still with him.

Canadian Machine Gun Depot

Crowborough, Sussex, England

Gladys was amazed that George had written so much because she knew that he did not like the task of writing. It was sweet that he wanted to be here skating. Maybe it was that hot over there and the thought of those bitterly cold January nights on the creek or over at Cootes Paradise skating among the reeds just cooled him off. She would write to him on the weekend and wondered if she should knit socks for him. With such hot weather would they be wearing wool socks? Of course they would have to wear boots, so they must need the socks too. She wanted to remember to tell him about the new hospital, St. Joseph's on the Mountain that was just finished in April.

Gladys wanted to tell George about how her swimming was improving this summer, and about the bonfires, picnics, and musical events which she and the girls had attended. She didn't want to make him homesick, so she didn't give too many details. She wrote about how many pairs of socks she had knit, and about Ellen's training as a nurse. She wrote about Annie's classes at night for typing, shorthand, and English grammar. She talked about the new female trainees where Myrtle worked. It was not very exciting, but she hoped it was enough to help him keep in touch with what his friends in Canada were doing.

Seaford July 24th 1917

Dear Gladys

As I got your letter a day or so ago I better keep the record up with you but I'm not quite as good as you yet for I never wrote back the same day as I got yours like you did but I do so today if I can find anything to write about now as I have wrote to Myrtle and Annie so I guess it's not fair to write to them and not write to you. What do you think about it? Well I am pleased to say I am getting along O.K. now hope you are all the same now.

We are moved now to another camp down the coast so you see we are getting a little nearer to France every move we make now we are only 69 miles across the Channel so we are not far now but we are near enough for near every night we can go up on the cliff and hear all the big guns go off so you would begin to think that there was a war on some place in the world but it's to be hoped it will soon be over. And then I like to go to France and see what has been going on all the time over there for there must be somebody getting hurt every day over there now. I was sure glad to get your letter when I did for I often wonder you was still Miss or Mrs. But I' m not saying anything in the way of tease. So I'm not being anything like that but any way I would like to get back in Hamilton for this next winter but I don't see how I am going to work in now for the way it looks we are goin' to be France for the winter but I will let you know as soon as I got to go out. This is a much nicer camp than the one at Crowborough for we only have to look out of the door of our beautiful hut and see the water all what is between us and Canada. You say Canada is the place for Canadians and if I am an English man I would like to be back over there again now for a while but I don't think it is my luck. I have all I want. Say I am writing you three girls today so you wanted to see which got yours first now but most likely you all get them together. I got the socks Annie sent and I think it a good one of your girl but Annie not in it at all is she for I only know you two by what I see.

I hope you will excuse this writing now And hope you all are well now. So I will have to make a stop for now. So good bye now.

Yours Sincerely

Geo M

Gladys smiled. She was glad George had written again, and happy he was writing to Myrtle and Annie as well. They would see which letter had arrived first. To-night she would begin another pair of socks and perhaps she would send them to George too, or to Bill who had also asked her to write when he left the office at Freeman's to enlist.

Gladys received a letter from Robert Telfor which she read with interest and amusement.

Somewhere - in - France
In the firing line
Sept 17/ 17

My dear Miss Hannaford

I am writing to thank you for the beautiful pair of socks which I have received from Q M S today.

You can hardly realize how much such gifts as these are appreciated out here in France. I had run short of socks for a few weeks and tonight I feel almost as tho' I was back home in Canada (if only the huns would stop shelling us)

I was beginning to forget how it felt like, to have a dry pair of socks on one's feet as once a pair gets wet, the difficulty arises, how to get them dried.

It is really a very difficult letter to write, but one which is a great pleasure for any boy who is lucky enough to receive a gift such as I have.

We are amongst war day in and day out, in fact there is nothing else except war all the time, so I don't think it would be at all pleasant reading for you, to write about it.

I only hope that it is my luck to visit Hamilton one day in the near future and to call to thank you personally for the gift.

In the mean time I once again wish to thank you very much.

With kindest regards
Yours sincerely
R W Telfor
1261727
No 7 Canadian Siege Battery
B E F France

It was heartening to know that her hard work on a pair of socks was so much appreciated. She knew that Myrtle was writing to several soldiers too, one in particular being a dark-haired young man by the name of Harold Forrest. Gladys just wished she didn't still feel so bad about not hearing from Jack. She sadly contemplated what he might be doing, and was annoyed with herself for thinking perhaps he was courting another young woman. Well, she was free to do as she pleased, wasn't she?

II

Jack was aching after the vigorous drill at the armouries last evening. His joints ached with the dampness of late fall. He managed to get through the day with two aspirin tablets, and was checking over the last edition of the *Hamilton Daily Times*, on October 31. This was Gladys' birthday. He had sent no card, no note, written no poem. His love for her was like a hard lump in the middle of his stomach. He could control it by keeping busy. Then it would be kept down, out of the way of everyday living, but he was not happy.

One-hundred point headlines read "CADOENA SAVED BULK OF HIS FORCES". Two explanatory leads followed. "Was another proud day for Dominion of Canada/ Thrilling story of the Great Work of Our Troops About Ypres Tuesday." Jack wondered if George were in this action. He had been shipped to France in late summer and had survived so far. He heard from his sister Annie, who was one of three young ladies to whom George wrote, Gladys and Myrtle being the other two, more about the weather than about the conditions of camp life. Jack was sure that it was much worse, knowing George not to be a complainer. Most of the men he heard about just wanted to be home.

Under the "Help Wanted –Male" notices was "RETURNED SOLDIERS should have your first considerations when requiring Help." Yes, if they were able to walk, and talk. There were too many unable to work, and many were crowded into hospitals, some hardly able to breathe after having been gassed. A Washington report from a speech in the German Reichstag was quoted in the paper: "You have not evidently, gentlemen, an exact conception of what war means. We have had 1,500,000 dead, three or four million wounded of whom 500,000 are crippled for life and two million absolutely invalided. That makes altogether six million men lost during three years."

"This," said Jack, "should have been on the front page!" Ed at the next desk looked at him curiously. Jack looked back at him, realizing he had spoken aloud. He bent back over the paper. The Hannaford Bros. had a good sized advertisement in the column beside the Music and Drama. What was playing? *Jack and the Beanstalk*, and *Polly of the Circus* were at the Grand and *Gay Morning Glories* was playing in Toronto at the Savoy.

forty-seven

GEORGE LOOKED AT THE SMILING FACE OF THE YOUNG MAN LEANING ON THE wooden frame of the quartermaster's store.

"Well, I'll be! If it isn't Mel Silk. Isn't it nice to see a friendly face?"

"Well, George! I was hoping to see a body that I knew. When do you think they will have us out of here?" referring to the British camp in which they were training.

"In some ways I'm not too anxious to get going. Have you seen some of those sergeants who have been over?"

"Yep, they look pretty grim, don't they? I almost miss my stuffy little office. Are you still farming?"

"Not at the moment. They want to make me into a soldier." Mel Silk laughed in response. He was quite cheerful at the aspect of a friend from his neck of the woods. He liked this strong British born soldier and they had friends in common. Life was a little saner with someone to talk to.

"Have you picked out a girlfriend yet George, or you still stringing them all along?"

"Well, I try writing to Gladys and Myrtle and Annie, Jack's sister. The girls keep me posted about what's happening in Hamilton, but what can we talk about? The weather?"

"Ya, it's a problem. I just try to get a letter off once in a while to mother and the three youngsters just to let them know I'm still alive."

II

HAMILTON, ONTARIO: 1917-1918

Jack was tired of watching the younger recruits strutting around the streets in their uniforms. They walked with their noses in the air some of them, looking down at him apparently shirking his duty to be fighting overseas. If only they knew how many times he had tried. He was still on the wait list at the armouries and should they get desperate enough, they would recruit him. If he had had better eyesight, he would have tried to get in as an aviation observer. In the meantime he was serving after his working hours in the Canadian Army Medical Corps.

Jack had a fairly clear picture of what was going on in Europe. Articles poured in; wires were sent; photos of destruction in the aftermath of battles arrived daily at the news office. He read everything. He read the headlines, the articles, the political views. He read between the lines. It was an inhumane slaughter on land, at sea, and now in the air. If he were able, the flying corps would be for him.

"Jack," Ed called to his co-worker. Ed was always calling out, over the noise of talking, typing, phones, and the general din of a fast-paced workplace. "Did you get your war badge yet? When are you going to get married so that you don't have be drafted? Your time is coming." Ever since the *Military Service Act* a few months ago, unmarried men of age were being drafted. Special requests for skilled railway workers had been made. The Military Police stopped anyone they suspected of trying to shirk from their duty, so an exemption from duty badge had to be worn.

"I'm not getting married, and you know it," Jack answered with a smirk. He knew Ed was married and happily so, always anxious to get home to "the little wife", he would say. He noticed in today's paper that the Australian government had defeated the vote for conscription. He always took home a copy of the paper, but today there was one particular page he would bring to his mother's attention: "War-time Cookies for the Home or Overseas", and the Maple or Brown Sugar Drop Doodles sounded delightful, especially if some of them found their way into his lunch.

III

The letters Gladys had been receiving were from France, no postage, censored, officially stamped, and re-sealed. Information was vague she thought, but that was as it should be.

France, Jan. 21/18

Dear Gladys

So I guess you will be thinking I am not going to write any more but the same old excuse not any time but I will have to find another way to tell you not time to write but I will write as much as I can.

Well I received a letter from Myrtle and you the same day so I have the both of you now so you both should get these the same day.

I think before you get this letter you will have had lots of the winter and you should have had lots of skating but we have had no winter here yet but we had lots of rain here so I guess we will have the rain instead of the snow but I think the snow would be much better. We have not had any frost here. It is very wet and dirty for us but we will have to put up with it for a while yet. Not long ago had a letter from Mel.T and Li is getting along fair and told him to try and find himself a little time to write you. You will hear from him before so very long. Say this is a very poor place to find anything to write about but I will try and find a little more to write about the next time. So hope you are all well now as I am O.K. now. So hope to hear again soon and I will try and write sooner next time so must close.

Yours sincerely,
Geo. F. Mountford.

P.S. How is Annie B and all of them now as I have not heard from her for about the same length of time as I have from you but I wish they are all well now.

Gladys was finding it more difficult to answer George's letters. She had a number of young soldiers with whom she was corresponding, and while she quite enjoyed this, there was little they could say. They couldn't describe the countryside, or the people, or their manoeuvres, so there was little except the weather and their health which they could discuss. She was very busy at work since the implementing of the draft because many of the young men were now enlisted. Women were being considered for just about any job that men used to do. She missed the balance which the men provided in the office. Some of the girls got wrapped up in their concern for finding suitable clothing, silk stockings and other home products, and started unnecessary squabbles. Everyone had to make do with the shortages.

forty-eight

CHRISTMAS HAD BEEN A LITTLE DISAPPOINTING THIS YEAR. NO GIFTS FROM HOME had arrived, not to say that they hadn't been sent. The king and queen had been good enough to send the troops greetings, but all the troops got them, right? George laughed when he recalled seeing the enemy troops dressed in white on New Year's Day. It was frosty, but they stood out in the mud so clearly that several prisoners had been taken. George had Gladys' letter in his hand while enjoying a few puffs from a cigarette. He hadn't smoked at home, but when he could get a cigarette, it helped calm the nerves in all the din and horrible smells. People looked at him and saw an easy-going fellow, but they didn't know how his innards got tangled up the minute there was machine gun fire. George wanted to answer Gladys' letter quickly so he began:

> B.E.F. France, the twenty-fourth of February, 1918.
>
> Dear Gladys:
>
> As your letter came today in which was dated Jan. 17th and to-day is the 23rd but putting a day on this to allow for tonight for am writing this at night and the mail will not go out before tomorrow. I was very glad to receive your letter as I had not heard for quite a while but the same old saying better late than never I guess. I also got one from "Myrtle" today in which was dated 19 so two days don't make very much difference at that end when we get them both the same day. Well Gladys, I was very sorry to hear of your mother being sick but hope she is quite well though before this letter gets to you for I always think if one's mother is sick in bed it does not seem like home at all. So I hope she will soon be quite well and in best of health again.

George wondered what else he could write about. He couldn't write about the night firing of the guns to harass the enemy. They did the same thing to them. Since the twenty-third of January when the guns were mounted where they were at present, there had been increased firing. It felt like, no- it really was all morning, noon and night. On a clear day there was the added danger of aerial activity. It was quieter by day with fog and mist, but that chilled him to the bones. Bully beef and ration biscuits and water was all he expected when he was relieved of duty for what seemed too short a time. There were a lot of fellows getting sick too. He was a bit concerned about Mel who had been coughing for some time, and he wasn't any too hefty to begin with.

I was talking to Mel Silk last Sunday night and he has been feeling kind of sick for quite a while now but he said he's beginning to feel much better. I know he is not looking as good as he did the winter we was in Hamilton, but to say the truth and nothing else we have to work much harder out here, but we are sure risking as much as anybody for it. I hope for the war to end but it don't seem very much nearer the end yet to what it did when I came out here, but it is only about six months since I came out here and I will say that, that is near long enough for me to be in this place. By your letter you must be having some pretty cold weather over there now and lots of snow. But we are pleased to say that we have not had very much cold weather here yet, but we have all kinds of time for it to come here yet before the winter is out. You should have lots of good ice to go skating on this winter but I guess there be too much snow on the Creek to go there now but there will be other places besides that, but there was a place for fun, for you could run up against the stone wall and wear out your gloves as you sure did. But I believe I enjoy myself there as much as ever I did and to finish up the day you even took me home with you in the car which I will assure you was very kind of you. But if I could only come there now what a difference there would be and things that I could tell you I can't now. But as we have said before wait patiently and we sure will get back home again.

I guess by the time you get this letter that Harold Forrest will have had a leave and will have been up to see you all once more for I know it must be hard of you not see all the boys in which you have known so long and then for them to go away and not be back for five and six months, but as you said there is one in all and hope he will spare all of us to get back home again. Say if I ever get back I'll not go far away from home again. I will stay- put a string on me and when they think I am far enough pull me back for I think that is the best way now. Oh, I say

Gladys it will be very hard on Annie and all of the Baileys to have to let John go but as I was told when I left North of Shelburne, the best off friend must part for a while but I tell you leaving all things aside that if he has to leave for overseas in which I hope he never has to, you and the rest of the people both in your family and in "Bailey" will have my sympathy, for I know how hard it was for me to leave, and it will be much harder for him for I had been away from home so much and he had not been so very much, But I hope the day never comes for it will be much better for him and so much better for us out here. Well now you tell Myrtle I will most likely write her tomorrow as it will be Sunday but the days make no difference to us out here. It's work near all the time, but will find time then most likely.

George wiped the perspiration off his brow. He would have liked another cigarette, but he didn't want to have to go back down into the bunker. He missed his friends in Ontario, but he was stuck where he was. Truth be known, he would rather be turning hay during the dry, hot summer days with bits of the dried grass scratching the places exposed, or poking its way under his shirt or pants. He thought of his family, sisters, brothers sitting around the kitchen table in an evening, reading, or chatting, his mother and sisters mending. Evenings he could go outside, look up at a star-filled heaven and thank the good Father for being alive. He thought of Myrtle, Annie, and Gladys laughing and talking a mile a minute. What he wouldn't give to be there among them now. Quickly he finished his letter.

I have near forgot to ask how Annie and all the people are now as I expect to hear from her in a few days time now and I will be writing her then. Say Gladys I hope you will excuse me for not writing more than I have done but I will try and do better in the near future and before so very long I will have a leave to England if all goes well so you will hear from me then. So now hope your mother will be O.K by now and also you and all the rest of the people and also remember me to all of them now. So write as often as you can as I am very glad to hear at all times and I will try and write more than I have done.

So best Wishes to you all.

Yours Sincerely
George Mountford

II

Gladys studied the signature. It was the first time he had written his full name. His hand writing seemed to have improved since his first letters. All the practice he was getting corresponding with so many young women, no doubt, was the reason. He was very sweet thinking about when mothers were in bed sick, it didn't seem like home. That was true. The illness which had been so hard on her mother was common. There usually was some kind of influenza every winter, but this year her mother had taken it quite badly. She and Myrtle were both trying to look after the housekeeping, the business end, meals and tending to their mother.

She was thankful there were indoor water closets. She could not imagine having to deal with illness and having to go outside to the toilet. Cleaning up would be such an added burden. She knew that her grandfather and uncle had planned well ahead, installing indoor toilets during the construction of the house. Plumbing for sewage and clean water, as well as wiring for electricity had also been modern and up to date. She had been appalled to hear of the outdoor privy, the outdoor water pump, and no hydro-electricity in Saskatchewan where the Bailey relatives lived. They had a wooden house now, but for years had lived in a 'soddy' with packed dirt floors. Oh, they were fortunate being in the city, indeed.

forty-nine

Jack Bailey, seated on right, Texas training field.

GLADYS PICKED UP THE OPEN NEWSPAPER TO CHECK THE CONTENT OF THE *Hamilton Daily Times*. It was an old one dated the twenty-sixth of February, but she liked to keep up with news which she might be able to send when writing to the soldiers. She read of the $600,000 scheme for the Waterdown Road Bridges. That was just too much money. She remembered when her great-uncle Alfred was on the water board and people complained of spending six thousand dollars on a job. "STRONGER BEER/ Workmen Plan to Petition Government". What did the workmen need beer for? Wasn't water and milk much better for them? Of course a nice cup of coffee never went amiss either. People of her mother and father's generation liked their tea too, but coffee was popular with all the young people. She glanced over other headlines: "German Drive Sweeps Ahead; Chinese Quake killed 10,000; New Head of Russian Army; State of Siege Now in Poland." Nothing about politics could be discussed. She wanted to have something of interest which she could write about to Mel, George, and now Jack. Since he had been called up, Annie asked if Gladys would write to Jack.

"Gladys, it would cheer him up. He wanted to enlist for a long time you know, but they just wouldn't take him with his glasses, of all things. He was terribly disappointed he wasn't accepted for the Royal Flying Corps, but he wasn't alone. He said almost half of them didn't make the first cut. He's remaining at Fort Worth as a medic though. We received a picture of the Medical Corps. See, here it is. Too bad he's not wearing a hat. The men look so smart in full uniform." Gladys hummed. She studied the picture, and tears gathered in her eyes when she saw Jack's humble, sweet face, looking beseechingly at the camera. How she had missed him! She couldn't admit it to Annie just yet. Annie was her best friend outside of family, but Gladys had moments of pride which would not allow her to have made the first move at reconciliation before this.

"Do you have the address, Annie? What do I call him?" Annie had looked over at her friend. Oh, she was pleased. They were all so worried about him having to go overseas. The war should have been over by now. Her mother was most anxious. She would sit on more occasions than was usual, staring out the front window, letting her tea in its cup grow cold.

II

Jack spent hours making a linen envelope with which to send Gladys a souvenir photograph of the Royal Flying Corps. Its sepia coloured picture of a single plane had an elaborate border, and "Greetings from Texas Christmas 1917" was written below with silver ink. He included, partly for protection of the card, a piece of linen on which he had sketched the caricature of a sad looking soldier. The pencil smeared, so he used pen. On the back of the envelope he sketched the Royal Flying Corps badge, the dates 1917-TEXAS-1918. It would not arrive until the New Year, but Gladys' letter had taken him by surprise. He thought she had all but forgotten him, but it was apparent from her Christmas letter that she had not. In response he wrote in "their language" as they called his poetry.

Judge not the gift alone as
measure of affection,
Though it should be a precious
gem or other rare selection,
But rather let the gift
bespeak what of times to impart
No tongue can tell
-the depth of love within the heart.

He continued with another verse and signed his name "Jack 1917". He felt a quieter joy in doing this than he had as a younger man because he felt there had been a change in him, not in the way he felt about Gladys, but mainly in how he looked at life. He had made the firm decision for one thing, that he would be a reporter.

III

In the Robinson Street house kitchen, Gladys was studying *The Hamilton Spectator* and read the headline: "SOLDIERS WALK OUT AT BRANT HOUSE" and wondered.

There was a novel and what may be a serious strike at the Brant Convalescent home for soldiers this morning. Shortly before noon about fifty men walked out as a protest over the way they are being used there.

The fifty men are practically all who could walk... "They treat us like children. We have hours imposed upon us and rules and regulations that would be all right for an orphan asylum or infants' home, but for men who have been shot to pieces in their country's defense – well they'll have to change those rules."

221

This was something she could write to Jack about. The other article on venereal disease was certainly not something she wished to discuss. After dinner she would get out her collection of letters and poems and read the last birthday poem he had sent, and his Christmas gift. She had never responded to his birthday poem the year before, but she had at last written to him this Christmas, and was grateful to Annie who had encouraged her to do so. She had been stubborn with Jack for far too long. For her, there really could be no one but Jack. She must learn to temper her impulsiveness, because she often regretted the words that came out of her mouth before she had finished her sentence.

fifty

FRONT LINE, FRANCE: MARCH 1918

GEORGE HEARD THAT MEL HAD BEEN HOSPITALIZED, SO HE COULDN'T HAVE BEEN improving too much. There was no faking illness in this business. George had been happy for a while when things seemed to have quieted down. There were two new lieutenants attached to the Fourth Machine Gun Battalion who were doing training courses for the ranks. Of course, there was extra duty cleaning and checking the equipment, but a fellow didn't want to be stuck with a jammed gun when shells and shrapnel were flying at him.

He thought it a bit pessimistic that they began working up ten acres for potatoes and some smaller vegetable gardens because it seemed plain to him that the war was not going to be over soon, and that the thought of some fresh food was a real stimulating idea. Maybe it helped with their morale.

In January they had been firing about fifteen to twenty-thousand rounds every night and George could feel the increase. He didn't know how many more, but there were more rounds being fired on each side.

In mid-March there were several low-flying enemy planes and then on the twenty-third of March all leave stopped. The guns were realigned. George began to have a nervous tightness in his gut. He wasn't easily intimidated, but he felt he hadn't yet lived his life, and it could be over before it began. Gunfire started at 5:30 am the next day. There were eight extra Vickers guns and tripods sent in and firing in response to an S.O.S. flare. The next day all ranks returned from courses. Heavy firing occurred all day and harassing fire all night. The days and night got mixed up for George. At eleven o'clock one night, gas projectiles were successfully sent into enemy lines. Heavy artillery fire was sent in retaliation. On the twenty-ninth the fourth division were reorganized. Now 250,000 rounds were brought to each dump. George felt numb with the increase. His hands continued tingling for hours after he left his gun. Eighty-three reinforcements were brought in. Four observation balloons were destroyed by enemy airmen. Thirty signallers proceeded to connect all phones. Heavy rains set in. On his next break George scrawled a note to Gladys. She hadn't mentioned Jack as of late, so be damned, he would tell her how he felt. He didn't think he would live to see her or Annie or Myrtle again anyway.

II

Myrtle looked with curiosity at the envelope addressed to Miss Gladys Hannaford. She thought she recognized George's handwriting, but it didn't look quite right. It was definitely a soldier's letter on active duty, censored, from overseas. She put it aside because she wanted to spend a little extra time with getting ready for Harold's arrival tonight. He never said boo about his work or where he was, or what was going on. 'Mums' the word was his only answer to any of her questions. They would be going to the pictures, and he would then walk her home in his very gentlemanly way. She had become quite excited when he wrote to tell her of his leave. Harold was the oldest of seven children, mainly brothers, and he was ever so sweet. Oh, she would use her best toilet water to smell enticing.

Gladys was late arriving home that afternoon, having to do some extra typing, then offering to clear up some receipts which had been collecting. She flung off her scarf and literally threw her hat onto a hook. She would have only a few minutes before dinner which was fine with her, because she was out of sorts. The evenings were so long now that Myrtle was busy with Harold. She felt like a third wheel, although she was happy enough to be included at times. Her mood lightened when she spied the envelope with her name on it, but hardly recognized the hand writing. It wouldn't be from Jack just yet as she had only written to him yesterday.

She took it into the den for privacy and opened it quickly. The ragged piece of paper had been written in such a hurry she could make neither head or tail of it. She looked at the signature. George. She read through it with cheeks flushing. He was telling her he loved her. He didn't think he would make it home. The firing was so heavy, everything around them was in chaos, he wasn't sure he would live. So many around him were dead and dying. He had to tell her. Gladys burst into tears. None of his other letters showed that he cared any more for her than he did Myrtle or Annie or... did he write to anyone else? Did he send this just to her? She would be heart-broken if he was killed, but she loved Jack.

"Gladys, are you home?" called her mother as she came down the hall from the kitchen. "Oh, there you are. Will you please go and tell Myrtle that dinner is about to be served, and then call in your father from the yard." Her tired mother hardly noticed Gladys wiping her eyes hurriedly as she turned on her heel and retraced her steps back to the kitchen. Gladys made one more attempt at drying her eyes without making them red, then did as she was bid. She would write tonight of course, clear up any misunderstanding, explain that she and Jack were corresponding, seriously, more than just friends.

France, April 8/ 18

Dear Gladys

Your letter of Mar 5 came a few days ago in which I was very pleased to get for I had not heard from you for quite a while. I was also glad to hear you were all in the best of health as I am fine myself at time of writing and have been nearly all the time. Well Gladys I had a letter from one of our other boys a few days ago, and he was saying that he heard that Mel Silk had gone back to England and he was very sick but have not heard what was wrong with him yet but if I hear I will let you know but I think he must have been pretty sick for they have to be that way to get over there but hope he will be well again for I know it is not very nice to be sick all the time but I always thought he was not very strong and would not stand the noise all the time.

I guess you will be having lots of warm weather over there now but we are having lots of rain here now, but we have had lots of nice weather all winter so we have not so very much to kick about now. You will soon be going out to the country now for the summer so if you go out and get some more snap-shots taken please send me some for I always like to have some of all you girls for you were all so good to us while in Hamilton for we did have some good times there. Now I hope you will excuse this short letter for now, but will try and write you more before so very long so hope this finds you all in the best of health now and remember me to all of them.

So will close for now.

Yours Sincerely
Geo. F. Mountford

Gladys was so relieved to see the Geo. F on the signature this time and a return to talk of the weather. She would make sure that he got some snap-shots of the "girls" as he called them, but would also be sure Annie was prominent in them, as well as the surrounding countryside.

fifty-one

JACK HAD TO SCRIBBLE ON ACTIVE SERVICE OUT AS HE WAS STILL IN SCOTT Barracks. The red triangle behind the Y.M.C.A. initials stood out colourfully. When he was rejected as a candidate for training as a pilot, the officer studied Jack's records in front of him. Jack stood at attention waiting.

"You've been in the medical corps for two years?"

"Yes, sir. Nearly three."

"Can you run?"

"Yes sir."

"Do you know how many injuries these practicing pilots get learning to fly? Too many! You'll report to chief petty officer Ralph to outfit for the Medical Corps. Dismissed."

"Sir!" said Jack, saluting smartly. Well, he would be here for a while then.

He began this day to put pen to paper.

When the day's work is over and we put away the gun,
And gaze away to westward, where we see the setting sun,
'Tis then we think of loved ones, especially the maid
With whom we used to linger and watch the twilight shade.
So, like many other soldiers, this evening here I sit
And revel in the mem'ries of that time gone by a bit
Just longing for the old times, and making strong my will
To be the same as ever, as I know you love me still.   April 16/18

Jack turned the page over and wrote another poem, thinking of his one true love with glowing images.

Lying in the bunkhouse, where tobacco smoke is thick
And the soldiers spin their yarns in a manner very slick
One falls to meditation, perchance 'tis good or bad,
According to the past life each single soldier had.

That's why for me 'tis pleasant to just lie there and think –
For I can form, with greatest ease, a charming binding link
With happy scenes, and joyful thoughts, and ringing, thrilling words,
When I and my sweet lover lived like the happy birds.

So you, my love, remember, while in barracks I must stay,
That you at home must buoy me up with prayers by night and day.
And when I have the chance, dear, to visit you once more,
Remember to be loving and refill my memory's store.   April 16/18

Gladys answered immediately. She read and re-read Jack's poems, re-folding each one carefully and returning it to its envelope. She looked at the box holding her treasure trove, smiling, wondering when Jack might get his next leave. She had no trouble remembering him in her prayers. She earnestly prayed, too, for all the young men over in Europe, especially the ones she knew.

II

In June, the warnings were to swat flies. On the twenty-eighth of the month Gladys read what Dr. Roberts had to say: "Flies...are responsible for a great amount of sickness, and the best way to keep them down is to have a liberal supply of swatters in the home, and the moment one of these typhoid distributors appears, turn the whole family loose and run it down." She knew her mother was taking this to heart.

"Myrt, can you get in and close that door. We don't want flies in the house." Myrtle pulled the screen door and latched it quickly behind her. Their father had seen to it that screens had been put on all the doors and windows years ago. Her mother had never liked insects. There hadn't been many in the old country, not like there were in this wild place, she would say.

"How is mother, Glad?" Myrtle asked, dropping her cloth bag of groceries on the table.

"She's a little better, I think. I'm just making her a cup of tea, and I'll take it up to her just as soon as I finish this row." Gladys was again working on her crocheted pieces for a tablecloth. She was still simmering from quarrelling with Jack. It seemed each time they met when he was on leave, things were not going well. Both had short tempers. Was it this war? Was it the weather? Was it love? The next day, she smiled as she saw the envelope awaiting her on the hall table. Would it be a poem? In the privacy of the den she read:

The Maiden's Confession

Growling and grouchy the whole day long
Scowling or else rebukes with his tongue.
Nothing will please him, so far as I know
So what can I do? Why! Nothing but go.

So I left him in anger yet hoped we should meet
When he in a quieter manner should greet.
Then away to my slumber I wearily stole
And he to his bed like a bear to his hole.

Then morning succeeded the quiet of night
And I woke to discover that all was all right –
As so far as I was concerned,
For in fact, for that rascal I actually yearned.

And, curious to tell, so he afterwards said,
The first thought he has as he jumped out of bed
Was, 'Why do we thus so constantly fight
When I want her so much and everything's right?'

So we met the next evening and mutually forgave
And promised each other from then to behave.
We crooned and we spooned, were lovers again
And to our old passion we gave fullest rein.

When the good sun had set, the twilight apace
To the dark shades of night quickly yielded a place.
But heeding no time we did fervently love
So passionate each yet gentle as dove.

But Time on His Wings we two lovers bore
To the place where each night we kissed o'er and o'er.
When alas! Just a word, like the flash in a pan
And once more a 'Lover's Quarrel' began.

So we parted again– My life seemed so dark.
Thére seemed of true love to be not a spark.
And Oh! How bitterly in bed I did weep
And wish forever my own heart to keep.

But Love is so queer, it leads one away,
Into his arms the next day I did stray.
That evening our love was of Heaven a lease
And for once in our lives we parted in peace.

But Alas! I awoke– and not as they seem
Are things– for always contrary go dreams
So, though I now love him tonight 'tis my fate
A little of Heaven – then parting in hate.

But strange yet so coveted, affliction called Love,
Encouraged by men and sanctioned Above,
If, when Thou art True, Thy course must be rough
Then not even yet will I confess I've enough.   21-6-18

Gladys smiled. He knew her thoughts so well. Oh she wished this war would end and they could settle down. Would he get a newspaper job? Where would they live? She thought most likely Myrtle and Harold would beat them to it.

The summer passed slowly. The waiting was nerve-wracking for Gladys. Jack showed impatience over simple things that did not work out, but was so quick to apologize, she always forgave him. She could be impatient herself. She knew that. Her father had always said Myrtle was the patient one.

fifty-two

BY THE END OF SEPTEMBER THE DREADED SPANISH FLU HAD MADE ITS APPEARANCE at the armament school of the Royal Air service, West Hamilton. It apparently wasn't as serious as the outbreak in Eastern Canada or the United States, but the cadets would be isolated at the King Street Military Hospital. Gladys was prepared, under her mother's direction, with eucalyptus oil which, or so it was thought, if applied to the nostrils, would check the illness in its early stages.

The seriousness of *la grippe* or influenza was challenged within a week. On October the seventh, Gladys read the list of nine more people who had died of the flu. It was recommended making a mask to wear in public and on street cars. Gladys preferred to walk wherever possible. She worried about her mother who was already in a weakened condition. Myrtle had been sniffling, but kept up with smelling the eucalyptus oil dabbed on a hankie. Aunt Mary next door appeared as strong as a horse. Though white-haired, she remained straight-backed, and bright-eyed.

Dr. James Richard Nixon of Georgetown had died. The Burlington schools were closed where two hundred cases were reported. Strangely, schools in Hamilton remained open. Then Dr. Clarence Graham died, having been treating hospital patients with flu. On the twelfth, over 500 cases had been reported during the week. The flu led to pneumonia in many cases, causing death. Hospitals were closed to visitors. On the fifteenth, nineteen more deaths had occurred. There was a request for private funerals. The authorities wanted volunteers to help with nursing, and many doctors were themselves becoming ill. The Victoria Convalescent Home, Barton Street, became the new flu hospital.

On October 16th, Gladys read that on Monday, all public places would be closed. No gathering of more than 25 persons was allowed anywhere. She had not been to the office for two days herself. Business seemed to hover in a standstill position, waiting for things to improve. With over 6,000 cases in the city, the doctor shortage was critical. She read of the sad death of Mrs. McGibbon who left five children under the age of twelve, and her husband who was very ill in hospital. Many returning soldiers had returned sick with influenza. Many more had already died in Europe's military hospitals, increasing the casualties of the war. She would phone Jack's parents tonight to see how they were doing. She was so pleased that they had finally installed a telephone; although Jack had not been around to benefit from its use, it was very handy in this instance. As far as she knew, the flu could not be transported down the wires.

II

Gladys received a letter from France written Nov 20. 1918 by George.

Dear Gladys,

As I guess you will be wondering how it is I am not going to write you but I guess you know how it is so I guess I will not tell you but any way I hope you will excuse me and I will try and not let it happen again. Well now I guess you will be having still a good time as John is still near to you so you are in luck. What do you think I only wish I could have stayed there a while longer and then I would have had some time, but if I am lucky to get back it would take me so long to get to Hamilton. So you will depend to see me if I am lucky to get back as I feel pretty lucky so far and I guess I will be now as there's not going on now. I guess you are quite proud of your new dog you got so I hope you still kept it till I get back, so I can see it and it must be some dog. Let's hope so any way.

What do you say now? I hope you don't think I am fooling you by saying it is some dog for you know I am still the same as ever if not worse but not much now. I guess you know I have been on leave but I know you will be mad at me for not getting any photo taken but I never had any time to get any.

Now I hope this find you all well and in the best of health as I am fine at time of writing you so I wish to be remembered to all of the people at home and tell them I may be lucky sometime as I hope so anyway. So now I think I will have to close for now so hope to hear again soon and I will try and write you again soon. So will close for now.

Yours Sincerely,
Geo F M

Say I have not heard from Mel but I don't where he is now.

III

Jack had several of the men in their housecoats ready to go outside. The ones on crutches could manoeuvre through doorway themselves, but the ones in wheelchairs needed assistance. There was just enough sun on this spring day at the Brant Military Hospital to allow some of the men some fresh air. He had to shout at the assistant to catch Nick's chair before it went careening over the edge of the cement patio and down the embankment.

"There are no brakes on these chairs, Ed. You have to watch you don't let Nick go down the bank there, although I know he wants to escape." Jack looked over at Nick and gave him a wry smile. Nick's sad eyes just looked at him with the pain of hopelessness. Both legs had been blown off from under him in an attack, and he had still been in the field when the deadly gasses came creeping along the ground, over him and around him. It was miraculous that he was still living, that he could breathe, and that he had made it back to Canada. Jack patted his shoulder kindly. It didn't do any good to let these fellows wallow in hopelessness too long.

"Alright, men. You have fifteen minutes to bear that fresh air and sunshine before I come back with my camera, and I want you ready to turn those smiles on, and that's an order!"

"Yes, Sergeant! But did you forget to whom you are speaking! That is Captain Smith and above your rank," joked Allan.

"Good thing I didn't forget to whom I was speaking and that you don't rank with me when it comes to your health! Step smartly there, Smith, and help your comrades!" Noticing that two on crutches were getting entangled trying to get out the door, Jack motioned to Smith who quickly stepped over to help the two men. Jack always tried to make them feel useful. These were his boys.

IV

Elizabeth met her son at the door when he arrived for a short leave.

"What's wrong, Mother? Aren't you happy to see me?"

Elizabeth gave her son a gentle hug, and nodded towards the sitting room. It was extremely quiet and Jack was puzzled.

"Your father just received news from England and he's quite upset. His youngest uncle Emmanuel Bailey lost his son and step-son in the war this past year and a half. Harold was in Palestine last year, and Arthur died in September. That leaves him with three daughters and his second wife. They are all very upset by it."

Jack nodded. Of course they would be. Arthur was about his own age, and Harold was even younger. What grief they must be feeling. Conditions were so much worse in the Old Country, and the war was very close at hand compared to Canada.

fifty-three

JACK WAS EXHAUSTED FROM THE DAY'S WORK. NOT JUST THE DAY, BUT THE interrupted sleep at night with men calling out, some crying in pain. He knew he had to write Gladys. When was the last time he had written to her? He didn't even date it. What was the date anyway? Jack didn't like to think of his work when he could think of Gladys, but the list of diseases that the men were bringing home to the military hospitals was astounding. Obviously conditions continued to be so terrible that every manner of infection and vermin had plenty of fodder. There were the usual childhood diseases like mumps, measles, and scarlet fever, but there were also the German measles, meningitis, diphtheria, erysiphis, trench mouth, dysentery, lice and scabies. Above and beyond that the men were trying to forget the trenches and find physical comfort in the arms of willing French girls. They often ended up with gonorrhoea and syphilis. He had seen the trainers' medical warnings, but they apparently went unheeded and they paid the price. He had heard that men would sleep outside the tents when there were epidemics going around like influenza. He worked his best so that these men who had served overseas could rest in a bit of comfort. He pulled out a scrap of paper and began a note to Gladys:

> Must I settle down to write? Of all burdens this is the greatest. Surely you know that. Too well you do. Only bear with my tardiness and I will tell you all when I see you face to face. For the cold page is <u>all</u> too inexpressive. I remember you each night. Years seem endless but Time gets tired. Every effort I make shall be to return. A few months more and who knows what may happen! Rest as easy as possible. Not that I think you will ever forget any more than I shall never cease to think of <u>you</u> Tootsie.
>
> My message is brief, its
> contents I keep
> And just wish you now

Love's rosiest sleep.

Jack X L.C. Y. 5:30 pm

II

"George, it's me, Mel Silk." George stopped short. It was Mel, but not the Mel he knew. They were on the main street in Shelburne.

"Mel, I didn't know what happened to ya. When did you get back? Are you alright?" George anxiously inquired.

"Well, they thought I had, I guess I did have pleurisy, but I wasn't getting better. They had me in the hospital for almost nine months and found that I had T.B. After that, they sent me back to the Spadina Military Hospital. I'm much better, thanks. What about you? Never a sick day I bet." George looked at the small frame of his friend who used to be his own size when they enlisted.

"Oh, a few days at Harfleur with a bit of the flu." George had actually had two bouts with the flu. After ten days he was sent back, but was still ill, and his anger towards the sergeant was construed as misconduct, which when he became fevered and ill again soon afterwards, was struck off as legitimate complaint. He didn't talk about the fact they were taking out the bodies of many, not so lucky soldiers who had against all odds, survived heavy shelling and gassing, only to be struck down and die from the Spanish flu that killed hundreds each week. He had managed to resist the bug all during the fall of 1918 when so many were admitted to hospital, and so many buried, but he guessed his body just got tired of resisting and let him have it in May of 1919.

"When were you demobbed?"

"Oh, I got out just before last Christmas. And you?"

"Just got back a few weeks ago in July. Got to pick up a plough that my dad had repaired."

"It's been really good to see you, George. You get hooked up to one of those Hamilton girls yet?"

"Na. Gladys and Jack, and Myrtle and Harold are getting married this fall, so ya missed out there, Mel. See ya again, eh?" and with that George headed down the street to the blacksmith's shop for his father's plough.

III

Gladys could see her sister getting more and more excited as the day for her marriage to Harold Forrest approached. It was to be the tenth of September and here it was already the sixth. Gladys truly hoped the nice weather would hold. She and her mother had been making wedding cake and wrapping the fruit filled slices for the guests. They had had a lovely picnic just this past Sunday afternoon in the back yard. Annie, Alfred and Elizabeth Bailey came along with Jack, her mother and father, Myrtle and of course Harold. It was still that warm they had worn their summer whites. Mac sat on the blanket with Myrtle, Harold and Gladys, the white stripe down the middle of his face and over his snout made his eyes stand out in contrast to the black fur of the rest of his face.

"Gladys, I know that you love Mac, but I've been thinking that since Harold and I will be living in our house out at the new survey, I'm afraid I'm going to be lonely so far away from the city centre. It's rather isolated, you understand, and I would like to take Mac," Myrtle said, interrupting Gladys' daydream about her own wedding.

"You can't take Mac. He follows father around like a shadow. He's our dog! Really, I had hoped to have him when Jack and I have room. I pay more attention to him than you do." argued Gladys.

"But Harold will be away all day working in the city and I'll be lonesome. Mother thinks it will be a fine idea," insisted Myrtle. Gladys hopped off the bed and went to find her mother.

"Mother, I'd have appreciated it if you had asked me about Myrtle taking Mac. You know how I love him."

Her mother looked at the unhappy face of her daughter. She was such a softee when it came to dogs, or horses, or any pets for that matter. "I know you will miss him, Gladys, but really it's not practical for you to have him when you're moving in with the Baileys. They won't have room for a dog. Myrtle is going way out in that new subdivision and needs company. Besides, Mac will enjoy it out there," responded her mother, pleading with her eyes.

"I'm sorry to upset you, Glad," apologized Myrtle as she entered the room. "I know you will miss him, but you will come out to see us often, won't you?"

"Oh, I suppose so," reluctantly agreed Gladys. She bent over to rub his ears and pet the sweet Border collie who liked to be with Gladys, whenever the master of the house was not in. "I'll miss you, Mac," she whispered.

IV

The weather was a fine day for Myrtle and Harold's wedding. They were so pleased with everything. Gladys had given her sister the hand crocheted tablecloth which she had finally finished after three winters. There had been many pairs of socks for the war effort so that she didn't get much done at times, but it was finished at last and would be lovely on the table for a Sunday meal.

Once Harold and Myrtle were married, Gladys and her parents would occasionally go out on a Saturday afternoon in the Model-T Ford. There was a great deal of landscaping around the house to do and they all pitched in. Gladys laughed when she saw Mac sitting in the empty wheelbarrow.

"Has he done this before?" asked Gladys.

"Oh, my, yes, Gladys, and when we are using it she chases us, running back and forth after it. He loves to be free out here, running in the yard. Thank you so much for letting Myrtle take Mac. It's a comfort to know that she has some company while I'm away." Harold's smile told Gladys that he knew how much it had taken to give Mac up. She did miss him, and would have even more had her own wedding not been coming up in November.

Once Gladys had written to George who was now on the Mountford farm, near Shelburne, to tell him of her upcoming marriage to Jack, she rarely heard from him.

"Annie, do you hear from George at all?" she asked her close friend and almost sister-in-law.

"Not very often. I try to write to him on a regular basis; I think he works from sunup to sundown, and is sometimes up in the night with calving. He really is a good farmer. The war has changed him, though, Gladys. He's lost a bit of spunk somehow. He never was much for writing, but now he has even less to say, unless of course it's about the crops or animals. We should go up there and visit someday."

fifty-four

Gladys and Jack Bailey, 1919.

GLADYS EXAMINED THE POSTMARK CANCELLATION STAMP: TORONTO NOV 11, 11 pm, 1919. She had received this at her office the next day and wondered why Jack would be sending her a letter so close to their last visit because it certainly was his handwriting.

3 Collahie St.
November 11, 1919

Dear Tootsie,

I am not writing because I expect to be away long but that you may have a souvenir of a memorable occasion - the first anniversary of Armistice Day which means so much to us. As a matter of fact I shall be home, I expect, before you get this.

At present I am at Mrs. Yeo's but will likely be going to Ossington Ave. before very long, returning here for the night and home in the morning. There is every reason to believe that I shall receive my discharge as anticipated on Thursday, but as I have a return fare issued me I may as well come home for the day. Of course as per usual procedure there was no need for me to have come to-day. Merely wanted some documents which they found without my assistance. However, I eased my mind by giving my tongue a little exercise.

It is very homelike here, and, as Mrs. Yeo says, "It's too bad Gladys isn't here". I am looking forward to the time when she will be. They seem to take quite an interest in me and Mrs. Yeo was much pleased when I told her that I was a Knight of the Trowel yesterday. She seems to think I ought to stay at it, as a near relative of "Lavinia's" would like me to. It is needless to say I am extremely stiff to-day as in addition to working hard yesterday I did the same job over again in my dreams. Still, I shall be ready for the fray when I get my ticket, as we need a little more "honeymoon money."

In closing this little note, my love, D - - - y can only say that a repetition of last night with B - - - y with the addition of 12 more nights is his sincerest wish. When next I write it shall be my happy privilege to ascribe myself "your loving hubby" but in the meantime I must be content to close with a heart full of affection from

Your loving sweetheart
Jack

This world may be filled with beauty, as the one -- we are told, is above,

But the most beautiful thing of the beauty is the power of the love that begets Love.

II

The dress Gladys had made for her wedding day was not quite to her shoe tops. Long-fitted sleeves were trimmed near the cuff with lace. The gown was daintily embroidered marquisette. There were several layers in the skirt, and the one below her knees was edged with four inches of satin. She had wanted a veil as such accessories had become popular. It was attached with a wide band of orange blossoms across the top of her head, some hair showing beneath it, and the rest drawn behind into a bun. She had gracefully walked up the aisle of the Charlton Avenue Methodist Church with her father, while Evelyn Walker played 'The Wedding March'. She nervously carried a bouquet of white roses and sweet peas which was as simple as she could get. She had wanted a church wedding, of course, and she was so pleased that her cousin Bill had agreed to sing "O Perfect Love" during the signing of the register.

Jack was handsome in his new suit and leather gloves. His high, rounded collar allowed a white cravat to be knotted in the opening at the front. A single rose was pinned to his lapel, and his pocket watch from his parents and Annie was draped from the inside button of his vest to the pocket.

At last they were Mr. and Mrs. John Bailey. Harold and a friend of Gladys' had signed as witnesses. Everything was settled for a delightful supper party back at her parents' home.

"Ah, Mother, don't look so sad," Gladys said, trying to put a comforting arm around her mother. Lavinia shook her off.

"Oh, go on with you. You go and join the others in the parlour. I'm just a silly old woman who can't control her tears," and Lavinia turned her back on Gladys to watch the kettle, which wasn't anywhere near boiling. Charles came to the doorway and gave his younger daughter a hug. He was proud of her, and so pleased that at last she and Jack had married. It wasn't going to be easy for Lavinia this winter with both the girls suddenly gone, though she wouldn't complain.

"You look lovely, my dear, now go into your husband, and let me help your mother with the tea." He knew Lavinia just needed a few minutes to compose herself, so he was only somewhat surprised to find her sobbing over the stove.

"They won't be far. Gladys will visit often, you'll see. You'll get some of that peace and quiet you've always wanted." Lavinia wiped her eyes and nodded. She felt foolish. This was a happy day, and she couldn't spoil it for anyone with feeling sorry for herself.

"We need to leave for the station by five-thirty," Jack reminded Gladys.

She looked up and smiled at him. Her small overnight bag had been packed for at least three days, but her mother had insisted on taking the suit out which was to be Gladys' going away outfit, and hanging it up until today. She had remained in her dress until now so would need to hurry upstairs, hang up her wedding dress, change her undergarments, put on her new suit with the wide collar and buttons, then carefully fold her extra suit in the case on top of the unmentionables. Myrtle followed her up the stairs as soon as she saw Gladys go. She wanted to help Gladys pack, but also give her some older-sister advice, as she had been married nearly two months herself.

III

"Oh, Jack, I can hardly believe we're finally married," Gladys said to him, leaning towards him in the plush train seat. Their still gloved hands were clasped tightly.

"I can hardly believe it myself, but it's not a day too soon. You know I dreamed of this day years ago, and then I had to stop thinking about it because I didn't think it would happen three years ago." He looked down on her beaming face with affection. "I hope married life will be everything that you expect," and squeezing her hand, he let it go in order to remove his glove and loosen his collar. He still had on his wedding suit because he had no other at the moment. It was six-thirty and there would be a little time yet before the border crossing at Buffalo.

"I hope Mother won't miss us too much. The house may seem so empty without either Myrtle or I. She may be lonely, but I can come over and visit with her often. Father has always been very attentive, so now they can enjoy each other, alone. You know, the two of them were only alone for a matter of months when they were first married, and then my grandparents wanted them back at 232 Robinson Street. I hope your parents won't expect you to move back home," smiled Gladys as she looked up at Jack, knowing that he had no intention of moving back in with his parents. They would be renting a duplex on Johnston Street until they could afford a house, which might be some time.

The two-day honeymoon was everything the young couple could hope for. The weather was gentle for November, and there was no snow when they returned to Hamilton. Gladys had wanted to keep working at Balfours, but of course married women were expected to stay home, now that the war was over.

"Isn't it lovely, Jack?" asked Gladys as she opened the drawer of the brown leather-covered silverware cabinet which had been a parting wedding gift from the staff at Balfour's office. She would set the table with the silverware only on special occasions.

"It's a lovely gift for a wonderful woman. They must have appreciated having you work there these past few years, and they must have thought you very special to give you this wedding gift."

"'Gladys L. Hannaford, from Balfour, Smye Co. Hamilton, Nov. 22, 1919.' Oh, I will miss working for them you know. They were so kind, and very generous," Gladys said rather wistfully. Jack knew she would have kept working, and perhaps financially that would have been easier to get them started, but he had walked into the job at *The Hamilton Herald* with no difficulty. He was just happy to be married at last, and to his Gladys. He really had thought she had parted from him forever, and the desolate memories were still harsh, but now he wished to forget that time, and all the frustrating wait until he was demobbed.

"Well, Mrs. Bailey, what do you say we retire for the night," suggested Jack softly, and Gladys, glancing over at the single bed they shared in the only bedroom, giggled.

"We're like these two spoons nestled in a cradle," she said, placing the utensils she had been holding back into their bracket. Oh, being married was wonderful. She didn't think anyone could be as happy as they.

fifty-five

HAMILTON, ONTARIO: 1920-1921

GLADYS SPENT WEEKS THAT WINTER MAKING CURTAINS, TABLE COVERS, CUSHIONS. Her mother had let her borrow the old Singer treadle sewing machine, but wasn't going to let her keep it. Myrtle had wanted it as well, but for now Lavinia thought that sharing it among the three of them would be ample. She no longer used it as often as she once had.

Once the rooms had been decorated simply and tastefully, she began to plan what to make for Christmas. She already had one pair of socks made each for her father, Jack, and Harold. She and Jack had found lovely gloves for their mothers at Robinson's Department store, and she had the wool to knit mittens for their nephew and nieces, Maggie and Alf Miller's children. Perhaps she should make her father-in-law a muffler. She could also give Annie a new scarf for the winter. She still worked at the Federal Building and walked to work every day. That was the thing Gladys missed -- the camaraderie with co-workers. Oh, she missed the office. She even missed the work. It kept her mind stimulated. She must try to get busy and read more, but first she would get her recipes in order, and typed on filing cards for future reference. She would see about getting the old Brother typewriter from her father's office. She didn't think it was used anymore.

"Jack, don't you think a few cedar boughs over the doorways would freshen up the apartment, and maybe a little Christmas tree?" asked Gladys hopefully.

"And where would we put even a little tree?" laughed Jack, looking around the already crowded space. "How about a few boughs as you suggest, over one or two of the doorways? I'm sure we can cut a few branches from the overgrown hedge next door, and they would thank us. I'll see about it tomorrow after work."

Jack sat down with the newspaper while Gladys, only slightly deflated at not being able to get the cedar boughs right away, boiled the potatoes and carrots, and fried the meat. She was doing well with only two burners, she felt. If she had had a third, she would have used the potato stock to make a bit of gravy. The pudding she had made this afternoon would be a nice extra, because Jack had looked so tired.

Jack was tired. Days at the paper were long, but it was a great change from army hospital work. He missed some of the fellows he had met at the convalescent hospital. Some had major impediments to overcome once they were released: missing limbs, injured spines, and lungs which hurt even with only shallow breathing. These were dreadful handicaps which would challenge them, their wives, and families. It would be worse in Europe. There were so many widows that it seemed the population would keep shrinking, what with the war and flu epidemic.

"What do you say we go over and see if Mrs. Weston would mind if we cut a few cedar boughs?" Jack asked Gladys, after the pudding. He was feeling refreshed, and could feel that tinge of disappointment lingering over Gladys. She brightened immediately, the way he liked her to, the way he knew she would when she was pleased about something.

II

During the February flu season, Gladys had been ill. She didn't think it was the flu, but she didn't let on to anyone that she thought she had been with child. She was so long in recuperating, that Jack insisted they start taking short walks every evening, the way they had when they courted. Gladys was still very thin, but became much brighter as the days went along. In early spring Jack came home with a surprise in the pocket of his overcoat. He trudged carefully up the wet outdoor, staircase to their apartment. He wanted to surprise Gladys.

"Oh, Jack, you're a little early. I haven't yet started dinner," and then Gladys squealed with joy when out of his pocket Jack pulled a little black and tan terrier.

"Oh, a puppy! Oh, Jack," Gladys beamed up at him. "Oh you've known how much I wanted a dog. Oh, isn't he sweet! Oh, thank you Jack!" Gladys spouted, taking the tiny ball of fur from his outstretched hands. "What will we call him?"

"How about Pat?" offered Jack, and Pat he was.

III

By summer Pat had grown enough to climb the outside stairs himself, and would run around the yard excitedly until Gladys either followed him down, or called him back up. They enjoyed each other, and it helped Gladys adjust to the long days with Jack away.

This Christmas Jack gave Gladys a little extra housekeeping money a few weeks before the holiday. Gladys knew of something that she wanted to get for decoration. She would wait until she had made the Christmas cake with her mother and sister, then what was left over after regular expenses, she would buy some glass ornaments for the branches.

It was thrilling to go to the busy downtown where people were excitedly shopping, street cars were picking up and dropping off workers, housewives, mothers and young children. There was a spirit of happiness in the air that had been missing since the war started. The worries of receiving a dreaded telegram were over, and after years of restraint, people were feeling flush. They wanted to purchase gifts, ornaments, and delicacies which they had done without for what seemed so long.

Gladys pulled her collar up closer as the wind rushed around the corners of the tall buildings. She could feel the excitement of those around her, and her heart sang. She and Jack were so happy. Pat was a comfort. Both her family and Jack's were well. Life was good. The display which had attracted Gladys' attention was even larger. There were the glass ornaments she would get. A small box of six would do this year. There were bunches of grapes and apples. The fine glass had been painted on the inside, and the top had a small metal band with a loop. A person could tie a string to that and hang it to shine colourfully on a tree or in her case, the branches. Oh, she was excited.

IV

Gladys sat knitting on a quiet January evening, thinking about what to make Jack for his birthday in three weeks, when Pat began to fuss. Jack got up and let him outside, looking at the sky, thinking it was too mild for snow, but they might have rain. He watched Pat run around in the back yard, and stepped back inside for his jacket. Jack was down and back up the steps in a hurry.

"Gladys, I can't find Pat. Can you get your coat and help me look?" and Jack returned to the yard. The rain had begun, and both Gladys and Jack were worried. They couldn't find him in any corner, or on the street in front. They searched up and down, around the corner and over the main intersection. People were headed to afternoon Sunday Schools and church services. Gladys and Jack headed back home, deflated. Oh, the poor pup, thought Gladys, out in the rain and cold and he's still so small.

Gladys tidied up the kitchen, poking her head out the door and calling once in a while, but she was sure he was lost. Jack stood at one window and then the next, looking out. After an hour, when the knock at the door came, Jack had been reading and Gladys distractedly knitting.

"Annie! What? Where did you find him? Come in out of the rain," Jack exclaimed, ushering Annie and a wet, wiggling little terrier into the sitting room.

"I couldn't believe it, but I went into the Sunday School at Charlton Street, and there was this wet little dog, and I thought it looked like Pat, so I called him and he came right over to me."

Gladys had jumped up and taken the little bundle that wiggled from her and raced around the room. Gladys laughed.

"That has to be eight or nine blocks away," stated Jack. "This is a miracle that you found her. Well, come now for a cup of tea, and you'll have to miss class today. Thank you so much for returning with him." Gladys was so pleased. It *was* a miracle that Pat had found his way to the Sunday School room and that Annie had found him. She could hardly believe it, but it was a fact.

fifty-six

ON THE DAY OF HALLOWEEN, IN 1921, JACK LOOKED OVER THE FIRST EDITION OF the *Hamilton Herald.* Headlines in seventy point read "PREMIER MEIGHEN WILL SPEAK HERE TONIGHT". It was not a full headline across. Jack thumbed through to the advertisement: Hear Meighen at the arena tonight. Bands in attendance. Good seats for Everybody. Doors open at 7:00 p.m. Bring the ladies. Extra street car service." He wasn't sure how Gladys would take to going to hear the premier on her twenty-sixth birthday. Perhaps he could persuade her that the bands would be entertaining. If Annie would go with them, Gladys would enjoy that and he could focus on a review for the event. The premier had already spoken to the Rotary Club at a luncheon, but the evening presentation might be broader in scope.

He checked out the article accompanying "Woman Bandit with Gun," and the photo above the caption, "Dunking for Apples Still finds sway on Halloween". He was reminded that he wanted to pick up some aspirin when he saw the "Bayer's" advertisement.

II

For months now, Gladys could hardly keep anything down. Tea and dry toast was about all she could manage, and even then it might be down the drain. She felt so weak most of the time, and lay in bed usually until noon. Jack was very concerned. He knew she was in the family way, but couldn't understand why Gladys couldn't keep food down. The doctor confirmed the pregnancy, gave Gladys some powder to help with the nausea, and told her to drink plenty of fluids, soups, and such, but otherwise, things appeared normal. This relieved Jack somewhat, but the powder didn't seem to help much. He would often have to come home and cook up a little something for himself, because the smell of food cooking was enough to turn Gladys' stomach.

After months, Gladys was able to start eating something, but Jack had to cook it, after Gladys had prepared it. If it went straight into her mouth before the smells got to her, she could keep it down. Then they would take a short walk outside, and the fresh air seemed to help. Lavinia came over regularly to help tidy up and perhaps bring a pot of soup. The ice box needed cleaning too, and that was something Gladys could not stomach. Lavinia didn't remember herself being quite so ill, but at the time her mother-in-law was doing most of the cooking. She remembered her mother talking of feeling sick to her stomach, but then, they had a cook when she was young, and her mother wouldn't have had to be in the kitchen. Things had changed.

III

Finally, on October 28th, Ruth Eleanor was born after long hours of labour. She had a small tuft of blond fuzz on the top of her head, but she was beautiful. The doctor had been there for the delivery, as well as Lavinia. Jack was so relieved that he had a daughter, and handled her very cautiously for a minute the day she was born. Of course he couldn't help with feeding, but he could do washing up, and with Myrtle's and Annie's help kept up to date with some clean laundry. There was an endless amount of washing. The nappies, the blankets, the nightgowns, time and time again would be laundered. The fine embroidery of the nightgowns was beginning to fade, but then Ruth gradually grew out of them.

Ruth was young when they moved into the house which they were having built for them on Chedoke Avenue near the base of the mountain. It was to be number twelve, and at last, Gladys thought, she had her own address. Their mail had been going to her parents' or Jack's parents' addresses, and they would pick it up daily, or someone would drop it off when they were out.

Ruth was only three weeks old, but the house was finished, the furniture had been moved, and now they were in their own home. Pat had the whole backyard to himself as it was fenced in, but he didn't seem happy inside the house.

"Jack, I'm worried about leaving Pat with Ruth. He seems jealous. I caught him trying to tear the blankets off the baby this afternoon, and I was just in the kitchen."

"I've noticed it too, and it doesn't seem to be improving. I know how you love that dog, but I think we should be looking for a new home for him, one where there are no children." Gladys slowly nodded her head in agreement. She didn't trust herself to say anything, but she knew Jack was right.

IV

"I found a place for Pat, Gladys. Shall we take a run out to the village of Stoney Creek where the people have lots of property and see how he likes it?"

asked Jack one Sunday afternoon. They had been to service in the morning, eaten their noon meal and were finishing their cup of tea.

"Yes. I can call Father and see if they would like to go with us, or perhaps let us use the automobile." Jack had had a telephone put in the new house which made life so much easier when trying to arrange things with the family.

At that moment, Charles Hannaford was calling Regent 2761 to see if they could come to visit. Jack answered their telephone, pleased that he hadn't had to make yet another request for a ride. Their next major purchase would have to be a car. The arrangements were made, and Pat seemed more than happy to be free to run.

Gladys and Jack checked on how Pat was getting along a few weeks later. They took pictures of Gladys holding the baby in her lap in the overgrown field. They watched Pat run freely, and knew he was content.

"Oh, he's happy alright. He gets right down in them groundhog holes and chases the beasts until he has a bloody nose, but he loves it. He's doing the job he was made for," explained Pat's new owner. Pat came bounding up the steps to the back porch where he was patted affectionately by his new owners, but took one sniff of Ruth in Gladys' arms and growled.

"Well, I guess he's made his choice," laughed Jack.

fifty-seven

JACK LOOKED VERY PLEASED WITH HIMSELF WHEN HE ARRIVED HOME ONE EVENING in the middle of March, 1923. Ruth was just over four months old, old enough for her grandmother to be looking after her. Jack had already called his mother from the office, and Elizabeth had agreed.

"How would you like to see Jane Cowl in *Smilin' Through* on Thursday evening?" Jack asked a stunned Gladys.

"But the baby, who will look after the baby?" she asked, with hope in her eyes.

"My mother has already agreed, and Annie is available if she feels she needs a back up. You can feed her before we go. I have the review to do, so here are the two free tickets!" Jack gleefully replied. Gladys jumped up and hugged him around the neck.

"Oh, I'm so glad. Thank you, thank you. I've been feeling a little housebound these days, and this is such a treat. Does this mean you have the performance review job?"

"Well, this is just to fill in for Harry, but I think if I do a decent job, and you can help me with the musical end of it, I may have more opportunities in the future." Jack was actually quite delighted to be able to do some performance reviews for the *Herald*, because it would be a change of pace from advertising and obituaries, not that he wouldn't do some of those things as well, but it was a welcome change, and gave him and Gladys a chance to get out once in a while.

They thoroughly enjoyed the "Fantasy in a Prologue and Three Acts by Allan Langdon Martin" as it was billed, and loved the Edward German and Tchaikovsky selections as well as the surprise ending. It was very fun to attend an opening night at the Grand Opera House. Perhaps they might next see "The Dumbbells," the Boston Opera company in "Bohemian Girl," or "Irene," the supreme musical comedy. Any would delight Gladys. She wished she had a piano so she could come home and roll through the tunes once again, reliving the performance. Jack knew anytime that he could get tickets, Gladys would be game to attend. His mother and Ruth got along famously so there could be other evenings. Ruth had made it easy and spent all evening sleeping.

II

Judy was the newest addition to the Jack Bailey family. She was a purebred Airedale, and never seemed to mind the baby. In fact, she would stand in front of Ruth who was in her highchair, and let Ruth pound her back with her little soft shoes. She followed Ruth or lay near her when she was playing on her blanket. One day Ruth was sleeping in her carriage on the back veranda which was screened and glassed in. Gladys looked out the window of the back door occasionally, to see if the baby was sleeping or was waking up. She gasped when she saw a rat run across the veranda floor.

"Judy, a rat!" and Gladys opened the door so Judy could race out from the dining room and catch the rat.

"Oh, Judy, you good dog, good dog. Oh, thank you. You're such a good dog," praised a trembling Gladys. She opened the door to the back yard where Judy took the rat and shook it dead. All the visitors for the next while heard about the brave deed which Judy had done, as Gladys never tired of telling everyone who would listen.

III

Gladys was worried. According to what Maggie had said about her children, Ruth should be crawling by now. Ruth sat and cooed, she pulled on the dog's tail, or pounded his back, but she was not interested in crawling. At last Gladys got down on her own hands and knees and after placing Ruth in position, demonstrated crawling before her. Ruth would get her little bottom high in the air and rock back and forth on her hands and toes. Gladys would collapse in laughter because she looked so cute, but Ruth wouldn't crawl.

One evening Gladys stood in front of Jack with her back towards Ruth. She didn't want Ruth to hear what she was saying.

"Jack, I'm worried about Ruth. She should be starting to crawl by now. Do you think I should have the doctor check her over?" Jack leaned his head sideways looking beyond Gladys. Seeing that Ruth was making an effort to pull herself up to a standing position using the arm of the sofa, he didn't see a need to be concerned.

"I think she will be walking before you know it," he smiled, and returned to his paper.

Gladys was cross, but turned to see what Jack had been smiling so smugly about. There was Ruth, looking so nonchalantly at her mother, Gladys almost didn't catch the significance of the moment. Ruth was standing without aid.

IV

Jack's family were coming for dinner on Sunday and this included Alfred and Maggie and their four children. Young Alfred at ten, was the little man of the family, what with three younger sisters to help keep in tow. Five-year-old Margaret still had to be kept calm, but she would be in attendance today. Three-year-old Dorothy was the shy one, clinging to her mother's skirt, and baby Eileen was just a year old. Harold had arrived by himself, as Myrtle was under the weather.

Annie was quite pleased to be helping in the kitchen and helping to set the table. She hadn't mentioned to Gladys and Jack just yet that she was planning a tour in Europe late next summer. She was very excited about it. Her friend George, to whom she was still writing, didn't think too much about traveling now that he was safely home from the war. She thought he would have asked her to marry him, but she wasn't ready just yet. He was working hard on his father's farm, and didn't have time for such things. He enjoyed farming and always spoke about the satisfaction of the work. He rarely had time to come for visits to Hamilton, but on occasion, usually when there was a good freeze on, he would come overnight from north of Shelburne where the family farm was located. He was thinking of buying himself another farm nearby, but as yet had not made the move. He could flag the train down after its stop at Dundalk, go as far as Burlington, and transfer to the Hamilton line. The Baileys always welcomed him, glad to catch up on the family news.

Gladys was so pleased with her new dining room table that she had insisted on having Thanksgiving at their Chedoke Avenue home. She soon hoped to have a china cabinet, but more than anything, she wanted a piano. She was so pleased to be able to have her parents, Jack's parents and family, she would stop what she was doing and watch everyone talking or playing, smile, then continue on with her preparations. Jack was proud of the way Gladys organized everything, had the dining room beautifully set, and was beaming a smile across the room to him which he picked up and returned. His asking God's blessing over the meal was heartfelt and joyful.

fifty-eight

ON OCCASION ELIZABETH AND ALFRED BAILEY WOULD HEAR FROM THEIR relatives in the old country. The war had been very hard on them, but things were settling back to what they would call normal. Most of the women had left the factories and stores and returned to their places at home. Elizabeth's mother had died when Elizabeth was very young. Her father had died before they left for Canada. She was still in contact with her brother William, and often pleaded with him to come for a visit. Alfred's parents had died during the war; Anne first in 1915 and Thomas next in 1917. His younger brothers and sisters wrote on occasion, and sent news of weddings, births and deaths. Emily, Edwin's wife was good about keeping in touch from out in western Canada and let them know how their children Tom, Percy, Margaret, and John were doing. Emily ran a store, giving her a little social life which otherwise might not have taken place. Jack liked to hear about all his cousins, but there were too many to keep in touch with at regular intervals. He had been saddened by the news of his grandparents' passing, but didn't feel he knew them well, unlike Gladys, whose grandparents had lived with the family all her life, until their passing.

There was a knock on the door one morning and Lavinia was there with a few packages for early birthday presents. Gladys greeted her mother with pleasured surprise.

"Oh, come in, Mother. Ruth has just gone down for her nap," and she checked the baby's bed to make sure that Ruth was sleeping soundly. As her mother took her heavy, long coat off, Gladys put the kettle on.

""You look tired, Mother. Is anything wrong? Is Father alright?" inquired Gladys.

"Yes, your father is fine. He's terribly worried about his cousin Frank you know. Frank was off on one of his three day traveling sales trips, and when he returned, Anna and Enid had packed up and gone. She had train tickets to Buffalo, New York for Enid and herself. Francis told Frank when he returned."

"Did Uncle Frank and Francis go too? Were they just going on a holiday to visit her family?"

"Apparently not," sighed Lavinia, "They had trunks packed and took them along. Frances said his mother never left a message or anything for Frank. He is beside himself."

"Enid would be eleven now. You think she would be able to talk some sense into her mother. Poor Frank. I don't think he ever got over Alfred's death," replied Gladys thoughtfully.

"Which Alfred? His brother or his son? I don't think he ever really got over his brother's death, but when little Alfred died, he was not himself. He blamed Anna. Anna blamed Frances. It has not been easy for them living with resentment and heartache. We can't blame others for tragedies like that. God is the one who has control. It's His plan we have to follow, whether it pleases us or not."

"Oh Mother, I understand now. You must have been heartbroken when little Robert died. Now I have Ruth, I would be devastated if anything happened to her." Gladys tried to put thoughts of Ruth's apparent limitations out of her mind.

"How is Myrtle doing, Mother? I haven't heard from her or Harold in ages."

"I probably shouldn't say too much, but I believe your sister is going to have a baby. She has been in bed so often when I call early in the day, I can't help but feel that she is suffering from morning sickness. It's early days, so hopefully she will improve."

Gladys looked at her mother with renewed love. She knew that her mother thought she was boisterous, not refined the way Lavinia had been brought up. "Mother, I hope you are taking care of yourself. Have you heard from Uncle David lately?"

"Funny you should mention it. I just received a photo of him and he looks so dapper in his suit. I am not sure that he really married Jessie May, but they are living together. I wish he would send a picture of her, but he rarely mentions her. I still miss him." Gladys wouldn't ask about her Aunt Lou, her mother's sister. For some reason there was little contact between the two, although her mother talked of the early days when they were best of friends. Maybe they were just busy with their families.

"We should talk about Christmas plans this year," said Gladys, changing the subject.

II

Ruth was walking and trying her best to talk. Her speech was not as clear as Gladys and Jack would have liked, but Gladys kept speaking directly in front of

Ruth, exaggerating her lip movements. At times she wondered if the child heard her, but then she realized if she repeated herself enough, Ruth would catch on to the word or phrase. It is going to take her longer to learn, thought Gladys, but she's not hard of hearing.

"Let's go and visit Grandma and Grandpa Hannaford, Ruth," Gladys said, enunciating clearly.

"Go gramma's and pa's," Ruth answered excitedly.

III

Jack glanced at the clock. Nearly midnight before the first of January, 1925. He picked up a sheet of paper and his pencil as he felt a poem coming on:

> One more year had passed away
> And what have we done for Thee
> Who gave us life and health alway'
> And the Saviour who died on the tree.
>
> But let us now, O God, we pray
> Each other's burden's bear
> While walking alone with Thee each day
> Throughout this Glad New Year.

He closed up his writing drawer and went out to greet his wife in the traditional New Year's way.

fifty-nine

GLADYS WAS GOING TO APPROACH HER MOTHER ABOUT GETTING THE PIANO MOVED to Chedoke. It would be so much fun for Ruth to try learning to play, and it might help with her development. Gladys had been pining for the pleasure of playing the piano herself, especially when she accompanied Jack to performances which he would review for *The Hamilton Herald*. Gladys' sister Myrtle had no interest in the piano, other than listening to others play. She spent all her waking time with her new son David who needed constant attention. It had been a heartbreak for Myrtle and Harold to discover their baby was profoundly deaf, and had eyesight problems as well. Inspired by Helen Keller's story of overcoming seemingly insurmountable physical obstacles, they worked hard to teach him what they could. Ethel, who now lived on her own in a Herkimer Street apartment, had her family piano, and so enjoyed playing it.

Gladys didn't want to stay away too long because Judy was in the basement pacing, meaning that she could have her pups at any time. They had bred her with a male Airedale and now Judy would be having her first litter of pups. She walked from their Chedoke Avenue home to the familiar door of Robinson Street. Her mother was in the kitchen, standing by the stove.

"Are you sure now, Mother?" asked Gladys.

"It's only played when you come over. Otherwise, it just sits here collecting dust. I'll miss your playing, but you should have it. We may be moving out to the beach sometime soon, anyway. Your father keeps talking about it."

Later, after Judy's pups were born, the veterinarian came to dock the tails of the pups. Gladys was upstairs comforting Judy who had no idea what was happening to her puppies. Jack had taken Ruth for a walk as she wouldn't understand.

II

Jack took Gladys and Ruth up to Nanticoke for a late summer holiday. They were staying at Mrs. Charles Edsall's. A letter arrived for Gladys on the fifteenth of September.

Hamilton
Sunday, Sept 13th/25

Dear Gladys

I was glad to hear you were enjoying your holiday so much. I did not get your letter until Friday. It seemed a long time coming so short a distance, Ellen thought it must have got left in the box. She said Mrs. Brewer waits for the Postman and gives him the letters. Sarah was in last night with my dress she was fixing. I thought she was up with you all week. It seems the young lady that was to bring her up was delayed at the office on Tuesday. She had a new car and did not know the road and someone told her it would be bad if it had rained very much. She is a friend of Mrs. Lewis. I was to go up for company coming back. Mrs. Lewis was not able to go as she had some visitors come to stay that she did not expect and so the girl would have had to come back alone in the dark which she did not want to do and Sarah did not want her to. Sarah is quite busy for this coming week, so I do not know if she could come the last week. I did not know if you would be staying that long if the weather keeps so wet. It has teamed all day today, yesterday not much better.

Father and I went up to your place right after Tea last night to pick some flowers for the Cemetery as it is Decoration Day to-day. He took them up this morning. It is a bad day for them. Ellen put an ad in the paper this week and she got several answers. She had a Widow lady and her daughter coming to share the apartment with her. They have some furniture.

I am glad she has it settled before she is called out. She may have to go to an old lady tomorrow, but she hopes they will get somebody else as she is dying. It is hard for her to take those cases.

Father is keeping pretty well. He was not able to go to the Ex as Uncle George and Norman were up at Hespeler working and Tom Frears was not able to come as he expected for a few days. Jack Cameron got his eye full of stuff and there was several jobs all at once that had to be done so the Yeos have not been up yet. I had a letter from her yesterday. They are all pretty well. Evelyn White had a cold and came out in a rash all over her body. The Doctor thought it was from eating Tomatoes and Peaches caused to much acid in the blood. She is some better again. Evelyn Grierson is keeping fairly well also.

Myrtle and Harold hope to come up with you on Saturday afternoon if they can get away. I have canned your Pears. I did a large basket. They were 50 cts and made 18 small jars. We took them up last night and put them in your cellar. I took the sheets and pillow cases off your bed and picked up the bath and tea towels etc. and got them washed and put them on the bed again. I thought that would help you when you came home, as you would have a lot of dirty clothes to bring home with you. Mr. Walmo took up the Causwell coal that was in our shed. Ellen said you might as well have it for the Parlour grate. We had to get it out of the shed as Halls have quite a bit of wood in there, he gets from his boss. The cases that are around the baths etc. They seem to be nice tenants. I think we shall like them all right. Tommy Strel started to dig out ready for the cement wall between the houses and right around the back part. The posts were all rotten. I do not think it would have stood another winter. The back end would have sunk.

On the holiday Dad and Tommy took out 9 loads of clay between the houses. They are filling it up again, but it will not be so much as before. Mr. Forrest has not finished with the carpeting jobs in the cellar as he is building a garage for somebody. The furnace is not finished either as we are waiting for the 4 rads from Britain. We found we had to get them as Mr. Forrest kind of got cold feet about making them. We wish now we had got the 8 all at once. It would have been better. Father has to plaster the boiler also the pipes. I hope he will be able to get it finished soon. Uncle George is home again we hear. Norman has bought a (closed) in Cheo Car.

They have not told us themselves yet we may not have the Yeos up for a week or so. They can come any time. Jean has her sister and husband staying with her and her mother is going back with them for a visit. I hope John has left his cold in the lake somewhere. Give Ruth a kiss from me. I guess she and Judy are having some time. Judy will not want to come back to be tied up again. Did you know Mrs. F. Dunswood died at the back of us? She had 2 operations and had been home from the hospital a week and passed away quite suddenly.

I am feeling pretty good to-day. I was not very good last week those hot days. Thursday was a bad day for everybody. I hope to be finished preserving before the Yeo's come up. I am nearly done now. We were over at Locke Street last night and got some very nice sausages at a Pork shop that is just opened next door to the Regent. They were something like the Toronto ones 3ish a lb. You might like to try some.

Mrs. Bailey called up when they got home on Sunday night. How does Ethel like it up there? She will think the weather is poor for her holidays. Bill and Joy were up last Sunday as he and his wife were going away. I must close now and write to Aunt Kate.

With love from
Mother and Dad

sixty

IT HAD BEEN ALMOST TWO YEARS EXACTLY SINCE AUNT MARY NEXT DOOR HAD died. Ellen and Ethel had been the only ones living at home at the time, and the house was too large for just the two of them. They had not wanted to sell it. In fact, their brother Bill had been the one to suggest they rent it out and then there would be a small income for some of the family members who needed it, meaning his two single sisters.

"I hope the family next door will be happy there and some company for my parents," Gladys said to Jack and Ethel after reading the letter aloud. "My mother really has come to rely on Ellen and your company, Ethel, since Aunt Mary died, but Ellen is certainly keeping in touch. Of course she is not that far from Robinson Street now. I'm glad she had people to rent the apartment with her."

"She has been such a help. It's too bad she didn't meet a nice young man to marry," commented Jack.

"Oh, you make it sound as though she's an old spinster. She still could marry if she chose. I know of..."

"Yes, I know you know of other cases, and I've heard of them, but I think Ellen is devoted to her nursing and she likes to be independent, just like Ethel here."

Ethel smiled her jolly smile, and nodded her head in agreement. She had her own apartment and enjoyed the solitude after a busy day at the Bell Telephone Company. She enjoyed being a career woman, and had never yet met a man who could change her mind.

"Why don't we have a few tunes, like the old days?" laughed Ethel, as she sat down and let her fingers nimbly roll over the ivories in harmonic arpeggios. Within minutes Gladys had joined her, and Ruth bounced up and down to the lively rhythm.

II

Jack checked the birth notice: "BAILEY – TO John and Mrs. Bailey, 12 Chedoke Avenue, on Monday, August 11th, a son." What!? That was two days ahead. He would be speaking to Walter about this; gently mind you. It had been a busy day. Jack looked at his original copy: August 9th, a son. Well, at least it hadn't been his mistake in the excitement. People would know it was the 9th since it was in today's paper, the 9th, and they wouldn't be publishing a birth notice before the event! He laughed and continued perusing Monday, August 9th, 1926's *Hamilton Herald*.

The top headline on page three read, "DRIVERLESS BRITISH TRAIN WITH 200 ON BOARD RAN WILD, Heading right for station at Newcastle, Where it would have met Passenger Train. STOPPED BY FREIGHT – Only five passengers hurt; Driver had fallen from Train."

Now that was a strange and fortuitous event, Jack thought. Worse fatalities occurred when the fireworks factory at Providence blew up: "THREE KILLED- THREE MISSING, AFTER BLOW-UP", and the reported "35 WEEK-END DROWNINGS AT U.S. RESORTS."

At home Gladys looked down with relief, love and pride at her healthy new son, Robert Thomas, named after his two great grandfathers; Robert, her father's father, and Thomas, Jack's father's father. The nurse in attendance had filled out the History Chart from PARKE and PARKE. "Baby Robert Bailey born - 9:10 am weight 7 3/4 lbs. Birth normal."

Life was wonderful.

CPSIA information can be obtained at www.ICGtesting.com
Printed in the USA
LVOW13s0801300714

396602LV00004B/32/P